Vigilante

One man's Justice

The Story of a Man Gone Bad

and

Half Saved by a Woman

Ronald Edward Myles

Contents

About the Author

Ronald Myles is a Canadian author, a graduate of Concordia University and a retired Royal Canadian Police Officer and intelligence agent. He has more than twenty-seven years in law enforcement and intelligence gathering. He retired from this trade into Municipal politics. His transition allowed him to advocate for the same principles of justice, transparency and responsibility that highlighted his working career. He is also an avid reader.

Mr. Myles has always been a fan of novelists and is fascinated by the talent of authors such as Dan Brown, Steven King and Louise Penny, who are capable of weaving such tales of fiction that they have gained audiences around the world.

Mr. Myles is the father of two beautiful girls and four angelic grandchildren. Retired now, he lives outside Montreal, Quebec.

For any comment you may wish to leave, Mr. Myles can be reached at Vigilante22@Tutamail.com (mailto: Vigilante22@Tutamail.com)

Acknowledgements

Thank you to my wife, Christiane, who acted as editor, idea bouncer, critic and advisor, all nonpaying positions.

Chapter

I

I had it all. I was at that point in life where I thought that everything was under control and that it would last forever. I guess that that's just an illusion. You really don't know, do you? You just don't know what kind of beast lives inside of you until you are put to the test. Then, the things that you can do or, in reality, have done boggles your mind. Could I have been that violent? Is it really inside of me that I can take another human being and do those things to him? What kind of motivation does anyone need to become such a monster?

I was a quiet kid. My parents took good care of me. I had everything I needed. I was loved and had a group of friends pretty much like I was. Life seemed to be going along normally. Well, it seemed normal. But then again, I didn't know anything else, so to me, it was what everyone else was doing. I was taught by my parents that there is right and wrong and that I should show respect to the elderly and to ladies. The forces of authority were just and fair; criminals were always caught and punished accordingly. The world was a place where good prevailed.

I grew quickly, faster than most of my friends. This made me a natural for sports. I loved baseball but preferred football. It was the contact, the banging together of the equipment and bodies, and that thumping sound it made when they clashed that I enjoyed. I guess it was the roughness of the game.

To enhance my play, I bought gym equipment with my paper route money, weights to lift and simple machines to help grow my strength. Dad kicked in a large number of dollars to help. He would say, "A kid on the field is a kid not in the back alleys."

All my life to that point was normal or average. We'd hear on the evening news about injustices happening somewhere in the world, but it never seemed to be close to home. Still, the idea that everything needs to be regulated was deep in my psyche. The world doesn't balance itself, and there are forces of righteousness that keep us on a steady track. I kind of knew that they were there but never gave it a lot of thought.

I graduated high school with marks that were good enough to get me into the local college. I was pretty much average in most subjects but in math, I excelled. My goal was to be an architect. I loved math. I loved building things.

It was in my second semester that I happened to wander into a job fair being held at the college when I saw two Army sergeants at a recruiting booth. They looked really sharp in their dress uniforms. Curious, I went to chat with them. By the time that we were finished talking I was seriously thinking of enlisting. My goal wasn't just to be a grunt, a regular trench soldier, but to join the Delta Force. I believed that these were the people who righted wrongs anywhere in the world. I wanted to be part of that. I wanted to be the ying to counter the yang. I could see a glorious future to my dreams.

I went home after that meeting and discussed this possibility with my dad. Turns out that he was very supportive. He had been in the military when there was conscription and said that he had learned a lot about individual self-esteem and working with others. He said something to the effect that "Serving one's country is a very noble and necessary task. Someone has to do it, and in the U.S. military, you'd get the best equipment possible and the best training available. I enlisted the next day.

Boot camp at Fort Moore was tough, but honestly, I enjoyed every minute of it. I'd never tell the instructors that. They'd just dump more and more on me till I broke. No, best to be quiet about some things; this was one of them. Ten weeks of physical exertion. The comradeship among the recruits and the challenges were all elements that I enjoyed.

I applied for the Delta Force immediately after boot camp. I went to the first training session, where I met the drill instructor from hell. He almost seemed human the first day. He said very clearly that he was going to do his absolute best to drive us out of his Army. "This is my fucking Army, and I don't want any of you maggots in it." His mantra was "Panic and die.' He repeated this to us at every session, yelling it into our collective and individual ears.

I noticed a pattern in his rants and tantrums. He would choose one recruit, someone who may have shown a weakness, anything that caught his attention. Then, for two or three days, he would yell, scream, curse this one individual to see if he could drive him to quit. We started off with thirty recruits, and eleven days later, we were down to twenty-one. His method was working.

Sooner or later, it would be my turn. It wasn't long in coming. It started on a Monday morning after a weekend when six of us went out for a beer. One beer led to the next and then to another. Well, you get the point. We came back to the barracks more than slightly tipsy. Drill sergeant miserable saw us arriving while we were singing a Michael Jackson song way out of tune. Michael would not be pleased. I saw the look in his eye as he thought we were having too good a time. I could almost hear him say as he looked me in the eye. "Monday, you pay." I realized that he seemed to like three-word mantras.

On Monday morning, directly after roll call, our drill sergeant stated that he thought that it wasn't appropriate to be singing and having fun while trying to get into his army. The fact that we were already in the army didn't seem to occur to him. Nobody I knew was going to correct this little misunderstanding. It seemed that I was going to be the subject of his attention, and he chose me to vent his frustration. I was called every name in the book and even a couple I hadn't heard before. He was at least twenty minutes wringing me over the coals, doubting my ancestry, using every tactic that he could to get me angry, mad, and panic to get too excited and challenge him, curse at him, anything to break discipline. As he stood in front of me, his nose inches from my own, yelling at the top of his lungs like a mad banshee, with veins bulging from his neck, my lips moved a minor fraction of a millimeter into a smile. His voice stopped in mid-sentence. "Are you laughing at me, maggot?"

"No sir" was the required answer. I gave it. But he and I knew that that was a lie. No more harassment from the mad drill instructor. Off he went to search out another victim. I did not 'Panic and die.'

The beginning of the end of my military career happened three days later. We were learning unarmed self-defense moves when the two other recruits to my left were practicing body throws. One recruit was throwing the other over his back. He was then supposed to pounce on the thrown individual and succeed in the kill. Unfortunately, the thrown person came into my practice zone with flying feet that struck me on the side of the head, just above the temple. The blow knocked me out.

When I regained consciousness, the instructors were all around me. First-aid bandages were put around my forehead. Blood was flowing profusely from my nose, and I couldn't see through my right eye. I was rushed to the infirmary, where some ice and ten stitches stopped the bleeding. It was more the eye that had the medics and doctors concerned. I was diagnosed with a detached retina. To make a long story short, the retina was put back in place. I was told that in time, it would heal and that there would be no side effects, but that I should avoid any movement that could or would cause my head to hit a solid object. Unfortunately, in the army, this was not only a possibility but was more than likely to happen. I exercised my right to leave the military, canceled my contract, and left with an honorable discharge. My military dreams were over.

I took up my second passion, building. I had always loved designing and building things, from birdhouses to castles. I went back to school. I succeeded with flying colors. I wasn't really surprised that I had done so well. I was formalizing something I had been doing all my life. When you love what you're doing, it's not really work, is it?" I missed the Army life but realized that I had to move on.

Once I was out of the Army, I figured that I had to start a new life. My first step was to marry my college sweetheart. She'd been waiting for me, and getting married was just the expected next step in our relationship. I was never interested in anyone else and she showed a lot of patience with me while I pursued my dreams. It was a small ceremony with just family and friends.

She was an orphan, her parents having died many years earlier. She was brought up by an aunt. My mom died while I was training with the Army. Shortly afterward, my dad followed her. It created in us a certain bond. Two of us alone in the world.

I got my papers as an architect and tried that for a while. I worked for a large local company, and they gave me some interesting projects to work on. The problem here was that although I had designed the house or building, I was never involved in its construction. I enjoyed the design but there was something missing. I didn't experience the internal reward you get when you conceive a project and then get to actually build it. There's a deep sense of satisfaction when you stand in the driveway or parking lot and look at what you've created from conception to birth. When I mentioned this to Nicky, my wife, how I conceive and give birth as well, she just didn't think it was that funny. "You walk around with a basketball in your stomach for nearly a year and tell me that it's the same." She was not amused at my comparison. I told her that she had no sense of humor. Her comeback was deadly. "I married you, didn't I?"

The game was over, and I lost again.

I resigned from the company and hung out my own shingle. My logo was "From Design to Delivery." I thought that it was a catchy phrase. Anyway I did get a contract within the first week. It wasn't big, but it was a contract. The clients and I created a simple design for a ranch-style bungalow, and I was going to build it. They were in a hurry to move in, and I promised them a rapid delivery. It was, after all my only project for the moment. My life was unfolding well. Everything seemed to be falling into place. I was content and happy.

Nicky was a computer analyst and software designer. She did her magic and the computer would spit out the info you wanted. She did things with her computer that made my head spin. I just wasn't geared that way. I had to work in the real world. Digital land was not for me. But she loved the ones and zeros and could write a program in minutes. This talent of hers gained us a lot of money. We ended up being quite comfortable.

One of the applications she wrote was an inventory following a program that allowed the user to know at a glance where he was with his goods. Did he need more of brand "Z" or "How many of brand "Y" are left on the shelves? What product hasn't moved in the last, 'enter any number you want.' She was all excited about this new program, I couldn't see the advantages of it, but I did enjoy the income.

At first, she rented this software out and we made some good money with the income. She was then approached by an international firm that wanted to buy the program and keep her as a developer of this and other programs. The purchase price was great, and her new job with this company paid very well. We really did have it made. Just when you think that all is ok and that you're going to get ahead of the game, fate intervenes.

I remember that day vividly. It was a Friday afternoon. I was putting the last of the asphalt shingles onto the roof of that house that I was building for that couple, my first clients. I had designed it, and now I was the builder, too. I love this job. Only six more squares to go, but it was a little after four in the afternoon. I figured about ninety minutes more, this roof would be finished, and I could take the weekend off. I had promised the buyers that it would be ready by Monday morning. If I didn't finish this today, then I'd have to come back tomorrow. But by finishing it now, I'd have the whole weekend off to spend with my pregnant wife. I called her and asked her to jump in with Betty, our neighbor. They worked together and often shared a ride to work, so this request wasn't unusual. I called. "Honey, I've got some good news and some bad news. Which do you want to hear first?"

"Give me the bad first."

"Ok, I have to work late and can't pick you up. Jump in with Betty, and I'll be home around seven."

"Ok, so what's the good news?"

"Well, I'll be finished this roof this afternoon, and I'll have the weekend off. We can spend it all together."

"Great. Can we go shopping for a crib for the baby tomorrow?"

"That's exactly what I was thinking." I lied. "Ok, so I'll see you at home. Bye, love you." and I hung up. I didn't know it, but that was the last time I would talk to my wife.

Billy, my helper, was bringing those bundles of shingles over to me and I had the pneumatic nailer going like crazy.

My ninety-minute estimate was off by thirteen minutes. Only a little longer than I expected. We had put in nearly two extra hours, but the job was finished. I gave Billy a small bonus to help him make up for his fiancee for being late. He could take her out for a nice meal. My treat.

I rushed home, making up apologies all the way. I even practiced a few out loud. As I turned the corner onto our street, I noticed subconsciously that Betty's car wasn't in her driveway. I saw the absence but didn't put any importance on it. Hell, there could be a thousand reasons the car wasn't there. Really, it was a non-issue until I parked and entered my house. It was quiet. It shouldn't have been quiet. Nicky always had music on in the house. She would put it on the second she entered. The place was silent. A cold shiver went down my spine. I just knew that there was something wrong. I went over to Betty's place. Fred, her husband, worked shift work at the plastic plant. He wasn't home. "Probably at work," I told myself. Still, that feeling of impending doom stayed with me. I went back home.

As I entered the house, the phone was ringing. With a terrible feeling in my gut, I ran to answer. It was the emergency room at the hospital. My wife was there with severe injuries due to a motor vehicle accident. I should get there as fast as possible. I didn't make it in time. She and my baby had succumbed to their injuries, and both were pronounced dead about three minutes after I talked to the ER nurse.

As I ran towards the ER, a doctor met me in the hallway. "I'm sorry," he said. "We really didn't have much chance of saving either.

The injuries were extremely severe. My sympathies, sir." and he turned and left. What a way to tell me that my world has come to an end.

I stood there. I stood there some more. I continued to stand there until a nurse working at the admittance station noticed me and came to see if I was Ok. She asked me the same question a number of times. "Sir, are you ok?"

I didn't answer. I just stood there. She took me by the arm, led me to a bench, and sat me down. I let her lead me. I was confused. I sat there with the thousand-yard stare. "She asked again. "Sir, are you ok?"

This time, I looked at her and quietly said, "No." I sat there some more. The nurse brought me a glass of water. Eventually, I went home, or to what used to be our home. I sat on the sofa, staring at a blank TV screen. What the fuck do I do now?

Chapter

II

Eventually, I must have made all the proper funeral arrangements and done all the right things because Nicky and the baby were buried together. I guess Billy took care of the Monday morning customers. I really don't remember a whole lot. Neighbors would stop by to express their condolences, and the ladies would leave casseroles and other foodstuffs. I ate them without tasting anything. Everything seemed to be robotic. I was still waiting for Nicky to come home.

The Police came by one day sometime after the funeral. I don't recall when. They explained to me that Betty and Nicky were heading home along First Ave. They went through a green light at the intersection of Tenth Street but were hit by a car going through the red light. The individual was arrested and given a Breathalyzer test, which he failed. He was to be charged with Criminal negligence, causing death, and driving while impaired. I didn't really care.

Betty was still in the hospital with severe injuries. They didn't know if she was going to make it. I was silent.

They talked. I listened. They asked no questions. I asked no questions. They expressed their condolences and left. I continued staring at a blank TV screen. I could still hear her in the house but when I went to the room that the noise was coming from, she wasn't there. I didn't cry. It was seven days before I realized for real that Nicky wasn't coming home. We were only children to deceased parents. We were alone, but we had each other, we'd would be ok. "Two orphans against the world." we'd say. Then, laugh at the idea of loneliness. "We had each other," I'd repeat in my mind. Now, she was gone. She can't be gone. I still didn't cry.

What the fuck do I do now?

Chapter

III

Time has no relevance when you are in pain. Every minute seems like a lifetime. Your beautiful wife is gone. It's time to accept that. The next question is a killer. "Why did she leave me?" The answer will be in Court next week. You want to see who destroyed your world. You want to ask, "Why?" It still doesn't make any sense, but you have to know. Thus, you end up in the Courtroom with three other spectators who look like they are half asleep.

The Judge and all other relevant people arrive and take their places. After much incomprehensible talk, the case is put off for some reason you don't understand. I couldn't hear well enough to figure it out. I did get the next Court date. "Why is this taking so long? The guy was drunk. The breathalyzer proved that. This should be a slam dunk for the prosecution. But no, there's another Court date and then another, and finally, after four adjournments, the trial will be held. Finally.

The first on the stand is one of the Police Officers who answered the call and was first on the scene. He describes the impact, how the defendant's car had smashed into the passenger side of Betty's car and no, there was no indication that the defendant had even touched his brakes. He had, in the Officer's opinion, driven head-on into the other vehicle. He used the expression "T-Boned" the other car. The Officer demanded that the defendant submit to a breath test. The defendant complied and was found to be well over the legal limit. The Prosecution rested.

The defense lawyer then asked the Officer if he had seen the accident. The response was, "No."

"Where was the defendant when you arrived?"

"He was standing beside the car he had hit, trying to get the woman out of the driver's side. The door was stuck and wouldn't open."

"What time did the accident happen?"

"My car got the call at sixteen thirty-five hours, and we drove directly to the scene."

"That's not what I asked. What time did the accident happen?"

"I don't know the exact time."

"What did my client do between the time of the accident and the time that you arrived?"

"I don't know. Like I said. When I arrived, he was at the driver's side door."

"Is it possible that the defendant took a drink of alcohol between the accident and your arrival?"

"Yes, I guess it is."

"So, Your Honour, I request that you not allow the breath test into evidence."

The Judge responded "I have no choice but to not allow the test into evidence."

The Prosecution did not have any other witnesses. The case was dismissed, and the defendant was free to go. He had killed a woman, my wife, and our baby, put another one in the hospital, and was now walking free. "This is not right."

My wife's name had hardly come up in the whole proceedings. The whole affair was held in a nonchalant atmosphere. I screamed in my mind. "My wife is dead. You, you bastard, killed her, and now you're shaking hands with your lawyer, smiling and leaving here a free man. This is not right." I had no idea what this single statement was going to do to me. I was angry and had no place to vent my feelings. Anger is a sneaky thing. It sits in your mind and grows without you even realizing that it is festering. The pressure builds and builds, and you are not even aware of it.

I went home mad. "This is not right." I read the statistics on the number of accidents and people dying as a result of booze. It really is a scary number." Then I put the TV on and there was the documentary that was going to lead me down the road to hell. Simply entitled 'Missing Kids,' they talked about the number of children that vanish every year. To my astonishment, I learned that it's in the tens of thousands. Something like fifty thousand kids a year leave home and never come back. I sat there with my mouth agape. I repeated, "Fifty thousand." Where are they?" I asked myself. They just disappeared? Something is wrong there, too. That's not right.

The investigative reporter on the TV went on to say that many of these children are sold into sexual slavery and that pedophiles often purchase and then trade these young people like they were sports trading cards. Certain features bring the owner more money. Others are less valuable. An undercover officer said that many criminals prefer kids to drugs. You sell drugs once, and it's over, but kids are sellable over and over. When you're finished with them, you sell them to another pervert, and the abuse continues. The time comes when the abuse is so intense that the child is not sellable. Then, they are simply disposed of. "What does that mean 'disposed of'?" The short answer is they are murdered if they haven't already committed suicide. The anger festering from my baby and wife's death, no I'll call it murder now, remained with me. Drunk driving was bad, but pedophilia was worse. It was the planned and executed exploitation of society's most vulnerable, our kids. I wasn't there to protect my unborn child. In my mind, the two melded into one idea.

I was already in a depressed state. I really didn't need another depressive trigger bouncing around in my head. I can't save the world. I had to get control of my situation, take my own future in hand, and do something, anything, to break up this depressive spiral I was in.

I sold our house, and since Nicky's death, now my house and took my truck and started driving. We lived on the East Coast, so the West Coast sounded good. I would stop along the way, meet and talk to people. The whole idea was to detach from my old, now ruined life and get something else going. Where? I didn't know. So I just let the cards fall where they may and drove on. Money wasn't a problem. The anger was still there, seething. I asked myself that same question that was becoming the mantra of my life. "What the fuck do I do now?"

Chapter

IV

I couldn't stay here. Too many memories. I said goodbye to my friends and headed out. I have never seen the Rocky Mountains so I thought I'd go west to Colorado and then north on the interior of the mountain range. Once I hit the Canadian border, I'd cross over to the Pacific side and drive south to Mexico. There, I finally had a plan.

The drive west was a somber one. I was still in the anger stage and honestly wasn't very sociable. By the time I arrived in the mile-high city, my mood had taken a swing for the better. Denver is best when listening to John Denver's "Rockie Mountain High." I had the music going and I was singing along with every word. At the end of the song, I realized that I felt much better and that somewhere along the way, I had left my cares and woes behind. I still missed Nicky but was at peace with her passing. The mountains are both impressive and beautiful and maybe a little bit healing. I turned and started driving north. In Idaho, I entered this town, like many others I'd see all along the way. There was nothing special about it. I checked into a small, cheap motel and brought my overnight bag inside.

Supper time saw me in the restaurant just up the highway. Hamburger steak with fries was on the menu as the special of the day. Ok, I like steak. The order went in. The steak was good and as I was finishing up, I heard some music coming from next door. I paid for the meal, went to where the music was, and ordered a beer.

The singer-guitarist was an older guy. He'd obviously been around a long time but never had been 'discovered.' The bar was nearly empty so I was singing out the old songs with him. I was having a great time all by myself, and the singer was getting a kick out of me, too. "Hell," he said, "You knows the words to all my songs?"

"So far," I said. "When you're done, come over, and I'll buy you a beer."

"Well," he said, "I'm kind of thirsty, and this set just finished." With a little chuckle, he was at my table in a flash. Amazing what a free beer will do sometimes. "Name is Bob, Bob Barber.'

I responded, "Don, or as I'm called when I'm in trouble, Donald Minson. Nice to meet you, Bob, and I love your music. Is that a Martin you're playing?"

"Ya, believe it or not, I won it in a poker game a few years back. The fellow couldn't cover his bet and offered me this in exchange. Best deal I ever made. I love the sound that comes out of it. Where you off to?"

"Nowhere special. I just have to travel a bit."

We spent the rest of the evening and into the night talking about music, traveling, and the things we'd seen and enjoyed. He mentioned that just to the west of here, there was a ranch that gave tours into the Rockies. He said that he'd seen a lot of beautiful places in his travels but that this place was extra special; "If you ain't in a hurry and you got a hundred bucks, then I recommend it highly." "Green Horn Tours," I think he called it. The conversation went on from there until we closed the place. I promised to be back tomorrow night and that a visit to the mountains would be a good thing. Get "Some real fresh air." I was looking forward to a change in scenery.

All that was innocence on my part; I didn't know that I'd be spending weeks and weeks here and that my life path, as it's called, would be radically changed. For now I planned to go into those mountains. I was excited.

As I had told Bob last night, I was going to take the Rockie Mountain tour. I was there early in the morning and managed to go out with the first group. Apparently, they do four tours a day. I had never been on a horse before. Something that my new friend Bob didn't mention was that the tour was on horseback. I looked at it. It looked at me. I suspect I heard a small chuckle from it. Obviously, it recognized a greenhorn. Oh well. I'd paid my money, now take the ride.

We returned to the ranch ninety minutes later. Do you know that there are five thousand four hundred seconds in ninety minutes? I swear that horse jumped up and down every second just to see if it could squeeze my balls to the saddle. My privates were sore, my legs were aching, and I swore that I would never ever ride a bloody horse again. That beast gave the same chuckle again as I was walking slowly away. I turned to look at it. I'm sure it smiled at me. I turned my back and continued to walk away. I'm gonna find a store that sells horse meat, and I'm gonna eat your cousins, you bloody sadist. I hate horses. The horse looked on unimpressed.

Given the condition of my groin area and the rash and soreness on my upper legs, I decided to spend a quiet afternoon recovering. I picked up a newspaper, ordered a cup of coffee and a piece of apple pie, and sat in a booth reading the local news. There was the regular scandal you see in most small towns, an attempt to create a controversy over a new road project and an article on a pedophile that had just got off on a legal technicality. As I read the paper, for reasons I don't know or understand I could feel my blood pressure rising.

This bastard, Sacks by name, was suspected in a whole string of child abductions. I read on, and as I did, the anger returned. I don't know these people. I'd never been here before, but still, I could sense that the anger rising in me demanded that I do something. Another bastard getting away with murder. It has to stop. "If the Courts won't do it, then I will." Just saying that to myself surprised me. Then I asked myself, "What the fuck do I do now?"

Chapter

V

Shit, what did I just say to myself? Am I thinking that I should get revenge for a kid or kids that I didn't even know? Should I be taking the law into my own hands? Why do I think that it's up to me to be a vigilante?

I still had a couple of hours before I was supposed to meet Bob, so I read on. The article was long on speculation and short on facts. I wanted to know more about this sickness that kills kids and destroys families. A trip to the library. Their book collection was short on these medical studies into the cause of pedophilia. But the saving grace was that it did have an internet connection. I sat down at one of the terminals and signed in.

I started with the basics. There is no pattern for the offenders. It cuts equally across all races, colors, and creeds. It's prevalent among the rich, the poor, and the in-between. Some of the common traits of pedophilia were the tendency to own their own small business, live alone, no or very few friends. They are secretive and, once discovered, tend to be arrogant. I wondered if this guy Sacks fit this profile. Before I arranged to see him, I read on. According to investigative journalists, these arrogant S.O.B.s are everywhere. And when they are finally discovered, even if they have been hiding it for years, once it's out of the bag they're proud of what they are. That was the case with this clown. He'd been at it for over two decades. Never did he get caught in the old days, the days when he was younger and more careful. But in reading the discovery documents that his lawyer and the investigating journalist had obtained from the prosecution, it looks like he (Sacks) was once spotted near a park where a kid vanished.

The journalist speculated that the fact that it took them so long to catch up to the suspect probably gave the suspect the impression that the cops didn't really care. Pedophiles believe that they are so much smarter than those asshole cops.

As I read on about these very special people and for reasons unknown to me, I felt that I had to do something. Scathing anger eventually needs a target, sometimes a scapegoat, to focus the hate. Was my anger at my wife's death making me do something a thousand miles away? These guys, or maybe this guy in particular, were just too full of himself to concede. My anger was focused on him. He was responsible for Nicky's death. He was why I didn't have a baby in my arms tonight. It was all his fault. He's gonna pay.

But sometimes arrogance pays the price. And I decided that here and now, justice will finally done, justice that should have been served by the system. That fucking system that seems seriously intent on letting all the criminals loose. But that's another story for another time.

I was in the army. I should be able to kill a piece of shit like this guy without any problems. I made my plan and then did my homework. I learned where he worked, where he lived, and how I was going to do it. Fast decisions. Clean work. No evidence left behind.

Today is Snatch Day. Today's the day one of many wrongs will be righted. Today's the day that Jeremy Sacks pays the price for the eleven kids he's kidnapped and murdered. That's just the ones we know about. And after him, there are many more to come.

I followed him and learned that he lived in an apartment on the second floor, worked as a delivery man, and drove a beat-up old blue Ford Escape. The plan is simple. I'll wait for him in his parking lot, then use the taser. After that, we'll have a brand new trial, find him guilty, and administer the appropriate punishment.

I've been watching him for a while. Now, all the pieces are in place. If he follows past patterns, he'll arrive here at 7.05 p.m. This is Tuesday, so he'll have bought a small pizza from Mario's Pizza Palace around the corner. He'll park in the same spot. Hell, it has his apartment number on it. No brainer there. The spot next to his is usually vacant till after nine p.m. when the woman in apartment 305 arrives with her kid. As they say at NASA, it's a go.

At 7.07 p.m., the blue Escort turns the corner. It drives to its assigned spot, and he gets out. I'm parked beside him, facing outwards. He gets out carrying the pizza in his left hand and freezes when I hit him with the taser. I give him a good punch to the stomach, just in case, and he bends forward. I grab him by the hair and belt. Poof, he's in the back of the van. He's not hard to hogtie and hood. All's done in two seconds. Probably a rodeo record. Almost seemed too easy. Off we go.

I have a special place for him. Took me a week to prepare it, but I'm in the construction business. I'm very satisfied that this homemade dungeon will serve my purpose. I'm going to kill him in that basement. As a side bonus, I built a small gym beside the dungeon. I have to keep in shape and I do need the exercise to vent my emotions and keep me calm.

There's plastic all around, so no blood or DNA samples will be left, as I'll burn the plastic once I'm finished. The restraints are solid as hell. After I had tested them, I then doubled the screws in the ceiling and floor. Then, I set up the time-lapse camera. I put the remote by the door so I can easily and quickly activate the recording. Naturally, it's facing where the pervert will be hanging and dying soon. I've never done this before, but someone has to step up. These perverts are attacking our most vulnerable, our kids. And no one in power seems to care. It's all about the rights of the accused. The victim is an afterthought. No rights at all. I think that Nicky would be proud of what I'm doing.

By the time I get back to central control, I call it that to make myself feel good; it's really my house and garage. He was quiet the whole way. The ropes and tape have done their job. God bless duct tape. We enter the garage. I open the back door to the van and drag him out by his feet. There's a large thump when he falls off the end of the van's floor onto the cement. There's a loud moan or cry from his mouth. Too bad, pervert, the worse is yet to come.

He's not too big a man, so dragging him over the floor is easy. Plus, I have a ton of adrenaline pumping through me. He's a feather to my natural high. Into the special place we go. I hit the record button. I put on a hood. Then, as the directors in movie scenes say, "Action." I attached the pulley to his hand restraints and hoisted him up. His feet don't touch the floor. That's good. I don't want him to be comfortable.

I think about the children he's abused. I get madder. I think about his arrogant smile as he walked out of Court, smiling at all the reporters and spectators who had to watch this injustice. I get madder.

I can still see his grin as he walked passed the parents of some of the kids he murdered as they held each other, knowing that they were face to face with their children's murderer. And he was walking away, walking proud, a free man. I feel my face go red. If it's possible, I get even more enraged. There's thumping in my temples. I'm getting so mad; my blood pressure is peaking.

I walk around. I've talked myself into a frenzy. Over to his space I go literally screaming at him. In my hand is a small baseball bat. I use it on his legs, especially the knees. Next is the elbows. The swings have all the power I can generate. I'd be hitting home runs on any baseball field. They have all the power of my pent-up anger. I swing and swing. He screams and jerks non-stop. I'm so mad and swinging so hard that I forget to breathe. With this, my enragement has run out of energy, and I leave him there whimpering and crying. My shirt is wet with sweat. I'm panting heavily. Tomorrow, I will kill him. I leave the room as mad as I had entered, except that I am exhausted from punishing him. Tomorrow, one swing with the bat will do it. Maybe two, to be sure. He has to die.

Wednesday morning comes around. It's time. I go into the room. Turn on the camera. It smells terrible. He's still hanging where I left him. I can see that some of my strikes on his legs have bled. There's blood coming through his jeans and dripping on the floor. It's mixed with urine and stinks like hell. Pervert, that's what I have named him, has pissed and shit himself. He hears me coming and talks, then screams through the gag in his mouth. He's jerking himself around trying to get free; good luck with that, I say to myself. "Gonna run on broken legs?"

I stand in front of him, thinking of all the pain this person has caused. I think of the kids, the abuse, and the torture. Then, killing them. Not one of his victims ever survived; he killed them all. My anger returns.

I stand there for an hour, silent, thinking, building up hate, pushing myself to do it. He doesn't deserve to live. Kill him. Do the world a favor. Kill him now. But I can't do it. I accuse myself of cowardice, chickening out at the last minute. Am I really that spineless, that cowardly? I've been planning this for weeks, and now I'm??? I'm what? Not capable?

Then I think. "What the fuck am I going to do now?"

Chapter

VI

I've never killed anyone before. How can I start now with this helpless piece of shit? He deserves to die. No doubt about that, but can I be the executioner?

I have no doubt that I would kill to defend myself. I know that I would do whatever I had to do to keep me from getting discovered in this my latest enterprise. I'd do it to protect my wife and my family. But this is something else. Killing a helpless person, even if he is the devil incarnate. "I'll come back tomorrow," I say to myself. I give him a swing or two with the bat. Just to let him know I'm still around. Let him suffer a little longer. I'll look at some of the crime scene photographs of the kids he's killed. That'll motivate me for sure. Tomorrow, you die pervert. And I leave the room. The camera is still rolling; I click it off.

Thursday morning arrives much too fast. I know what I have to do today, and as much as I know it needs doing, I'm not sure that I'm up to it.

I looked at the photos last night. They were horrific. As I went through the albums, I felt myself sympathizing with the kids. The hate was already there, but my mind kept veering towards the kids. I'll admit it. I cried. First time in a long time. I shook my head and cried. But I still can't kill this guy. I can't use a bat, shoot, or strangle him. Nothing that requires me to physically act and cause his death. I just can't do it. So call me a coward. I'm just not made that way.

So what the fuck do I do now?

Chapter

VII

It took a little thinking, but I believe I've found a win-win solution. It may take a little longer than I originally planned, but that's OK. I don't have anywhere to go anyway. Ya, meets all the requirements, so let's put that plan in effect. I put the adjusted modifications in place and watched my revised plan produce results. Plan "B" is now in effect.

It really is a simple plan. I'll just let him hang there. I'll give him water, nothing else. We'll see what happens.

There's an advertisement somewhere that says even if you can build a better mouse trap, you need marketing to let the world know of your new fantastic invention. And so, with this idea in mind, I commence Section 2 of Plan 'B', getting the word out. I don't have to change that part.

I have dealt with Sacks in a manner I think was even better than my original plan. I've very carefully edited my video recording so that they will not reveal my place, my 'control center.' I'm ready to show the world and warn the perverts what awaits them when I come calling. Now, I have to go public. And to do that, I need a publicist.

There's a newscaster on Channel 6 who is well respected by all. Chet Smyth is a tall, good-looking guy who dresses well and has a charming personality. He reports the news as events and separates the news from his comments. He is fair and unbiased. And he has the 'voice' of an announcer. The 'right pipes' they call them. Just the man I need. But I know what I want him to do will not be easy. He does have a boss, and even if he agrees to broadcast my tape, his superiors may just say no. He needs a motivator, gentle but clear. That can be arranged.

The next day I am outside the Channel 6 studios. I know that he is on screen from 10:00 to 11:00 o'clock, just before bedtime. I sit outside the studio's parking lot and watch as the news crew leaves for the night. It's now about 11:45 in the evening. Mr. Smyth comes out with the gang. There's joking around and his laughs can easily be heard some distance away. He has a special voice that carries far. He gets into a shiny new BMW. I see that he drives well. Not too fast, always within the speed limit. He's a cinch to follow. It takes 26 minutes from the studio to his home, a split entrance with double doors located on a large lot. The job is done for the night.

The next morning, camera in hand, surveillance begins again, but this time, photos are taken of his twins and younger little girl, about 8 years old as they all board the school bus. The name of the school is written on the bus so I'll stop by later to grab a few photos of that as well.

In the meantime I wait for Mrs. Smyth to come out. I don't have to wait long. Ten minutes later, she comes out of the garage, driving a minivan and goes directly to the hospital. The camera is clicking every chance I get. She parks in the ICU employee parking spaces. As she gets out of the car, I can see that she is in a nurse's uniform. She enters the emergency door and goes off into an area I can't see. I stick around for a few minutes, then take a stroll inside. I see her at the triage counter doing paperwork for some kid who seems to be bleeding profusely from the forehead. His mother seems very anxious to get to a doctor. More photos and off to the school I go and the day's work is done.

It's time to put the package together.

It's all done. I'm ready for delivery. It consists of three parts. There's the video of Pervert and his ultimate fate as part one. Part two is a simple video/photo montage of Smyth's lovely family. Then, there's a letter written and addressed to Mr. Smyth with instructions that the video contained in part one should be aired on his station. I've gone into great detail about why I want this done and have only slightly threatened his wife and kids. I plead with him to place himself in the shoes of the parents who have lost children to this sicko and to try and imagine how he would feel if it was one of his kids. I'm confident that this will be a good incentive for Mr. Smyth to do as I have asked. Maybe 'asked' is a little too gentle. I demanded his cooperation and threatened his family if he didn't cooperate. I'm sure he'll understand.

I put the instructions as to what I wanted done with Part One towards the end of Mr. Smyth's letter. He is to broadcast the video on air. I have allowed them to warn the general public that this video contains footage that will not be suitable for all viewers and that small children should not be allowed to see it. I suggested a Friday or Saturday night broadcast, but other arrangements were acceptable. It should be played after 10. P.M. when kids are supposed to be in bed. I've indicated in my letter that I am very reasonable and flexible in how they warn the public and give them the liberty of the final arrangements. The one and only area that I am not so reasonable is that the video has to be played in its entirety. After all, it took me some time to edit the hours of video I had it down into a thirty-minute sequence.

As a means of communication between Mr. Smyth and myself, I created a British email address for him and included the password. This will be our only means of exchanging dialogue. I should probably have used a Russian or Chinese email service instead of a British one, but I don't really think that it will go that far. After a computer search for free email servers, the British site was the first to come up, so I used it.

I've taken all precautions so that there is nothing in the package that would help the police identify me if it should ever come to that. I am concerned about my security. But really, I don't expect it to go that far. I couriered the package as "Private and Confidential" to the attention of Mr. Chet Smyth and waited for a response.

I can feel my anger generating positive results. "I'm doing something to better the world."

It was quiet at the end of the operation. Everything that required doing had been done, so I had some time on my hands. It was early in the morning, around 9:30 a.m. when I left my control center. I decided to watch the TV studio.

I set up in a secure, quiet place with easy visibility on the front doors and the parking lot. Surveillance around here was easy. A hot cup of coffee helped keep me alert, but it was very quiet in a normal kind of way. Luck was on my side. As I watched the front doors, the courier service I had used arrived, and the uniformed agent went inside. So now I knew my package had been delivered.

By my calculations, it took exactly seventy-five minutes for Smyth to read the letter, view the two videos, talk to his boss and then call the cops. They arrived in a hurry exactly seventy-five minutes after the delivery. I left my parking spot and slowly made my way back to the control center. "What the fuck am I going to do now?

Chapter

VIII

I hung around the center for an hour or so, trying to figure out what I was going to do now. To help release the stress from having my plan subverted, I went to my gym area to work off Smyth's betrayal. It's not good to make important decisions when the emotions are high. Remember 'Panic and Die.' I got going on the elliptical machine and worked till it was hot. The dead weights clanged together as I lifted, then dropped, lifted, then dropped. After a little over an hour I felt I was calmed down enough to start thinking correctly. The first action must be to assess the situation. Good Army training.

I went over to the internet cafe located near the university. It's a good distance from my home. I checked the email address I had given him, nothing. There were no notes from him. I fired off an angry email to Smyth. I accused him of being responsible for the death of any child abducted by a sicko. He was responsible for their torture and deaths.

In reality, I had no idea what I was going to do now. I had committed crimes, murder, for fuck sake. I'd gone to great lengths to right the world, sacrificed my life for the betterment of humanity by ridding it of this one sicko with the promise of more to come. How could he not see the purity and righteousness of my cause? I finished with a note of how disappointed I was in him and then signed off. I won't be back to this site. I could feel my anger rising. "What the fuck is wrong with people? This guy, above all others, deserved to die. I did it. I did it for you and all of the other parents who don't want to see their kids abducted and murdered. Can't you help just a little bit?" The anger was rising.

I pondered for a long time on what I was to do now. The initial shock of the turn of events had subsided, and I was looking for a way to save my project. As I said, I've done some serious crimes, and if I'm caught, I'll be in prison for a long, long time. If there is anything that the Courts hate worse than a child abuser, it's someone who does their job for them. To them, a vigilante is worse than ten murderers because it shows the shortfalls in the justice system, and they are the ones responsible for maintaining and enforcing the laws; thus, the blame falls on them. Never a good thing to be a caught vigilante in front of a judge.

Criminals are stupid people. That's why the cops catch them. And now, I have to include myself in with the dumbest of them all. How could I have been so naive, so stupid? The cops here must have contact with England and would not have too much trouble tracing my email to Smyth. Interpol, for god's sake. Russia or China would have been just as easy, but the English site came up first on my internet search, so I used it. Dumb.

And thinking that the cops would not investigate this properly because of who the victim was, well, that wasn't too bright either. A murder is a murder. They'll try to trace it down and catch the murderer. Not taking the precautions I knew I should have taken may cost me years in jail. At my age, I'll come out in a box. Dumber

On the other hand, my optimistic side sees the situation differently. I did use a bit of personal security and so now I'm left wondering if it was sufficient. I nabbed Sacks fast enough, and I don't think anyone saw me. He lives alone, so who's going to report him missing? Well, I guess I'll find out soon enough. If my door comes smashing in, I'll know I fucked up. So, in the meantime, I'll go ahead trying to get publicity for my work. Whatever it is that I am going to do has to be done with more of my self-preservation in mind. I'm going to stop using that traitor Smyth as my public voice and the British email is out. A little research has shown me how to use anonymisers, to hide the real identity of anyone. They are free to download and use. I practiced by sending myself messages, and they seem really simple to operate, and if the security they provide is real, well I'm a happy camper. I am concerned that the cops can bypass or, in some other way, find out who's behind an anonymizer message, so I'll use a Russian or Chinese email server just to make their work a little more difficult.

Then, I assigned Smyth to a Russian email service. New communication protocol. I believe that the British email was my biggest mistake. Now it's been fixed. I also intend to be more careful when dealing with the future. I don't know what or how yet, but I'll think of something. That something has to be secure and safe for me. I guess time will tell how successful I'll be…or not.

Smyth's email was on the TV station's website. I sent him a new message bitching about his lack of cooperation. I didn't get an answer.

I was calmer now, but a solution to my dilemma still eluded me. Obviously, Smyth was not going to help. My situation was even made worse because now I knew that the cops were involved and that they would be investigating. After all, they were part of the justice system, too. Vigilantes were not welcome. So much for avoiding the police spotlight.

It took me a while to realize two things. One. Maybe the cops weren't looking too hard for me. Every press conference they gave they seemed less and less aggressive in their search. Maybe my security measures were efficient and effective. Were they running out of leads, or were they just losing interest in a file they really didn't want to do anyway? Wow, that would be great. Or were they just hiding the truth, and their investigation was still ongoing? I had no way of knowing or even finding out, so I let that idea die.

Two, I would need a motivator to force them into action. The death of a scum bag wasn't enough. The disappearance of Sacks had hardly made the news. It had to be more, something that would get the public's sympathy, a public outcry for more aggressive action. When the idea first struck me, I dismissed it as being too harsh, too dangerous for me, and too extreme. After hashing it over in my mind, I realized that my life was on the line here. I had already gone the distance. Nothing I could or would do would be too extreme. Unnecessary violence was out. Had to be something the public sympathizes with. This has to be done with a minimum of force. I have to get the public on my side. Otherwise, the second abduction becomes the story. I don't want that.

The next question comes a little easier. Who or what does the public have the most sympathy for? Someone that would be a good target for me and raise public awareness of Pervert and his friends and the harm they do... A handicapped person? No, too much chance of harming them passed their injury. A child? No fucking way. A politician? No. They always have some sort of security around them and the chance of a violent confrontation is likely. Someone from the clergy? No, he'll try and save my soul and probably talk me to death. Again, it diverts the focus away from these perverts. No, go. A soccer mom? Well, the public does love these people. Kidnapping one would not be too difficult. It would sure get a lot of attention. So the question is, would it be enough to force the authorities to broadcast my video? Yes, I think so. Put a plan together, and from now on, be very careful. No stupid movements. Play smart.

The plan develops. I need a place to keep this lady while the authorities come around to my way of thinking. I'll refer to her as a lady to help keep me focused. I have to build a secure but comfortable room. Food in the required quantities for her and for me. I see myself spending a lot of time in hiding with her while the wheels of official justice turn. They turn really slow.

I need a safe place to grab her, something without security cameras or old ones that don't work so well. Something analogue. I know the perfect place. It's a run-down strip mall over on Broadway. It has a tattoo parlor and a couple of other fly-by-night operations, but the anchor is a large food mart. Ideal place for moms.

The van will work ok, but I'll have to liberate a new set of license plates. No problem there. The color is everyday dark blue. There is a zillion of these on the road. They all look the same. Transportation arranged.

After what seems like an eternity of thinking, planning, and arguing with myself, I realize that this abduction will go down just like the original one. Except that in the first one, I didn't care if I hurt my prey. This time, gentle force will be required. It is more the after times that will be different. Lucky for her.

I had used a plumbing service to help disguise my truck during the first kidnapping so I'll use the same signage this time. Speaking of the last kidnapping, I haven't heard a word about my last victim. Nothing on the news about him missing. The cops must know by now that he's dead and gone. My video would prove that. Wonder if they'll throw a party for him. Of course, him being dead and all, he won't be attending. Sometimes, I roll over at my own jokes. Back to the real world, everything seems to be coming along well.

The preparations are complete, and it's time to act.

I know what I'm going to do now.

Chapter

IX

I detach myself from my mind and body and hoover over the operation like I was an announcer on TV describing a baseball or football game. I believe that thinking like this will help me remain objective and hopefully warn me of any mistakes or miscalculations I may have made. I imagine this as having a partner, even a guardian angel, watching over me. He will keep me safe. And with that comforting thought in mind, I started to announce my own activities.

He drives the van into the shopping center parking lot. It is detailed in the way he hopes to avoid detection. Last week, when he did his initial survey to make sure there hadn't been any improvements to the camera/security system, the van was totally nondescript. This time, the vehicle is all dressed up, with new plates and plumbing info on the sides, and ready for the capture. His camouflage is great; initially, it took hours of research and preparation. He laughs at himself. Today, according to the truck, he's a plumber working for *Brian's Plumbing and Service.*

There really is a Company by this name and they do have an office on the west side of town. Only he doesn't know one end of a plunger from another. No, he's just a tired, angry, pissed-off loner frustrated at how the system works—or, in his parlance, doesn't work. Today is step 3 in the correction of these injustices. At least, he hopes so, but whatever the outcome, he will have tried to change something,

something that really should have been corrected a long time ago. And if he dies trying, well, he did his best, and fuck the rest.

He drives over towards the entrance, where he can see everyone coming in. It's very important that he gets the right person. Pick up a nobody and the whole scheme falls apart. Patience and observation are important. He becomes a watcher. It takes about 45 minutes, but here she comes. A mom in a minivan. Stickers on the back window indicate three children and a dog. Typical. She drives into the nearest parking spot, gets out of the van, and walks quickly towards the grocery store, clicking her keys to lock the van behind her. Now, he thinks, "Luck has to be with me." He waits impatiently at a discrete distance. It is not long before an old guy arrives with his cart and loads the trunk of an older-style Ford parked directly beside ' Mom's' van. The older guy then backs up and leaves his spot.

The watcher slowly drives into the vacated space. He puts on his hat and sunglasses, covers his arms, and grabs his shopping bags full of last week's newspaper, all crimped up to make the bags look full. The watcher becomes the hunter. He leaves his vehicle, parked beside the 'mom's' van, and walks slowly towards the store, discretely looking around and watching for 'mom' Pedestrian traffic is light today. He doesn't have to wait long. He barely gets halfway to the main doors when he sees her coming out, almost running towards her van. He falls in step behind her, keeping pace with her near jogging advance. She arrives at the van and slides open the driver's side back door to place the groceries on the back seat. He arrives as she is halfway in the vehicle, arranging the groceries. His side door is electronically controlled, and the one closest to his target is opening. She does not notice this. Her ass is half out. Great target. As she arranges her bags, He pulls out his taser and shocks her in the upper thigh. She shakes, not vibrates, as the volts pass through her. Before she can recover, he's on her and grabs the belt on her jeans and, through the blue blouse, grabs the back bra strap and throws her gently into the back of his truck. He is strong. He looks around. The whole capture took less than three seconds. No one seems the wiser. By the time he's looked around outside, inside she's stopped shaking. He hogties her arms behind her back, a hood and gag go over the head, and duct tape keeps her from kicking. On the outside of the hood, he wraps tape around her mouth to limit the screaming that he knows will start any minute now. He grabs her food and throws it in beside her. The next small step is to close up her van and lock the doors. It wouldn't do to have her doors wide open. This would cause suspicion from the next passing shopper. Closed-locked doors are best. "There are criminals everywhere, "he mumbles to himself. "Can never be too careful". The scene is cleaned up to his satisfaction, and he slowly drives out of the parking lot and heads for home. Phase three is successfully complete.

Now, he has to get her to the hideout, which he still prefers to call his control center. It is from here that the plan was developed and directed. Most of the activity will take place from here now that he's got his catalyst. That's what she is. Doing nothing but causing something to happen. Driving at the exact speed limit and making complete stops, he arrives at the control center, opens the electric garage door, drives in, and disappears from the world.

Chapter

X

Pam was in a hurry. As usual, she had ten things to do with time for only five. She had to pick up the oranges for her daughter's soccer team. It was their turn to supply the fruit at the end of the game. That meant she had to be at the field by four o'clock. It was only two fifteen, so she figured she had plenty of time and would get some of the groceries she needed at home to feed those growing boys who really seemed impossible to fill with food. "Robbie, the eldest, was the worst. It seemed that whenever she saw him. He was chewing on something. Carl, the younger brother was growing so fast, he was going to pass his mother in height pretty soon." That took a lot of groceries. "Well, she thought to herself, at least we can afford it." They eat nonstop like one of those 24-hour car races. Never ending," she thought. She was convinced that eleven and thirteen-year-old boys could, in fact, eat a horse if they could get the beast to stay still long enough. But they were healthy, doing well in school and they were her pride and joy. Off she went to get the food.

"Wow, lucky me," she said as she drove into the lot. A spot opened up right in front of her, not too far from the door. "Another few minutes saved," she thought. Locking the doors to her van, "There are thieves everywhere," she thought as she made her way inside. The aisles were clear, so she was able to use her high gear through the store. More luck when she saw cashiers waiting for her. She was out in record time.

As she approached her van, she noticed that some asshole had parked very close to her own van and that maneuvering between them would be tight. But she was able to do so without too much inconvenience. She opened the back door and was putting the bags inside on the seat when intense pain ran through her. She couldn't move. Flashes of lighting, thunderous pain in her lower back, uncontrollable shaking she couldn't stop." What's happening?" "I don't understand." Then there was someone grabbing her jean belt and her bra. He lifted her out without any problem and threw her into that truck or van the asshole had parked. Still shaking and in total confusion, she lay on the floor. Commands to her limbs were going unanswered. Whoever had thrown her into the asshole's vehicle came in with a hat and sunglasses. He tied her hands, placed a hood and gag over her head, and then tied her feet. By the time she was thinking at least a little bit straight, it was too late. She was a prisoner to some sicko. When this realization came to her, she started to shake again, cry and the tears flowed freely. She tried to talk, no beg, but something was blocking her mouth, and only gibberish came out. "I'm going to be raped and murdered. She thought. My kids, Tom, my husband, what are they going to do? I don't want to die. Please, Please, please," she mumbled through the gag. No answers, just the forward movement of the van. She rolled over and started kicking the side of the van. "Please, someone, hear me. I need help from this crazy." But by this time, the van was rolling along at a good speed. No one could or would hear her pleas. She was doomed.

The drive continued. Her mind was getting clearer now. She'd been kidnapped by a rapist and probably a murderer as well. "Well,' she thought, "I'm not going down without a fight. I'll do whatever I have to beat this guy; this asshole is gonna pay dearly. Keep calm and be ready."

Chapter

XI

Back to him and his over view buddy keeping tabs on everything. He used to call it a truck, but I guess a van is more accurate. It was a Company vehicle that someone used for work, getting material, meeting potential clients, etc.

The van rolls quietly into the garage. He is alone there, and inside the van, it's very quiet. She had made a lot of noise at the beginning, mumbling something totally incoherent but it was easy to guess what she was saying. Then she'd been quiet for a bit then started kicking the side of the van. By the time she tried that trick, he was rolling along at a good but legal pace. No one would ever hear her. He felt a certain sympathy for her. She was, after all, an innocent victim. He had not planned to kidnap anybody else. He had who he wanted and dealt with that situation. He had made a plan and then carried it out. It should have been easy.

The problem was that the damn TV station and the Authorities wouldn't cooperate. All he wanted them to do was play the video he'd made of his revenge, of his attempt to put society straight again. But no. Too sanctimonious to show real justice at work. Well, they'll listen now. His anger is simmering.

He shut the motor off and opened the door to the special room. It had taken him three weeks to build but it did meet all of his requirements. It was, of course, totally soundproof and had all the comforts of a small apartment. Laughing to himself, he said, "I could probably get a couple of hundred bucks a month for this place if I rented it to a student.". He looked at the van. His prisoner was very quiet inside. "She's probably going come out swinging," he thought. Better give her just enough distance to let the kicks or punches hit nothing but empty air.

He opened the back doors of the van slowly. She was more or less where he had thrown her. She was curled up in a fetal position, legs facing him. He took out his knife and cut the tape holding the feet together. "Don't try anything stupid," he says. No response. He grabbed her by the foot and pulled. She slid easily over the plastic covered metal floor, put there to help avoid later DNA proof that she was ever in this van. He intends to torch it anyway, but you can't be too careful. As her legs passed the ledge of the van's floor, she took a wild kick towards where she thought he was. Total miss. The kick was so hard that her entire body followed through, and she rolled over from the force of her efforts onto her stomach. A sob came from beneath the hood. He stepped towards her and gave her a hard slap on the ass. Then he pulled her up onto her feet. More kicking, but still in vain. He was able to dodge them all and did so with a small chuckle.

His hand went into her blond hair, and he pulled her forward and down. "There'll be no more of that nonsense," he said. Shaking her head, he asked, "Do you understand?" There was a whimper that he assumed was agreement. He released her hair, took her by the arm in a gentle but firm grip, and led her toward the room.

The door opened silently, and they passed through without any issues. She seemed to be cooperating. "There's a chair behind you; stand still." He re-taped her feet together and cut her hands free. Any swing she might take would be harmless. But she tried anyway. But by the time she took it, he had moved from her side to the front and watched as her closed fist swung at him and into thin air, striking hard at nothingness. With a raised hand, he gave her a small finger push to her chest, and she crashed into the chair.

Her hands were attached to the chair's arms. She was secure again. Time to have a short talk and give her time to cool down. "Do you hear me?"

She shook her head, indicating that she understood.

"Do you know where you are?"

A shaking head indicated no.

He removed the mouth gag, leaving the hood to sit free.

"More importantly, do you know why you're here?"

"You're gonna rape and kill me. That's what all you asshole sickos do, isn't it?'

"Not going to happen. I promise you here and now that you will not be raped or even touched inappropriately. You definitely won't be murdered. In about seven to ten days, I'll release you to your family, and this will all be an ugly memory, but you're going to help me. You just don't know how yet".

"Fuck you, asshole."

He continued, despite the interruption, "You're in a room that I built. It is very soundproof, so it saves your voice. There's only one way in and one way out, and I have the key. You can try if you want, but I'll see you on the cameras and you'll just be wasting your time. There's food in the fridge, and you'll find a bathroom and a TV for you to watch while I do what I have to do."

Then he notices that she has gone limp, whining or crying. He can't determine which, but she is quiet, and that, after all, is what he wants. He wants her attention so he can talk to her. "In a moment, I'm going to cut the tape on your hands, and you'll be free to undo your feet. Now listen carefully do not take the hood off your head until you hear the door close and the lock click. Then you can remove it. Understand?"

A nodding head said, "Yes."

Chapter

XII

Pam lay in the back of the van. She was totally incapacitated. Arms were tied tight behind her, so no punching or scratching, and feet attached, so no kicking. "I'm helpless," she resigned. But this fight isn't over. He's got to move me, strip me to get what he wants. Somewhere there, I'll have my chance, and I'll make him pay. The cops must be looking for me by now. What about my kids? I'm supposed to be at the soccer field. Who'll bring the oranges? Why is he doing this to me?" Fear leads to questions. Questions lead to Confusion. Confusion leads nowhere. She was still tied up in the back of a van moving along now at a good pace. Then it stopped. Pam could hear the rolling up of a garage door. Then, the van advanced. "Get ready," she thought. He's got to move me now. This is my chance.

The van stopped, and the back door opened. A strong hand grabs Pam by the shoe and cuts the tape. He pulls her towards the doors. She slides easily over plastic. As she feels her legs arrive at the back door she's careful to listen to figure out where he is. He makes a small grunting sound as he pulls on her foot. The foot is released. "Now you're going to get it" she thinks and swings her leg with all her might towards the grunting sound. "Nothing, God, I missed nothing." The force of her attempt causes her whole body to rotate and she ends up stomach down on the rear edge of the truck. Then she feels it. A slap on the ass. "Are you serious?" she thinks to herself. "You fucken sicko."

"No more of that' nonsense.' he yells in my ear. Who is this guy to be talking to me like that? He's going to rape and kill me, and he's talking to me like I'm ten years old" I drive my head towards the sound of his voice. I try to bite him through the hood. I miss.

"Are you trying to bite me? Through the hood?" His hand is then in my hair, and he pulls me down and forward. I stumble along beside him, always off balance, until he finally stands me up straight. We enter a room. Then he retapes my feet and then cuts my hands free. Another chance, and the swing goes out hard and fast into mid-air. :" Fuck" I say to myself, "Missed." There isn't much time between the punch that fingers arrive on my upper chest, and a gentle push sends me flying backward, and I trip into the chair. Arms are immediately taped to the chair. "Fuck again," I say quietly. "Then he starts talking to me like we're buddies, that he's not going to rape and or murder me: that I'll be home again in ten days?" When I took the wild swing at him, nothing, no negative reaction, and the push, ya, the push. It was soft. He didn't punch me, didn't grab a boob, or even push on a boob. And that slap on the ass when I tried to kick him, what's all that about? Who the hell is this guy? Is he just playing with me? I'm captured by a real sickie. What's he got in store for me? Oh God, pray for me to keep him away." I'm not a religious person, but I start to call on God for help. "My kids," I whimper. "My kids," and with the realization of the hopelessness of my situation, tears return. Soft, silent tears of desperation and terror. I'm starting to realize that my situation is desperate approaching hopeless. I don't have much chance of surviving this.

Chapter

XIII

The tension and fright of the last couple of hours finally catches up to Pam. As she sits tied in the chair, fatigue and fear start to work their way into her mind. With the realization of the hopelessness of her predicament, she starts sobbing uncontrollably. She hears only pieces of his little speech. "Don't worry, you're going home". She thinks that he is only tormenting me with false hope. He's torturing me. Then he grabs her arm. "Oh no, He's starting." and he cuts the tape on her hand and then nothing. There's no contact. She can hear him walking away, and then she's alone. She works the tape free and removes the hood. Her feet are still taped, but she quickly loosens them finally freeing herself totally. Rubbing her wrists, she looks around her prison cell.

The lights are bright; there's a TV playing behind a Plexiglas screen, a small sofa, and a bed off in the corner. The fridge is in a small enclave, along with a hot plate and microwave. "What the fuck?" She feels like she's in a student's apartment. Then she sees it, them, the cameras on the walls in the corners. She counts four of them, red lights blinking. She's being watched. "Well, he's not going to get a show from me. Screw you, asshole," she says, but only in her mind. She raises her middle finger. "So far, he hasn't hurt me, so let's not give him reason to until I have a real chance to escape. Then bang, make him pay and get the hell outta here wherever here is." She stays put, pondering. She's fluctuating between anger and fear.

Chapter

XIV

There's an acronym for some Police forces. It's called "RAD" or, more precisely, "Retired on Active Duty." As a cop approaches his retirement, he gets transferred to the "Cold Case" squad. His new job here is to review old files to see if there are any leads that could be discovered because of a new eye looking at the evidence. With the advent of DNA analysis and other scientific advancements, many unsolved crimes were being resolved. Really, it is a kind of thank you from the bosses for years of service. So it serves two purposes: thank you to nearly retired cops and puts an experienced eye on some old files that may have leads that were missed.

Detective Sergeant Donald O'Harris and Detective Sergeant Michael Ashley had gone through the academy together. Their paths had rarely crossed during their twenty-four and some years of service, but as classmates do, they keep in touch with each other. Both were divorced, a common thing among police officers. O'Harris had spent his recent years on the Major Crime Unit while Ashley had been with the organized gang intelligence squad. Barely six weeks apart, had they joined the other three RAD comrades.

Their first day that they were working together gave them a huge surprise. "Holy fuck" was the comment from O'Harris. Ashley just stared and laughed. "Thank the chief for this." Files nearly two feet high were waiting for them. Everything from old murders, assaults, and B&Es to missing people files, some torn, dirty, and earmarked from repeated reviews. Still motivated to serve and protect as best they could, they started with the top file. The bond was re-established very quickly. A murder of a prostitute twenty-three years ago. No physical evidence at the scene. She was found beaten to death in the back of the bar she frequented. No prints, no semen, no body hair, and no blood. No chance to solve this one.

Off to number two and so on till boredom doth you part. The job was to look for something different, something others may have overlooked. Look for something else, some clue that was hidden. Is there a possibility that new investigative methods can be used in this file? Look, weigh and think, look, weigh and think. There may be something there. Well, that chance was about to come.

Chapter

XV

He watched her for about forty minutes. She didn't leave the chair. She sat there looking around and did a double take when she noticed the cameras. "Did he really see her give him the finger? Oh well, let her have her moment of pushback. No harm to me."

He had been dozing, snoring quietly when she finally got up and walked towards the bed. He could hear her footsteps on the floor, so the mike was working well. Sleep had eluded him since he had executed this part of his plan and dispatched Sacks. The memory of the begging, the screaming in pain, and the final outcome, which he had planned well in advance, had kept him awake for many nights. He knew that there would be a psychological cost to himself but felt he had to do it anyway. His anger was being fed. This is a good thing. "Right?" he asked himself.

This plan was supposed to be so much simpler. There was the communication with the reporter at that dam TV station and their refusal to help. "I don't understand why they wouldn't help."

"Wasn't this like a public service announcement?" Then cops got involved, and the final refusal was to announce to all the weirdos and sickies of the world that there was someone who would bring justice to them. "And I am coming after you, perverts. "

He was sure now that she was asleep. The breathing pattern and the slow rise and fall of the blanket told him she had finally passed out. Probably all the stress and shock she had endured.

He'd been having the same problem. Visions of Sacks twisting body and screams replayed in his mind's eye. And then there was the disposal of the body and the clean up afterwards. That wasn't a cakewalk, either. A small taste of fifty percent proof rum might help him. He took a mouthful and curled up on his old army cot and tried to relax, perhaps to sleep and hope the nightmares disappear.

The over-the-counter sleeping aid combined with the rum seems to have done its job. He wakes up refreshed with only a slight headache. She seems to be moving around. He can't see the monitor from where he is, but the speaker is telling him that there is movement inside the room.

He goes over to the monitor and can see that she is over in the kitchen area, apparently making herself a coffee. "Good idea," he says to himself. He gets his peculator going and returns to the seat in front of the monitor. He watches her for a few minutes. Everything is quiet. She really is a good-looking woman. She's big but proportional, almost Viking-like. She must be five foot six or seven, with naturally blond hair and those eyes. They are not just blue; they sparkle blue, like a White Mountain glacier in full sunlight. He fantasizes that they are playing a little 'slap and tickle' together and that he could even force her to play. But these little intimate games are only fun when both parties are playing. To force this on her wouldn't be fun at all. And besides, anything like this happening to her would change the focus of the publicity he is seeking. The media would talk about the rape and not the elimination of a cancerous part of the human collective. But she sure is a good-looking woman. She must have some Nordic blood in her family tree. He comes back to reality. Is she adjusting too well?" he thinks. "I have to be careful with this one."

Chapter

XVI

Pam wakes up with a start. She doesn't know where she is. Confusion. As consciousness returns, she remembers. Her predicament is real. It's not just a bad dream. She lays still in bed. "I don't want him to know that I'm awake." She starts taking inventory. I've been kidnapped. I'm locked in a room and I don't have any idea of where I am. It's not too far from home; we only drove for about twenty-five minutes after he grabbed me. He's exceptionally strong. He picked me up like I weighed nothing but was gentle when handling me. He didn't retaliate when I tried to kick or punch him, and his hand on my arm when he brought me in here was firm, but "I think it was gentle as well. "Is it possible to be gentle and a monster?"

Then there's the short conversation he had with me. I didn't get to talk a lot, but what he said. "Is it possible he's telling the truth that he will return me home?" Or is he just fucking with me, giving me false hope so I won't try to escape, not give him any trouble:" Well, asshole, I'm going to give you all the trouble I can." Then, more morbid thoughts entered her thinking. He's going to rape and kill me. Given the extent that he has gone to with this room, he's not going to kill me soon. But the rape could go on for days. Wasn't there a recent case where the kidnapper kept his victim for years? He's already started with the psychological torture with the promise of going home. His tormenting is just beginning. He plans to keep me here for a while. "Oh God, I'm in hell. I'm going to die here." Tears return, and she weeps silently into the blanket. "I don't want him to know I'm awake."

"I don't want to die."

Finally, thirst and hunger get the best of Pam. She rolls over and looks at the cameras and then the kitchen area. The cameras are still blinking red. She's being watched. He said something about food in the fridge, so I'll have a look. Pam walks over to the fridge and opens the doors. She repels in fright. There on the shelves are the groceries she bought yesterday, so long ago. The oranges for the soccer team are prominent on the top shelf. There's bread, butter, and that blueberry jam that Robbie loves. "He stole my groceries too, the bastard."

Along with the stolen goods were bacon, eggs, milk, and a wide assortment of food. Pam stared into the fridge. "Christ, there's enough food here to feed an army." Then it hit her. "How long does he intend to keep me here?" There's easily a month's supply.' He lied to me about returning home soon." "No, he's going to keep me a long, long time before he kills me." The hunger was gone. "I'm going to die here." Pam returned to the bed and sat down. The quiet was unnerving.

Chapter

XVII

Outside he was watching her. She lay there for a while. He knows that she's awake. Her breathing has changed, but she's not moving. He can hear it on the mike. "Wonder what surprise she has in store for me today." A little chuckle.

She finally gets up and looks at the cameras. "No middle finger this time. Maybe that's progress."

He noticed her double take when she opened the fridge. "What caused that?" he thought to himself. Hell, it's the food she bought. What can be wrong with it? Plus, I put a little bit of everything, stuff people eat all the time. Bacon, eggs, sugar milk, what the fuck does she want?" Time for our chat.

He keys the mic on the desk, activating the speaker in the room. "Pam," he says, "It's time for our talk. I want you to put the hood on and go sit in the chair. You're to put your head down and look at the floor. I'll come in and tie you to the chair for our talk. Please don't do anything stupid that will cause me to harm you or have to punish you afterward. Do you understand?"

"Yes." He then sees her place the hood over her head and sit in the chair. This is a critical time. If she's going to try something, this will be her best shot. Proceed with extreme caution. He plays some music into the intercom system. This will hide my approach to her. She won't hear me coming.

He unlocks the door, puts on his own hood, and places the extra in his back pocket. She's sitting in the chair as instructed. The hood is on, and the head is down. So far, so good. He re-locks the double deadbolt on the door and puts the keys back around his neck. She doesn't move. He walks up behind the chair as quietly as possible. The music is hiding his approach. She is quite agile, so he has to be careful.

He draws near her from behind, puts his left hand on the hood, and seizes it along with a tuff of her hair. "Don't move," he says. Tape is used to secure her arms to the chair. He releases the hood and her hair. "Close your eyes and don't open them till I say it's OK, understand? "Keep looking at the floor." In one swift movement, he yanks her hood off and replaces it with a new one. Just in case, she put a hole in the hood in the room. Once her hood is secure, he removes his own and pulls up another chair to sit beside but towards Pam's back. He can easily talk into her ear.

"Ok," we have to talk about you, me, and why you're here. You're going to have questions, and we can have a kind of dialogue. Is that OK with you?'

"Ok"

"So, let's start at the beginning. Ok? We're going to be together for a week or so, so first, tell me about yourself. I want to know more about you."

"What? What do you want to know?"

"Where were you born, where did you go to school, your favorite pet, how you met your husband, your first kiss. I want to know everything."

"Did you have a nickname as a child?"

"Why?'

"Just call it personal curiosity."

"Do you do this with all of the women you kidnap?"

"Well, you're the first, so congratulations on that, but please tell me.

Thinking what choice do I have but to listen to you, asshole, and the more he talks to me, the less he's going to abuse me. Talk on asshole. These words are only in her mind. She pretends to listen attentively.

Outwardly, she agrees with a little anticipation in her voice. He catches this and wonders what it means. But whatever, he continues with his questioning of her past.

"I was born in Chicago, I met my husband at university, and we never had pets 'cause we lived in the city; why do you want to know this stuff?"

"I'd like to get to know you better. I understand that the way we met isn't the ideal way to make friends, but I'd like to make up for the rude introduction we had."

"Is he out of his fucking mind? A rude introduction," she says to herself. Outwardly and with an increasing voice of exasperation, "Are you serious? You fucken tasered me. Tied me up and brought me here against my will. Now you're going to rape and kill me, and you want to chit-chat. Know that I don't want to be here. I want you to leave me alone. I want to go home." Finally, in a more calm voice, she whispered, "my nickname was Tubby."

"Tubby?" he says as a question. "I'll bet those guys are kicking their asses now."

"Why? What do you mean?"

"Well, you're the ugly duckling."

"I don't understand. What are you talking about?"

"Well, you were overweight as a kid and bloomed into a good-looking woman."

"I'm just a normal woman. Nothing exceptional about me. I look like a thousand other moms."

"No. You're not, but anyway, continue. Sorry for having interrupted you."

"Ya, when I was younger, I was a little overweight. So what. Does that mean I can go home now?

He can tell that this conversation is not what he had hoped for but something he half expected. "Had to try and put her at ease anyway."

"Well," he says," Later we'll talk about your kids, what they do, you know, that general shit. We'll be having a lot of these little chats. I like hearing them. I don't get to talk to a lot of people. Now, so much for small talk. Let's get to the real reason you're here."

"Do you know who Jermery Sacks is?" he asks.

"No, I don't think so. I've never heard that name." Now that she's started talking, questions fly out of her mouth. "Are you going to rape me? And then kill me afterward? How long are you going to keep me here? You have enough food in the fridge for an army. You said you were going to let me go? When? I want to go home now. Why are you doing this to me? I don't even know you. I haven't seen your face, so I can't identify you. I don't know who Gerry Sacks is. Please, I want to go home?" As she starts to talk, the nervousness and fear come out, and words fly faster and faster from her mouth until her words are nothing but mumble jumble, totally incoherent. As she runs out of breath, her voice fades, and she breaks down in tears and frustration.

"Wow, that was quite a mouth full." He gives her a moment to recuperate then continues as if she had just answered his question in a totally normal fashion. No need to get her even more excited than she is. It might blow a gasket. Then I'd have to start all over again. No thanks.

"So, to answer your questions, one at a time. No, I'm not going to rape or even abuse you sexually. That would nullify the focus of this plan. People would remember that and not remember why I'm doing all this. Murder is out of the question. I can't murder someone in cold blood. I thought I could, but it ended up otherwise. In a way, and because I can't do that, kill someone, that is, that's why you ended up here. So forget that idea that I'm going to harm or kill you. It's not going to happen."

"As far as how long I intend to keep you here, I think about a week, ten days at the most. It all depends on how the Police and media react to my demands. The faster they do what I want, the sooner you'll get to hug your kids. In the meantime, you'll be well treated; you'll have all the food you need and the TV to watch. You noticed the cameras in the room here. Yes, they watch you 24/7, and everything is recorded, so I can go back to see whatever. But I promise you that there are no cameras in the toilet and shower area. You can wash without me seeing you, BUT" he raised his voice to empathize" if I catch you abusing this privacy thing, there will be consequences, very unpleasant for you. Understand?"

"Yes"

"And I'm going to need some help from you to make this kidnapping look serious. Are you gonna cooperate?

"Yes, of course," out loud but silently. "What choice do I have, asshole." said silently.

Well, that was a little too fast he thinks. But we'll see when the time comes. Let her play her games as long as I get what I want and need.

"Can I get back to my story now?"

"Ok, but I don't understand how I'm involved in any of this. I don't know, Barry whatshisname" I wanna go home" in a pleading voice.

"If you let me finish my story, you'll see how you're involved. Please stop with the questions. Just listen. We have plenty of time to talk later." There was no response from her. Quiet at last. So he continues.

"His name is not Barry or Gerry; it's Jeremy, Jeremy Sacks. And he's a child rapist and murderer. He's abused and killed at least eleven children that the authorities know of. How many more he attacked, we will probably never know. But he's dead now, so the question is moot. But four months ago, he was freed because of a stupid justice system and some incompetent cops. Well, maybe they weren't incompetent, but the system forced them to do things in an unprofessional way, and Sacks was released because of that. But justice has been served on him."

"There have been kids disappearing for years. Do you know that there are over 55,000 kids missing in the States alone? Where the hell are they? Well the answer is many of them are with Sacks and his sort. These are sick people who really should be in an institution, or somewhere they can't hurt anyone. But no, let them go because it's expensive to keep them locked up and they do promise to be good. How stupid is that? They promise to be good and take their meds. It's really unbelievable. But no one cares. It's only when it affects a family directly that they ask questions. The media will sensationalize a kidnapping for a day, maybe two, depending on the news cycle and what other story they can over-sensationalize to up their ratings. Real justice is an illusion, and we only find out how helpless the people and system are when we need it most.

Each of these perverts will abuse 200 kids in their lifetime. That's 200 children that will grow up traumatized. Many will become abusers themselves. Others take to alcohol and drugs to ease the pain and suffering. Suicide is very common among these victims.

But enough generalization. Let's talk about Sacks. The sicko pervert. He's been abducting kids for over 22 years. He goes into fits. He might take three kids in a year and then lie dormant for a year, maybe two. He is very difficult to catch as he leaves nothing behind. Most of the time, the bodies are not found for months, sometimes not at all. Then, for unknown reasons, he stops abducting. With the lack of leads, the cops that were on the original file move on to other crimes. Resources are tight. The kids that were abducted are forgotten as other priorities arise. It's enough to make you sick."

She interjects, "But I'm not involved in any of this. I don't know these people. Why am I here?" Let me go home." He notices that a lot of the fight that was in her voice yesterday and this morning is gone. She has realized that she cannot escape and that whatever happens to her is up to him. Good for her to realize this and understand her situation.

"Patience Pam. You'll see in a couple of minutes" "And I did promise you that you will go home. Just not today. Shall I continue?"

"Ya"

"Thank you. Ok, so where was I? Oh yes, so Sacks takes a kid out of a playground while his mother was busy on her phone. Looking down at the screen and texting had diverted her attention away from her boy onto some frivolous subject. The next time she looked up, he was gone." She jumps up screaming his name, asking the other mothers there if they had seen him, all to no avail. None of the other mothers had seen anything. He has vanished from the face of the earth. The cops are called.

They started their usual manhunt but had so little to go on that they quickly ran out of leads. The FBI were called in because of the kidnapping, but after seven days of monitoring the telephone lines and waiting for a ransom call, they gave up and moved on to other crises. Sacks never took kids for money. There was never a ransom call with him. There was never a live victim found.

The FBI left after it was evident that there was to be no contact from the abductor. With no new leads and little chance of a successful conclusion, they had little choice but to go on to the next crime. There's no shortage of that. Is there?

There was something about this particular crime that had irritated the Chief of Police. He had been Chief for a number of years, yet this one irked him especially. Two weeks after the FBI left his Town, he called the Cold Case office. O'Harris answered. He and the chief had been friends before the new Chief rose to his present position. After that, the two drifted apart, but each still considered the other a friend. The Chief was especially aware of the dedication Don put into his work. In the Chief's mind, there could be no better man to review this file. If something could be found, O'Harris was the man. O'Harris asked for Ashley as a partner. Granted immediately by the Chief.

All the paperwork was called up, and the study began. They started at the beginning in order to maintain an easy understanding of how the events evolved. The first calls were responded to by uniformed officers in patrol cars, followed immediately by the detective crime squad. Two days were spent reviewing, and nothing out of the ordinary. The next step was to review the statements made by the other mothers present at the park on the day of the kidnapping. One mother, in particular, had stated that she had seen a man hanging around and at first thought it was suspicious. But when she looked again a few minutes later, he was gone, so she thought nothing of it. That is until the boy was taken.

She gave a description of the man to the uniformed officers. He was about 5 foot 7 inches, had a slim build, and was in his early 40's. It was a very generalized description. She also mentioned a particular baseball-style cap that he had worn. It was white but with a very unique crest or logo on the front. The officer originally interviewing this witness had noted this cap in the description, but no one had ever followed through on this lead. There was not really much to go on. And there was a lot going on all at the same time. Detectives were interviewing people; the uniformed officers were looking for physical evidence, searching the fields, garbage cans and whatever. The FBI arrived and made their grand entrance, taking the spotlight. Immediately there is a jurisdictional dispute between the Sheriff's department and the Bureau people. More distraction from the case at hand. The witness and the cap were forgotten.

All the possibilities were chased down and ended up producing nothing. The lead detective and his team put the file on the back burner and went on to something else. You know, the cops never really close these types of files, but they do run out of places to look.

Eight volumes of witness interviews, FBI comments, and profiler reports suggest anything and everything about this criminal but nothing of substance, nothing for an investigator to get his teeth into.

A few days later and still reviewing the file, Don came across this woman's statement. He was curious because of the general description and then the great detail she had given to the officer about the cap. Nothing else in the file gave them another place to look. They decided that they would re-interview this witness.

The next morning, but after coffee and donuts of course, they knocked on her door. She was on her way to work and had only a few minutes to give them. The question went straight to the point. "The description of the suspect is so generic everywhere except for the cap or hat. Why is that?"

She responded with the first good lead they had had. When she was young, she described herself as a rink rat. She spent a lot of time at arenas watching hockey. She replied that her brother played hockey at the midget level many years ago and that they had hats similar to that one made to celebrate some long-since-forgotten victory. The hat looked very similar to the one her brother had worn. He almost made it to the NHL she said.

"How long ago was that?"

"Oh, let's see. He's 41 now so that would make it about 20 years ago." They obtained the brother's address and phone number. She stated that she would call him and let him know that they were coming. She furthered that he worked the night shift at the car factory and was probably at home now, sleeping."

Pam was getting restless. "None of this shit has anything to do with me. I don't know these people; I don't know these cops. In fact, I've never heard of any of this. Why are you telling me a story that has nothing to do with me? Just let me go, and I promise not to tell the cops anything." He noted that a bit of the aggressiveness in her voice had returned. That's good, he thought.

"Please have patience." There was anger in his voice. "I've been involved with this shit for over a year; you can fucking listen for 5 minutes while I tell you why the fuck you are here. So shut the fuck up and listen." His pent-up anger was showing itself. Losing patience when it really wasn't called for.

Oh, she realized that her interruption had sparked a bad note with him. He had responded with too much anger in his voice. Her temperament changed as she realized he was losing patience with her.

This is the first time that he's raised his voice with me. "I'd better be quiet." Quiet thoughts as she understood her inabilities. Don't rattle him. He has a short fuse.

Upset by her constant interruptions and the way he had responded to the latest one, he decided to take a small break. Count to ten, and then do it again until you have calm control of yourself. She's just the catalyst. No need to traumatize her more than necessary. The plan is rolling along very well. I should see the results in a couple of days. I still have to make the video of her kicking ass on the outside, where the suits are making the decisions. They must have concluded by now that the video I gave Smyth and her abduction are connected. "I wonder if they've figured out the motive behind her disappearance. This will give them a good one to chew on.

And if they have reasoned that far, then the debate about showing my video is going on right now. Tough choices for some.

He turned towards her and said, "Look, I'm sorry I barked at you. There is a lot riding on me over the next couple of days. I'm wound up tighter than usual. Would you like me to give you a cut-down version? It would be quicker."

A meek "Yes, please" indicated to him that he had really scarred her. Ah, well, it's done. I apologized, and she was more cooperative, at least for the next couple of minutes. Let me get this thing finished, get the video of her, and be gone.

"Ok, where was I?" Yes. The brother was home when the detectives called and remembered the cap; they had won the city championship but stated that the team had disbanded 15 or 16 years back. When given the description his sister had given originally to the police, he remembered that there was a rather small player on the team. This guy was small but extremely fast, which allowed him to play full-contact hockey. This fellow was strange in funny ways. Although he was good on the ice because of his speed, he never really fit in with the rest of the boys in the locker room. He rarely took a beer after a game. And that was very unusual. At the time, they passed this off as him being shy, a loner. He couldn't remember his name. Seconds later he remembered that the coach might still have the info on this fellow. So now we fast forward over to the coach's house. See, we're moving along quickly, happy?"

"Thank you."

The coach wasn't a hoarder, but he had kept records of every team and player that he had worked with. He still had the roaster of the other players the brother had played with. Between the coach and the brother they identified this loner. A fast search of the driver's license bureau produced a photo. This was shown to the sister, who said that she couldn't be 100% sure, but yes, it does look like him. Finally, a decent lead.

In the major crime office of the Police station, the excitement was palatable. A good lead in such an important file was a godsend. Most of these cops had kids, and the idea that one of them would go missing was? Well was unthinkable. It was an idea that any cop would flush from their minds. You don't want to think about it. Too terrible. So now that they had something to go on, all hands were on deck. The name Jeremy Sacks was run through every computer database known to man. All open case files and criminal records were studied and re-studied. Attempts were made to connect this new suspect with other crimes. Attempts were made to know his whereabouts on days when crimes were committed.

No connections were established. Nothing new could be found. This guy looked like he was lily clean. It looked like another dead end.

An interview was suggested, even an interrogation, but the evidence was so slim that it was thought that this would alert him to the fact that he was now a suspect. This would drive him further underground and make the investigation even more difficult, if not impossible.

A compromise was agreed to. Surveillance would be placed on him for the next two weeks to establish his patterns, etc. Seemed like a good idea.

After two long weeks of watching him and his apartment, they established that Jeremy Sacks worked as a delivery man for a local pharmacy. Information already gleaned was confirmed. He had no friends that they could see. His main activity was work and TV. On the second Saturday of the surveillance, he left his apartment with an expensive camera and walked along the shore of the river, taking photos of birds. There were a few playgrounds, but only one of them had kids playing in them. To the surveillants, Mr. Sacks didn't seem to pay any particular attention to them.

He returned home for supper, and the glow in the windows told the watchers that he was watching TV again. Long hours of boredom had given them nothing. They settled down for more of the same.

Meanwhile, as Saturday afternoon moved into night, an emergency call came in from the officers on patrol. Two cruisers responding to a disturbance call had walked into a riot that was growing quickly and had called for immediate backup. A street party had gotten out of control. Neighbors were fighting neighbors, there had been shots fired, and the situation was totally out of control. Dispatch had ordered all cars on duty to respond immediately as there was a high likelihood of injury to their members. The two cold case cops were exempt and told to remain on surveillance while the others were to go to the disturbance. They left immediately.

Meanwhile, the cold case cops, Don and Mike, sat together sipping their fourth coffee of the evening, expecting absolutely nothing to happen. At eleven o'clock, the TV went off. As they had done for the last ten days, they waited for one hour after the lights went out. When nothing happened, they left for home.

The riot went on till the small hours of the morning, and the surveillance on Sacks was canceled for the day. Sunday was a normal day off, and plans were made to return on Monday morning.

Old cops have instincts that can't be learned. They just know from experience or old age or whatever, but they develop a sixth sense, a gut feeling when they are on to something. This was the case with these two. So Don and Mike decided that they were going in on their own time a watch this suspect.

No sooner had they arrived with their donuts and coffees in hand than Sacks came out of his apartment, again with his camera, and walked the same shore. Surveillance is a difficult job, and doing it with just one car and one footman is even more difficult. But because Sacks was on foot, they parked their car and followed him through the neighborhood to the river. Staying as far behind him as they could safely do, they watched as he photographed birds, trees, and flowers. The cops stayed well back, about one hundred yards, and watched through the trees and scrub that covered the shore. There didn't seem to be a pattern today until he arrived at the second park. There were dozens of kids on the swings, throwing balls, on the slides, on the merry-go-round, and in the sandbox. Parents were sitting together chatting, yelling at the kids to stop fighting, laughing, and semi-consciously watching the goings on. When a ball came over the fence and towards where Sacks was standing, a young boy about ten years old came to get it. Sacks looked around and no one seemed to be watching this kid. Sacks kicked the ball behind a tree and looked again at the parents. Still, no one was watching this kid.

The cops saw this and realized what was happening. They ran towards the park, but twenty-five years of a sedimentary life had drained their ability to run. Sacks grabbed the kid and dragged him to the shore and along the river bank. The cops were far behind. The parents had not yet missed the missing boy. There were no screams or calls for help.

A call went out over the police radio: 'Kidnapping in progress, need backup,' but Sacks and the kid were long gone. Not seen anywhere. Now, the mother is starting to call, then scream, and then go hysterical. Units started arriving from all directions. The sounds of the sirens, the yelling of orders, and the mother's screams lead to confusion. But still no Sacks. No kid.

Don and Mike re-traced their steps. He can't have gone far. You just can't vanish like that in front of our eyes. As they retraced their own footprints, they noticed a large, about six-foot storm drain hidden under some fallen trees surrounded by new growth. More importantly, the drain was dry, with only a bit of water running in the middle. A closer look revealed fresh shoe prints in the mud, large and small, and the small prints seemed to be being dragged along. Sacks had definitely known that this drain was there and had purposely kicked the ball toward it. With one scoop, he snatched the kid and disappeared from the area. The whole thing had taken less than ten seconds. The kid was under the park and under the roadway beside it. The drain pipe had to be sixty feet long. Sacks had the kid at the other end of the drain before his mother even knew he was missing. Not good was going from bad and then to worse.

Don and Mike ran to the other end of the drain. There were footprints all the way. About three-quarters of the way through, Sacks had picked the kid up. There was only one set now, but the foot went deeper into the mud. When they arrived at the other end, their eyes gave way to the frustration.

Mike looked down at his shoes. "These are Italian leather. I just got them last week. They're finished. Fuck"

There were six ditches of various sizes leading away from the drain. This drain must have been installed to empty the torrential rains that came in the spring. Don indicated to Mike, take the one that parallels the road, go three hundred yards. If you don't see any sign of them, come back and follow the next one. "I'll do the same," here indicating the other drain that followed the road.

Mike looked at his shoes. They were finished. "Well, I can stop worrying about them. They're done". Down three hundred or so yards showed nothing. He ran back to the drain and saw Don returning as well. "Nothing?"

"No."

"Let's try these" Indicating the next two gulleys. Don ran no more than a hundred feet when he saw it. A kid's shoe on the side of the ditch. It was still wet. He called out to Mike, "Gotta lead." Mike wasn't far away and jumped out of the ditch and ran across the field towards Don's voice. Then he spotted him, Sacks, running behind a line of trees. A loud yell went out of his throat. Now Don and Mike, with eyes on the culprit, were running passed their ability. Don slowed down for a minute to radio for help.

The neighborhood was already swarming with cops, so when the call went out seconds later, fifty cops were there. Sacks was caught by a younger cop who ran marathons for fun. The kid was located back near the intersection of the six ditches. He was in the third from where Mike had started his search.

Arrested and taken to police central, Sacks was being processed when the Mayor arrived with his entourage in tow. The recent kidnapping and a high crime rate had the Town on edge. The Mayor wanted to reassure the population that everyone, especially kids, were safe. The monster had been captured. Photographs and positive publicity were needed now. After all, the mayor was up for re-election this fall. Mike and Don, the heroes of the day, were ordered to accompany the Mayor for the photo shoots. The processing had not been properly completed. Sacks was locked up for the night. An appointment with a judge was scheduled for the morning.

The Mayor took maximum advantage of the flurry of interest and gave interviews to any and everybody who asked. Don and Mike were dragged along to each and every one. Smiling photographs were to be found in every newspaper. Video interviews were everywhere. Paperwork could wait.

The next morning, while standing before a judge, Sacks pleaded not guilty. He insisted that he had merely been out for a walk and was curious about all the police activity just on the other side of the field where he had been walking. No bail was allowed.

Search warrants were obtained, and evidence was gathered. It seemed a slam dunk for the prosecution. Three weeks later, the trial started, and during the defense cross-examination of the police officers giving testimony, no one testified that Sacks had been read his rights. Once the defense lawyer picked up on this error, he mined it to the extreme.

In the end, the judge had no option but to rule that the overwhelming evidence that the police had gathered was the "fruit of the forbidden tree." He ordered Sacks released at once. There was no appeal.

Even when the judge orders someone released immediately, it takes time to process him. The jailer must return his personal items, there are forms to sign, etc. And so it was that Sacks was finally out on the sidewalk about forty-five minutes after Court had been adjourned. Instead of walking away from the building, he walked passed the front steps where many of the people who'd been in the courtroom were standing, discussing the horrific events of the morning. Many of those in conversation were parents of missing kids. As he silently walked by, he flashed a little grin their way. Mothers wept, and the fathers sizzled in anger, but there were police everywhere. There was nothing to do. Sacks was free."

"This still has nothing to do with me. I don't know anyone who's lost a child. I don't know Sacks. I don't know you. Why am I here? Please, Please let me go home." Pam's voice was neither angered nor pleading, just calmly asking a favor like you would ask a friend.

He noticed the different approach this time. Not mad, not begging, just ?? Well, asking nicely. "Sorry, Pam, the answer's the same. When I'm finished, you can go home." "But my story's not finished. You see, I watched Sacks for a few months. I thought maybe I'd catch him in the act of lifting another kid. But no. I think that he got such a scare by being arrested that he will lay low for a long time, Maybe years. I don't have that kind of patience. So I kidnapped him."

"What?" Pam burst out.

"Ya, just like I grabbed you, I got him. I promise you that I was not as gentle with him as I am with you. My goal was to kill him and beat him to death with a baseball bat. I even went out and bought a Babe Ruth Slugger for the job. But I chickened out. I couldn't do it. I tried psyching myself out with the crime scene photos, and then I tried getting drunk, kinda releasing my inhibitions, but I learned something about myself. I can't attack and kill a helpless individual, even if he is the devil. And then I realized that I don't really have to do anything at all. I had already done it. Now, I just had to wait. Pam, do you know what the 'rule of three is?'

"No, never heard of it.

"Well, it's simple really. You can live for up to three minutes without air. Then you die. You can live for up to three days without water. Then you die. And you can live for three weeks without food. Then you die. All I had to do was wait. My problem was solved. I didn't want the bastard to die as quickly as three minutes or three days, so I rigged a water pipe to where he was hanging. He could drink anytime he wanted. But there was no food. I starved him to death. I also recorded the whole thing. I must have used ten USB sticks. Then, I had to edit it all down to thirty minutes. Now listen carefully because we're getting to the part that gets you involved."

"I'm listening, but I still don't understand. I don't know any of these people; I just want to go home, please."

"Patience, Pam, we're getting close. You see, I sent a copy of the video to a TV station. I want them to broadcast it. The perverts of this world have to know that even if they can fuck the justice system, there are others who are able and willing to do them justice. Kids and the weak in our society deserve a hero to speak and act on their behalf. "

"Anyway, that attempt was a total flop. The TV anchor I contacted, his name was Smyth, called the cops. They refused to air my video. So, I found myself having committed major crimes without the expected result. Sacks was a pervert; the world was better off without him, so why play the video? There was nothing in it for them. I was stuck without a solution until I thought of you. Well, not you precisely, but someone of importance, someone who will get the public's attention, someone the public will fight for and demand results from the cops. A person who can gain sympathy from Mr. and Mrs. every day. You, Pam, are that person."

Pam sat there in silence. She had never heard such a story. It seemed to touch on the impossible, but the reality was that she was in this, like it or not. "Are you going to starve me to death, too?

"No, what did I promise you? No rape, no murder, and home soon. Now, we are working on that. Right? Are you gonna help me?

What can I do? I don't know that many people that they'll protest in the streets…"

"Stop, you don't have to. You just have to cooperate with me a little bit."

"What do I have to do? I want to go home."

"Attached to this room is another that looks like a medieval dungeon. I will photograph you there and then release the pictures with my original demands. There will be a threat of death for you if my instructions are not followed. Death in the same fashion as Sacks, BUT listen carefully, I will not murder you. It's an empty threat. Are we clear on that?

Pam looked down. Her hood was sagging, hanging loosely on her head. This guy murdered Sacks; hell, he beat and starved him to death. He kidnapped me and is holding me here. Can I believe him? What choice do I have? "If I cooperate with you for the photos, what happens next? Can I go home?"

"Well, it takes us a step closer for sure. And the more miserable you look, the more frightened you seem, the more effect it is going to have on the general public. They are your friends and all those people who you don't know are going to help me get what I want and get you home. How willing are you?"

The question seemed to have an easy answer. "Yes, I'll help," in the hope that this asshole isn't lying to me and I do get to go home. Will I get home unhurt was the big question.

Pam, poor Pam, her mind was going in ten different directions at once. What do I do? I'm strapped to a chair by a murderer who's asking me for help and who promises to let me go once his demands are met, yet he has enough food in that fridge to keep me here for a year. He asks questions that make no sense. He keeps telling me I can go home, but there always seems to be still one little thing I have to do, so he'll let me go.' I don't really see any other option. She repeats, "Ok," she says. "I'll help, I'll cooperate. What do we have to do?"

"There's really no preparation to do. The corner is ready. I haven't touched it since Sacks was here. Let's go."

Chapter

XVIII

With that, he releases Pam's arms and guides her towards the door. He takes the key from around his neck and opens the deadlock. Together, they walk through the garage over to a shady corner where there is an old mattress, a shabby blanket and a relief bucket. More importantly, there are restraining chains that come out from the cement wall and ceiling. Pam is taking slow steps as she advances blindly. Her hood is still on.

He guides her to the edge of the mattress and helps her sit down. The mattress is low on the floor. She sits and almost falls quietly. He reaches over and gets today's newspaper, and places it on her lap. Next comes the hard part. She's gonna freak out when he does this. He grabs the chain and locks it on her foot. She jumps from him and away from the wall, but the chain is locked on her foot. She can't go much further away.

"You lied to me. You've got me in chains, you bastard you lied to me. Get me out of here."

"Relax, Pam, this is only temporary. Five minutes at the most. Now, please stay still. This is what is going to happen next. Do you hear me?"

"Yes."

There's still a lot of tension in her voice. Trembling has started.

"I'm going to back off behind the lights. Wait five seconds then take the hood off. Grab the newspaper beside you and place it on your lap so the camera will see it. Click click, and it's over. Then put the hood back on, and we can go back to your room. Understand?"

"You promise?"

"Yes."

Pam takes the hood off and looks around for the newspaper. Then she looks at her surroundings, and her eyes enlarge. This place is damp and cold. The mattress is stained by blood and urine and torn. The walls are cement. It has a certain smell that she can't figure out, but it's not a good odour. Smells like death. There are brown stains on the floor. Unmistakably dried up blood.

Then she notices the chains that are hanging from the ceiling. The chains have pieces of skin and muscle tissue ripped off at some point during Sacks' detention here. They are all dried and withered. She remembers the tale that *"He"* told her of starving Sacks to death. She's sitting under where Sacks died. To the side is a baseball bat. There are blood stains on it, too. He said he beat Sacks with a bat. Oh my god, is that where I am? I'm in the death room.

There is a flash of light that startles her back to reality. She thinks to herself, *Of course, this is where he killed Sacks. One photo is taken. He tells her to look more frightened. Rip your blouse off your shoulder, and mess your hair.*

"I'm already fucken scared to death. How can I can I look more frightened? She mumbles "idiot" under her breath, certain that he can't hear it. The flash goes off four more times, and then there is a lull. He photographs her, the chains, the mattress and the bat. He takes them all from different angles. The spotlights are blinding her. She can't see but hears him moving around her and the sound of the camera clicking and clicking.

"Is it clicking towards my death at this insane man's hands?" And then it gets quiet, deathly quiet. Minutes that seem like hours roll by and still no sign of him. "Oh god, is he going to leave me here? In this death room. Real tears are flowing. Her body is trembling with fear. "This can't be, please." She starts screaming, "No, No, No, Don't leave me here, please, please, I'm begging," and rolling around at the end of her chain.

"What are you doing? What's with the crying? Get the hood on, and we can get the hell out of here. This room stinks. Women, I'll never understand them." He approaches her from behind and checks the hood over her head. He releases the foot cuff and then he takes Pam by the arm and guides her back to her own cell.

She's pleased to be back, locked up in her own security. She realizes that she feels comfortable here, and she's glad to be back. There's a homey feeling that she has developed for this cell, and that thought frightens her. "I feel safe here? I'm happy to be back. Have I gone mad? I'm still a prisoner here. I'm tied up like a hostage. Seconds ago, I had a chain on my leg. That's what I am: a hostage. Why do I feel safe?" All these thoughts are crowding through her head at the same time. She keeps these thoughts to herself. Emotional overload is affecting her. He leaves the room and there's a click from the door. "Locked in and safe."

"There's something wrong with me if I think that way." Then, everything falls silent.

She turns on the TV just in time to see the news. There, front and center, is a photo of her while the announcer talks about how long she's been missing and the fact that there has been no contact with her abductor, and it's been more than twenty-four hours. An FBI spokesperson addresses the reporters on hand, stating that this is unusual. Contact is usually made within the first twelve hours, and the authorities are concerned that this may be a case of abduction for other than financial reasons. No more specific possible motives are given, so the reporters are free to speculate.

The photo they are displaying of her was taken by a professional photographer on the occasion of her tenth wedding anniversary after she had been professionally made up. She has a glowing smile and beautiful white teeth. The attributes of her body are on full display. She looks drop-dead gorgeous. The photographer has captured all of her natural beauty. Could that have been the motive? It doesn't happen frequently with women her age, but could she be the victim of a white slavery ring? The question is left to hang.

Another possible motive is there a possibility revenge angle to this? Has she offended anyone? Maybe as a bank manager in charge of loans, she turned down someone who really needed the money. This person feels that his misfortune was caused by the bank's refusal to back his loan.

Or what about taking her to get money out of the bank, you know, holding her while a partner of the kidnapper gets the cash from the bank? It was all the rage a little while back. There seemed to be dozens of them all close together. Then the fad, if you can call it that, died out. Maybe someone new is using old methods with a new twist.

What about the neighbours? Does she have any kind of feud going on? The neighbours are interviewed, but none suggest a local reason for her abduction. One neighbour in particular expressed 'his' sentiment perfectly. "They let the criminals go free and then wonder why there's so much crime. This is just an example of the ineptness of the justice system."

"Wow," he says. "I couldn't have said it better myself."

Given the free reign that they had, the reporters went off on a million tangents, not one of them hitting the nail on the head. Funny how that works. He was going to fix that.

Chapter

XIX

It becomes obvious to him that one of the other errors he made in his original approach to getting publicity was to go to only one resource. Smyth was a total failure. The idea of going back to Smyth doesn't seem to be the answer. On the positive side, "I've learned a lot from the mistakes I made with him. Live and learn.

"There are zillions of radio, TV and internet possibilities to getting my cause out there. I don't understand why I didn't think of this before. Next time, I'll flood all media possibilities with my message. Let's see them censor this from the public.

It doesn't take him long to add Pam's photos to the Sacks' montage. A quick survey of all the media outlets within the city. There are four TV stations, five a.m. and seven F.M. radio stations serving this community. It's more difficult to figure out what would be the best internet outlet. You never know where the hell they are.

To resolve this dilemma he surfs the web for the site that seems to be following the disappearance of Pam most closely. It's also the one that is working the 'kidnapped for sex' angle or the white slave trade to its fullest and beyond reasonable possibilities. Sex sells, so exploit it. Sensationalism gone wild with no possibility of negative coming back. "You gotta love that first amendment."

And as an added bonus, this site had almost one million followers. "Can't go wrong here," he thinks. Time to put the last phase into action.

After making twenty-five copies of his new USB stick, he hides one copy each in telephone booths and under park benches. Each close to the media offices he's chosen. Then he makes the calls to each telling them where they can find an exclusive. Cub reporters looking for a big break to make their careers rush out of their offices and find the pot of gold. Eureka.

Now, the challenge is to be the first on the air with their prize. Three hours after making his phone calls, Sacks' death and the photos of Pam are everywhere. It would almost seem that there was nothing else going on in the entire world. He was going to get the publicity he craved, no publicity he craved up to the yin-yang. The moment of truth was fast approaching. He had seen the early reports on his computer monitor. The media flood was starting.

He calls to Pam. "I'm coming in, and this time, I'll wear the hood, but don't look at me. We can watch our work together just like its Monday night football. Pam sat in her chair and didn't look towards the door even after she heard the click of the lock releasing. He pulled up a chair and sat to her right and behind her. The room is dark. She'd have to strain to turn and see him. She wasn't going to do that. She still didn't know what he looked like and didn't want to see his face.

The time stamp on the video being shown indicated that this was on the first day Sacks was taken. It shows a tied-up individual being dragged and then hoisted into the air. A hood over his head hides the identity but is soon removed. Sacks can be seen looking around with a horrified look on his face. There is no audio. Given what was about to happen, that was a good thing.

In comes a hooded man with a baseball bat in his hand. He can be seen talking to Sacks. What he says cannot be heard. Then, the hooded individual is seen lifting the bat and swinging it at Sack's feet, then the legs. He works his way up systematically to Sack's arms, taking special aim at the knees and elbows. It can clearly be seen that the swings are at full force. The look on Sack's face attests to the pain he's suffering. No blows go to the head. The hooded man then turns towards the camera. He holds up a sign that says, *More and Better to come.* He then leaves the camera's line of sight.

The video then breaks into a new time stamp.

The hooded man returns. No bat in his, but he has a knife and a pair of scissors. He approaches Sacks.

Together, they watch as a hanging Sacks cries and screams, then jerks his body around, trying desperately to free himself and get away from the approaching hood. The hooded man grabs Sacks by the shirt and cuts it off. Next is the pants, then the socks, until Sacks is hanging there totally naked.

You can see the coagulated shape of his knees and the effects of being hit by the baseball bat. The torturer slaps Sacks in all the bruised spots. The intense pain these slaps are causing is evident on his face. You can see the effects. Over and over and over, Sacks cried, then begged, then pleaded, all to no avail. Marks on the body testified to the beating Sacks had endured. Cuts and bruises everywhere.

"Thank God I can't hear the screams," thinks Pam.

A new time stamp shows that a day later, Sacks is still hanging from the ceiling. It doesn't look like he's been beaten any more, but the sinking of his eyes into their sockets is an indication of his physical and mental state. Then the video goes off. The next entry was made after the hooded individual had continued his torture.

According to the time stamp, it is two days later. Sacks is slowly swinging around. In some places, you can see that the skin on Sack's back had been torn away, and a rectangle still hung with the vice grips attached, muscles showing behind the blood. God, he was being skinned alive. Fish-style hooks, but much bigger, were still lodged in the skin. The sickly blue-yellow bruises from where he had been hit with the bat were all over his body but nothing to the head. No, nothing that would knock him unconscious. The torturer did not want Sacks to pass out.

Pam sees pearls around Sacks' neck. "Pearls?" That doesn't make any sense. Then, a closer look. "Oh god, they're not pearls. They're teeth. He pulled the teeth from Sack's mouth. Death did not come fast or easy.

Dizziness came first. Then, an empty feeling in her stomach. Then light-headedness. Pam first reached and then vomited her super on the floor. She watched in horror as the video progressed, understanding now that her captor was a very sick man. To be able to do this to another human being was beyond normal revenge. This was sickness at its worst.

"And now that he's accomplished what he set out to do, am I next? Will I die like Sacks? He has his photographs. He doesn't need me anymore." A fear so deep at this possibility crept through her innards, releasing her bladder into her jeans. Primordial fear. Fight or flight, but flight was not possible. "I am going to die a horrible death."

"Mama, help me."

The last part of the video that concerned Sacks showed him to be dead or near death. There was no movement in the body, even when he was poked with the bat. The easy conclusion was that he had finally died.

The last few minutes showed Pam in captivity. Over her head visible was some of the remains of Sack's skin and muscle tissue still hanging from the chain. Another photo showed the bat leaning in the corner.

He leaves the room for a minute. He is concerned and wants to know how widespread was this video shown. After all, that was the whole point of this exercise. As he surfs through the internet he is pleasantly surprised at the enormous response his video is getting. It seems that it is everywhere. There are indications that this video is going worldwide.

"I hope that every pervert sees this and shutters. I am coming for you."

Chapter

XX

Political and law enforcement pundits are all talking about the video and the message it has sent to the authorities. The police chief condemns vigilantism and states that the hunting is now on for Sacks' remains and his murderer. In his mind this whole operation has been a total success. Perverts beware. You've been warned. Celebration time. So now he returns to the room and speaks to Pam.

"We've succeeded, congratulations, and thanks to you, the world knows I'm here to protect the young, the innocent and the weak. You've done an excellent job, so thank you."

Pam resists looking back towards where he is sitting. "Yes, it looks like you got everything you wanted." In her mind, she's thinking, "Is this the end for me too?" She asks him straight out, "What are you going to do with me now?"

He responds, "We'll have to see about that, won't we? There are some things I have to pick up and other things to do. I'm still very interested in not getting caught. So, I have to make sure I don't overlook anything. We'll see."

She reels. "You promised to let me go. You promised!" Louder and with emphasis. With that, he lets out a sinister laugh and says, "I'm a murderer. Remember. Do you really trust the word of a murderer?"

She turns to look at him. Visions of her hanging naked from the chain that held Sacks visualize in her mind. The screams that she couldn't hear but imagined deafened her. The idea of enduring that torture causes her eyes to roll up as she twists out of the chair towards the floor. The last thought in her mind as she tumbled towards the cement floor was "Pearls" and then unconscious.

Chapter

XXI

"Fuck", he says, reacting quickly, as he launches himself forward just in time to catch her head from smashing into the concrete floor. The body makes a thumping sound as it lands on her shoulder. "Too much," he says. Then he grabs her under the arms and drags her over to the bed.

It's a struggle lifting dead weight like that, but he manages to get her onto the mattress. He removes her shoes, undoes the bra strap, throws a blanket over her and leaves the room, ensuring that the lock is engaged.

It's not too long afterwards that he can hear the soft sounds of the bed squeaking coming from the speaker. He looks at the monitor. She's sitting on the bed, back to the corner. Her legs are rolled up into her chest, with her arms hugging her legs into her. He does a double-take when he looks at her eyes. There's a distant look in them. The vibrant woman he talked to earlier is gone. She's been replaced by a zombie-like entity. There is no emotion in the eyes. Even the complexion has changed from rosy athletic to sickly pale white.

"Wow," he thinks. "How can a change come that fast?" Time to talk to her and get her back.

"Hi," he says as he enters the room with his hood on, pretending not to notice the change in her. "Time to prepare for your release." There is no movement, no reaction from her. She maintains the distant, detached look. He goes on as if everything was normal. "We're going to prepare you properly. Don't forget, I want to get away with this and you cannot have any clues on you that might help the cops identify me? Understand?"

Still no reaction. He continues anyway. "I have to go out and get some things. I'll be back in an hour or so; then we can prepare. Are you OK with that?" No reaction. He leaves the room without understanding or knowing what to do. Maybe just some time for her to come around will help.

He returns a few hours later. Immediately, he checks the monitor to see how she is. She's in the same place, same position but now she's rocking slowly back and forth and humming to herself. He reviews the camera recordings and confirms what he thought. She hasn't slept at all. The fatigue is evident in her eyes. They are sunken and there are dark lines underneath. Now, he really starts to worry. This new situation could ruin his whole plan. If he returns her like this, this will become the story. All of the positive press that he has been getting will divert to her mental status. This can't be. The only thing that he can think of is putting her to sleep. Maybe permanently. Either can be easily arranged.

He has noticed that she drinks a lot of tea. He didn't think much of it at the time, but now this little insignificant fact is going to help him. He prepares some Earl Grey and puts a sleeping potent into the hot water along with the tea bag. He enters the room with his hood on. She pays no attention to him and continues rocking with her legs locked by her arms. "I brought you some tea." No response. He puts the tea to her lips. She takes a small sip. Good. He touches her shoulder and gets no response. He sits beside her and starts to rock along with her. She very slightly leans into him. He puts his arm around her and squeezes very gently. She gives a positive grunt and leans in further. She calls out, "Mama."

He responds, "Mama says drink your tea," and with that, she releases her legs and drinks the entire cup. Then, she assumes the same rocking position and hums to herself. "Pearls, Pearls, Pearls," she says.

"There are no pearls for you he responds." Now, the sleeping sedative is starting to work. Her eyes become droopy, and the little words that she was saying become slurred. She falls asleep, muttering, "Mama."

He decides that the idea of using the third person as a guardian and overseer of his actions has outlived its usefulness. Time to revert to "I" and "me". Ok, that's another small decision made. Now, I can get back to being myself. Anyway, "he" was becoming a drag.

I didn't have much to do at this point. I was ready to let her go, but she wasn't cooperating." How long can a person sleep anyway? Shit, she's been out for fourteen hours. "I keep rolling her release over in my mind. Is it really a good idea to let her go?"

I keep going back to the internet and watching in grateful amusement the positive comments I've been getting. Jacob from Florida thinks that if there were a few more of me around, violent crimes against women and children would diminish drastically. Some guy from Britain wants to start a *"GoFundMe"* campaign to support me and my endeavours. I really like that idea even though I have enough funds to carry me on this crusade but I would have to reveal myself to get the money. Now, I'm not the coldest beer in the fridge, but I don't think that is a very good idea. Thanks for the thought, anyway. I appreciate the sentiment.

Fourteen and one-half hours and a few minutes later she finally wakes up. I'm in front of the monitor. There is a little confusion on her face, but the lines under her eyes are gone and she looks sharper than yesterday. I hope she's back. It does look like she's back to her old self. I key the mike.

"Good morning, Pam." She looks at the camera and mumbles something. I hope it's a reciprocal greeting. "Stay where you are. I'm coming in and I'll have the hood on this time. Ok?" She shakes her head with a positive response.

"Wow," I say as I walk in. "Did you ever sleep?"

She looks at me and asks, "What now?" There's extreme fear on her face.

When I look at her, I can also see that she is extremely fragile, that this facade I'm looking at could easily revert to yesterday's version of Pam. That I don't want. Besides me not wanting to hurt her, she is, after all, supposed to be just a catalyst, not a victim. It would distract from my mission. Internet support is great, but it can easily and quickly do an about-face and become a negative force for me. No she has to return home with a minimum of damage. Yesterday's events showed me that I have to walk a fine narrow line. But I ask myself, "If she were to simply disappear, never return, would that affect the popularity of my cause? Probably not."

To keep things light. "Yesterday, while you were pretending to be Rip Van Winkle, I picked up everything I needed to take you home. Are you ready?" I ask.

She looks at me with a doubtful face. I think that she thinks that I am just toying with her. Deep down I know that she is hopeful but is afraid that her dreams will cause her more disappointment when I renege. Whatever, I just continue.

"So that I don't get caught, here are the things we have to do. You need to change your clothes. I'm sure my DNA is all over you. You are going to strip, take a shower and put on the sweat suit over there.

Now, here you have a choice. One. You wash yourself very well. Especially your hair and under your fingernails. You have to rub so hard your skin is red. If you don't do that to my satisfaction, then choice number 2 comes in. You won't like this one. I get in the shower with you and do the job properly.

She looks over at me, "When do we start?" with a neutral voice

"Now would be good." She gets up and walks towards the shower. "Too much of this is robotic." I think.

I think of saying, *"Now strip"* but the sound of that would be too harsh. I have to keep it civilized. I'm still concerned about her mental state, so instead, I say. "Please undress and get into the shower," I say as politely and softly as I can. I wait for the response. This is the first time that she has not showered in private.

She acts as if I'm not even there. She strips and steps into the shower. God, she is gorgeous. She washes her hair and uses the washcloth to clean herself. I see that she is rubbing viciously. That's good. When she's finished, I say, "Now step out, dry yourself and put on the sweat suit." She does as she is told but is still robotic. I think that in her mind, she has resigned herself to Sacks' fate.

"Now that you've got me nice and clean, you gonna beat me like you did with Sacks?"

"Didn't I promise not to hurt you? Didn't I promise not to abuse you in any way, even sexually? Haven't I kept all of my promises?" I say with a little bit of frustration in my voice. "After all, I've kept my word. What more do you want?"

She feeds me back my own words, "Well, you are a murderer, aren't you? Can you trust the word of a murderer?"

"Yes," I think to myself. "She's right there, and maybe that response shows that she's recovered from the zombie I saw yesterday. The mind is working. "Good," I think. I leave her in the room, lock the door and sit by the monitor. I'm not so much watching her. She's not doing anything. I'm more going through my mind trying to see if I have missed anything.

I'm getting more concerned about getting caught. As long as we are here in my headquarters, my control center, we're safe. But the next steps mean that we'll be leaving here and taking the van to the woods where I'll free her, I think.

The drive from here to there is about thirty minutes. Is she going to cause a scene? Well, I knew this day was coming. I've prepared for it as best I can, so here we go.

I key the mic. "Pam, sit in the chair. Put the hood on. I'm coming in". She does as she's told. I unlock the door and enter. She's sitting quietly. "Don't get too comfortable with her.' I think. Her kick is strong. I arrive in front of her, take her arms and pull her up. She stands. I put duct tape around the wrists. Now I can talk to her. "You're going home now?" I say. Her head moves to look where my voice came from. For a moment there is no reaction. "What?" I think.

"Are you taking me back there? To the chains? To the pearls. No, please, I'm begging." She's losing it. She starts to cry, pulls away from me attempts to run, but with the hood on can't get far.

"Stop!" I yell and grab her. "You'll see in a moment, you'll be breathing fresh air." She's still fighting me with all her strength. I grab her by the jeans and lift her onto my shoulder. She's kicking and screaming all the time. Her arms are swinging in panicked desperation, punishing my back with all her might. I finally get to the garage door and electronically open it. I'm sure I have bruises all down my back, but when she breathes the outside air, she stops fighting.

"You're taking me out to kill me, you bastard. Just like you did to Sacks." The tied hands are flying in the air. She's striking at any and everything. A couple of the swings hit me in the head. "Ouch," I cry. "Stop it."

"You're going to kill me and just dump my body."

"It's getting tempting," I respond. But she's still on my shoulder, and this constant hitting on my back and head is getting tiresome. I throw her to the ground. Before she can move I'm on her. Knee into her chest. "You know," I say as she lays pinned to the ground. Her arms are in the air, swinging wildly, striking at nothing. The feet are going like crazy but to no avail. There's nothing to hit. "I'm trying to let you go, but Jesus, you make killing you a real good-looking option." I hold her down like this for a few minutes until she either runs out of breath or just understands that this is not doing her any good. She stops and breathes heavily. There are no cars on the highway, so my security hasn't been compromised.

Into the van she goes. Same routine. Feet and hands are taped, hood over head, and gag in mouth. Now for the biggest gamble. I have to take her twenty-two miles into the State Park, where there's an old logging road. That's where I'll leave her, taped to a chair.

I'm driving along the interstate. I'm doing the speed limit when I see a cop car coming up behind me, red lights flashing. He's coming fast. "Oh fuck" I say. "Did someone see me put her into the van? I didn't see any cars pass. Stay cool."

The cop car comes up behind me, slows a little and then speeds past me, around a corner and is gone. "Damn, and wow," I say to myself, "That scared the shit outta me."

We arrive at the logging road. There's no one else in sight. I feel safe. I drive down the road a little bit but can't go past the stream. I check around, but still no one is in sight. I park. Now I have to move fast. Out comes the new lawn chair. It still has the store stickers on it, and I've only touched it with gloves on. I check around again. Same result. Now I'm nervous. I'm shaking and praying she doesn't do anything stupid that will cause me to overreact. I cut the tape on her feet so she could walk to the chair. When I grab her by the foot to pull her out, she kicks out at me.

She tried this when I first took her, so I think I'm ready for it. But I don't move fast enough. She catches me square on the temple with the shoe. It hurts like hell, and I see stars for a minute. It knocks me over, and I fall to the ground, grabbing my aching head. She takes advantage of this and sprints up the road, blindfolded and hands tied, running like crazy. She gets the gag off. Of course, it's not long before she hits a small bump on the dirt road and tumbles ass over tea kettle crying and trying to get up and take the hood off.

She gets up and continues running. I chase after her and use a full-body tackle to subdue her. I'm furious and pissed off. I grab her by the blouse using both hands. I pull her up. I shake her around like she's a rag doll. All the while, she's wailing, screaming and thrashing about. God, she's going to wake the dead with this fit and noise. Then I do something I hadn't done before. I make a fist and drive it into her stomach. That shuts her up quickly. Then I give her a hard slap across the face, then backhand her again. I put the gag back on, tighter this time. I'm seriously pissed off. Hell, with all that screaming she would have got the attention of anyone around. I look left, right, up the road into the woods. I look everywhere, but I still can't see anyone, no witnesses I think. But then I think anyone who saw what I was doing to her is going to hide for fear of me killing them.

I grab her. One hand into the back of the jeans and the other grabs the collar. I'm constantly shaking her back and forth, up and down. I'm still big-time pissed off. I can feel throbbing on the side of my head where she kicked me. That blow landed on the same spot where

I had been injured in the Army. I immediately thought of the retina injury. I checked my eye. Everything seems OK, but it doesn't help my disposition. Within seconds, I have her in the chair just off the road. I take out my box cutter knife. I look at her, then the knife. It would be easy to end this here. I think, *What a stupid thing to do, full tackle. I could have just as easily grabbed her by her hair with my gloved hand. Now she probably has my DNA all over her dam clothes. I think one stroke and any chance of identification by her is over. But I've already learned that I can't do that. Or maybe I can. After all, she is a live witness. She is a threat to my future if she can identify me.* "What the fuck do I do now?"

Chapter

XXII

But if I can't kill Sacks, then she's out of the question. All the bravado in the world isn't going to change that. The thought comes up again that this woman is a threat to my future. When I had Sacks, he wasn't. I don't want to get caught, and even though I don't think that she has seen my face she does know a lot about me. I think about the DNA again. "Fuck what a stupid thing to do. I'm back with the stupid criminals who get caught." Can I be sure that she won't one day identify me just by my voice? I'm not sure. Did she ever get a look at me through the hood that I never noticed? I'm crawling with indecision.

I sit her down roughly. Then, I wrap her legs with duct tape to the chair. I make sure she's well attached. She's moving and trying to get free to no avail. Another softer slap to the face reminds her that I'm still in charge. There are grunts and what I think are pleadings coming through the gag, but I can't make them out, and honestly, I'm getting tired of all this useless shit. I do the same with the left arm.

I attached the right arm to the chair using a different tape. This one is called 'painter's tape and it's made of paper, very easy to rip. I put just enough to hold her lightly. She'll be able to get her arm out, then the hood and the rest will be easy. This will give her a place to start unravelling her self. It'll take her at least fifteen minutes to get free. I'll be long gone and near the control center by then. "Listen to me carefully," I say. "There is a small knife between your legs" I push my box cutter under her ass. She flinches like I'm going to hurt her, but by the time she re-acts, my hand is back out, and I'm continuing with the instructions. "You're right arm is not fastened tightly. Work it, and it will come free. Use the knife on the rest of the tape, and "poof, you're free," I say. "Understand?"

"Yes."

"Now count to five hundred," I tell her in a threatening voice, "and don't move. I'm going to watch you, so don't move. What a stupid thing to say. She's going to hear the van leave, so why did I even say it? I guess my nerves were getting to me."

I stand looking at her for a moment. This whole adventure didn't turn out the way I planned or expected. Now, I have an innocent catalyst who is also a threat to me. I could leave her here, like I planned, call a reporter and tell them where she is. That would make their day, hell, maybe their career, sad as it may be. I set her up for this release scenario because that was my original intention. "Jesus, how did it come to this?" I ask myself. Now I'm not so sure. Or one stroke of the box cutter, and my future is secure. I stand in front of her with massive indecision. "Do I or don't I, now, what the fuck do I do?"

Chapter

XXIII

I revert back to my guardian angel buddy. He sits in his new rented house. The smell of fresh paint is still strong in the air. The furniture is brand new from the thrift shop. The fridge has a little food but mostly beer. There may be an apple or two. It's a good, quiet neighborhood. The neighbors would have a fit if they had any idea who their new buddy-buddy was. He still wasn't used to the friendliness of people in suburbia. They asked a thousand questions and were ready to divulge a copious amount of personal information. "Why the fuck do I want to know any of this shit?" he asked himself many a time. He concluded that this was just 'good America, friendly people welcoming a stranger into their fold. "Not bad, actually; when you get down to it, it was actually good. A great place to hide in plain sight."

He had spun the tale that his wife and child had been killed by a drunk driver back east and that he had come west to deal with it and try to get his own life back on track. The story is close to the truth with some details missing. He thought that when he first told this story, he may have gone into too much personal detail. It was at the first get together to which he had been invited to meet 'the gang'. It would have been too rude of him to refuse, and he feared that in doing so, he would turn them all against him, find him suspicious or too out of the ordinary. This would cause him problems in the future, so the reasonable way to avoid these possible future problems was to "deal with them today."

The hint that he was going too far with his tale of woe came as he noticed that half the women in the living room were sobbing softly into their sweaters while the others were absorbing tears with their handkerchiefs. "Shit, have I gone too far?" Not wanting to play the sympathy card beyond credibility, he toned his story down to acceptable levels. It seemed to calm them down. All was normalized, and his story was accepted as gospel. It really wasn't that uncommon of a story anyway. These accidents are happening all over the Country. And it wasn't far from the truth. Actually, when he thought about it, it was the truth.

Once the ladies of the community learned his "oh-so-sad story," sympathy grew, and they showered him with attention and food. Meat casseroles, apple pies, the works would show up on this door step or on the picnic table at the back. Maybe these noisy people aren't that troublesome after all. "And Mrs. Switch, yes, Caroline, is her name is kind of cute, and she does make a mean apple pie." He would have to complain jokingly that he was getting too fat because of all the good food that was being delivered to his doorstep.

As usual, when neighbors talk, the ladies huddle in the kitchen preparing food, exchanging recipes, and their kid's latest achievements. 'His' story was told and re-told while questions were asked and possible explanations were suggested. No one was so curious or impolite to ask him a direct question. Speculation, gossip and rumors are so much more fun.

The men were outside with beer in hand, surrounding the bar BQ, like the beef on the grill was going to try and escape. "The topics were the same everywhere." He thought. Same as back home when he was leading a normal life and socializing with his neighbors in what seemed like eons ago. Memories that he had long since extinguished and forgotten came rushing to the fore front.

First in the normal line of discussion was sports, with football leading the pack. NFL vs AFL and who's going to the super bowl. "Will Brady be able to do it...again?" There was talk about some rookie from Mississippi who was expected to burn up the league. No pressure on this nineteen-year-old kid who, in one game, will make more than this gang will in a lifetime. Rookie contracts with endorsements and signing bonuses took some kids out of the slums and made multi-millionaires overnight. No wonder these kids go wild.

Next on the usual list of sports was basketball. Even before the first game of the season was played, the 'gang' had decided who the winners and losers would be. "San Francisco would start hard and then fade by mid-season. No, the dark horse this year would be Boston. The Celtics look good. But what about that team-up in Toronto, Canada? They'll be putting it to some serious front-runners. Wonder if they'll ever win the NBA Championship?"

The response came fast from a fellow named Cliff. "Too fucking cold up there to play basketball. Went up there at a conference a few years back. It was the middle of winter, and God, it was cold. It must've been like zero degrees. Basketball there?"

"Never" was his own response.

Lately, ice hockey has become a favorite simply because of the speed and roughness of the game. And in ice hockey, the players sometimes dropped the gloves and fisticuffs began adding a new and exciting dimension to the sport. These fellows were mature and had settled down now, but you could easily see that in their younger years, they raised hell from the conversations that flowed around the room, and not really knowing them that well yet, 'he' wondered if there were any criminals here among this little group.

His next step to being integrated into the "gang' was to make sure he had all the names right. "Can't call Fred Joe. It leaves a bad impression." He paid special attention to the conversation, ensuring that he attached the right name to each of his new friends.

Once the varied opinions of these armchair quarterbacks were expressed debated, and with no solid conclusions made, the topic changed over to the high price of gasoline. "Those fucking Russians invading the Ukraine have caused all this turmoil making everything go up to crazy prices. Getting harder and harder to save for a small vacation or retirement."

He thinks that that was Mrs. Apple pies' husband talking while all the other shook their heads in agreement. "Yes, his first name is Burt, Burt Switch." Burt was an auto mechanic and worked for GM at the Centreville franchise. Silently said and accordingly recorded. He listened carefully to each guy relate some incident where the price had skyrocketed, and in some cases, they just put the needed article back on the shelf. *"We'll just have to do without"* was the accepted opinion. That was Clifford James, the fellow who's been to Toronto, recounting the conference story. He was married to a tall, thin woman; Diane was her name. He understood what these guys were talking about. They were middle-class Americans suffering under extreme inflation and trying to maintain their established life style. "A very difficult job these days."

The host this evening was Dick Richard Crandle. He owned and operated a small accounting/bookkeeping business that catered to other small businesses. His idea was to give a lot of good service to many so that his client base was always varied and solid. His wife Joan was one of the book keepers in the firm. He wondered, "What is it like to work with your wife, to be together nearly twenty-four hours a day? God, wouldn't that drive you crazy?"

"I wonder what Pam's doing?"

"Wow," he thought, "where the hell did that come from?"

"Yes, the war has created certain problems and has caused the price of some: ok, I'll accept most of the prices to go up, but have you seen the profits these Companies are making and the dividends they are paying out to their shareholders? The presidents of these Companies are making criminal-sized bonuses and all on our backs" This again was silently argued internally.

Dick realized that the mood around the bar BQ was getting too somber. "Ok, guys, time for another beer. But first, I need to piss the last one out, so I serve it to you at room temperature." The laughter from that joke raised the mood and lightness, and the friendly chatter returned. It wasn't too long afterward that 'He' was asked about how the prices of everything affected him.

"Well, these days, I feel the pinch just like you guys. Right now, I'm living off the proceeds of my wife's insurance. I was hoping to stretch that out over a year or so, but the way it looks now, I'll have to start looking for work soon." At the mention of his wife's insurance pay out, the mood crashed again. But his own demeanor caught it, and he smiled a friendly grin to release the tension. Smiles returned.

"What's your trade?"

"Well, I started in the Army. I had an accident there, and my eyes weren't up to standard. So I went back to school and trained as an architect, but I really didn't like it that much. Too much paper, too much under-the-table hand-outs, too many inspectors and the environmental people would have us all living in caves again if they had their way. That shit used to drive me nuts. I'm more of a hands-on guy. I like to get my hands into the work; I love the smell of wood, and a saw vibrating in my hand feels like heaven. At the end of the day, you stand back and look at a house you built or the renovations you did that take an old shack, and you reinvigorate it. There's a great feeling of self-worth, self-satisfaction." As he was recounting a part of his life that they had loved and lost, the 'gang' could see loneliness and longing growing in his face. Dick was again fast on the draw and told the Irish twin drunk joke, where the Murphy twins get to know each other all over again for the hundredth time. This joke was told at every get-to-gether but still managed to get a laugh or at least a chuckle. Dick decided to try a new joke he had picked up on the internet. It was a terrible flop. You could hear a pin drop at the gang's reaction. No one moved. No one even smiled. "Well, I tried," said Dick. "But why does it sound like we're in a church, and the church mouse is also so quiet?"

Burt, always first and fast on the reply, "Because we can all hear the fleas sneeze. It's blocking out the church mouse's foot stomps." Laughter from all quarters. And the noise level rose accordingly.

"Fleas, don't sneeze." This was Cliff, the quiet one talking. A massive debate occurred about mice, fleas and all other sorts of noisy little critters. Experts on the flea's anatomy suddenly appeared with considered opinions and charts drawn on paper towels to illustrate their point. Opinions were passed, and credentials were challenged. Bedlam prevails among the laughter.

The banter and ribbing went on forever until the ladies decided from inside the kitchen that the meat was ready, and everyone took their places at the picnic table. These memories of days long gone bye echoed in his mind, the way it used to be for him.

This was a close group of friends with a history of togetherness and devotion to each other.

Money has always been a sensitive topic of conversation with any group of people. A man like him renting a full-sized house to live in all alone raised financial questions among the group. The story of a wife's insurance money satisfied all their curiosities. And as for living alone, he just didn't like apartments.

The festive mood returned, and everyone now knew enough about his personal life to accept him into their fold. There were to be no more questions on this subject. Too sensitive. He felt the objective was achieved but at the cost of digging up hurtful memories. Well, he'd dealt with them before, and he'll just have to do it again. At least there would be peace on this front.

The bar BQ continued on into the evening till the ladies mentioned tomorrow's work and how early one has to be up to get the day started. He stood up and thanked everyone for a delicious and entertaining supper. At the gate, he turned to the crowd. Getting their attention, he said, "I don't know, please, if fleas can sneeze, but the breeze in the trees seems to whisper Louise." And with that, he did a little 'soft shoe' dance to conclude his exit. He had them in stitches laughing so hard. The day had gone off much better than he imagined it would. He thoroughly enjoyed himself, and for a brief period of time, he went back to his old self. "Yes, definitely a good day."

Chapter

XXIV

But his reality was not so glee and fancy-free. He was by himself with his secrets, a lone vigilante on the hunt again. He had read about another child molester living not far from where he now was. A mere forty-five minutes by van from Johnston's place to the future control center. And that was not a coincidence. The stalking had already begun. The info gained so far was really shocking. Two States south and one State east, this guy, Jim Johnston by name, had kidnapped a young boy, had abused, raped and eventually murdered the eleven-year-old. This all happened while he was dealing with Sacks.

The trial was widely publicized locally, but there were other international stories that carried more glamour for the Networks. Johnston's trial didn't even get a mention in the national media. He followed the story in archives of the local newspaper. There, they were explicit, sickening descriptions of what this young boy had endured before he died. The pathologist estimated that the little fellow had been murdered thirteen days after having been kidnapped. Imaginations ran wild on what little Richard had endured during his captivity.

The defense lawyer was very good. He was able to ask questions that put into doubt much, if not all, of the prosecution's theory of the murder and left the jury with little choice but to find Johnston not guilty. Then, a strange thing happened, and shivers went down his spine. 'He' saw it in the front page photograph of Johnston as he left the Court house.

It was a close up photo showing Johnston leaving the Court by the main entrance. As he is leaving the room, the photo shows him looking at the chief prosecutor with his head slightly bowed and on his lips is a malicious grin. *"Fuck you, I'm smarter than all you dumb assholes"* is written all over his face. He recognized this look as the exact same one Sacks had on his face when he was released and passed by the mourning parents so long ago.

Page two of the paper showed another photograph of someone attempting to get at Johnston. In the photo, three large sheriff's deputies are having trouble restraining this man. The article below identifies the man as Brian Estor, father of the murdered child, Richard. Even in a grainy black-and-white photo in newspaper print, this man looks huge. The article says that he is a contractor/construction worker and that at the time of the kidnapping of young Richard, Brian was away working on a new project. What a coincidence that both he and Estor worked in the same field when he was actually working, that is.

The question that 'he' asks himself now is, "Will the taser be strong enough to bring this giant down and keep him down till I can get control of him? He is going to be extremely important. I don't know if my handcuffs are big enough. This part cannot be screwed up. Better bring some strong tie-downs as well. I don't want to use excessive force on someone who is basically innocent. After all, he is key to my plan. And like I tried to do with Pam, I want to minimize their suffering, their inconvenience. "Shit, there she is again."

Shortly after the trial Johnston moved north to where he is living now. Johnston had always been involved with photography in general and digital cameras in particular. In fact, that's how he caught one of his first victims. Court records showed that he made the promise of some exceptional photographs for this kid who was himself an amature shutter bug. Johnston promised the kid to help him improve his skills so he could win a photo contest at school. The little guy was never seen again.

Richard was also into photography and this hobby eventually put him in direct contact with Johnston. He had dropped his new camera while photographing some birds near his school. The result was that the body of the camera had a slight crack that could easily be fixed by someone with a little know-how. Richard brought his camera to the only store in town that could do this kind of work. His fate was sealed.

Johnston could fix any camera worth over a hundred bucks. His repair work, along with some photography contracts, kept him busy. In reality, he was lying low, just looking for the right new victim. He had no idea that, as a hunter, he had become the hunted.

Surveillance and research on Mr. Johnston revealed that he lived alone, owned a photographic camera shop and was an official sex offender. This conviction had been from well before the recent murder trial. Details were sketchy and hard to find on the internet, but the fact that he was in the national registry laid to rest any idea that he was innocent. They must have had competent lawyers. Not like around here. This case should have been a slam-dunk if the theory and the facts had been laid out properly. But the lead prosecutor didn't consult with more senior staff for advice and he didn't study the file properly. Just plain incompetence. And a lack of professionalism. And probably arrogance. Be that as it may, and understanding that this poor excuse of a lawyer was ill-prepared, therefore Johnston walked. Knowing the generalities of the murder wasn't enough. He'd obtained a verbatim transcript of all the testimony.

He was reading some of the witnesses and shucked his head at some of the testimony he was reading. The first prosecution witness was the Police officers who had responded to the original call about a small body lying in a ditch on a dirt road. They described the scene as they found it, how they secured the area and called for the crime scene technicians. Very routine and competently done. After their testimony, the defense did not cross-examine. Off to the next step in the prosecution.

The technicians arrived and did their part. Photographs of any and everything. Mitts on the hands and feet of the victim, a small boy. Check under every blade of grass, turn ever rock. Look with microscopic eyes. In the end the only promising find was a short single hair which did not seem to be the same colour as the victim's. It was placed in a clean vial and marked as evidence to be examined later for DNA and anything else it could reveal. It went to the labs with the chief technician, the man who took control of all evidence to insure continuity of possession.

Meanwhile, the uniforms were searching the fields nearby by, looking for anything. It is amazing what these men and women found. Old news papers, trash of all kinds and the number of old beer bottles indicated that there was a lot of drinking and driving going on around here. Info for another unit. All were photographed, the location noted. The article was then tagged, protected and sent for forensic examination. Standard procedure.

As simple as that. The prosecution has but one shot at this, and if they miss, there is no coming back. A person cannot be prosecuted twice for the same crime. Point finale. The Prosecutors here did their job well but did not get a total conviction. Johnston was found guilty of luring children but not guilty of abduction or murder. The conviction earned him a year of supervised parole, and his name was put into the National Sex Offender Registry again. The case was closed. Johnston completed his year of supervision and immediately moved north to where he is now. For him, a new hunting ground.

When 'he' had heard about this case, he didn't really know if it suited his purpose. After all, the whole idea is to get publicity and scare the shit out of these sickies to the point that they leave kids alone. *"Was this a realistic hope?"* Well, maybe he was overly optimistic that his actions would stop all attacks on kids, but if it only stops one, if only one kid is saved, then his mission was a success. This whole mission is a tough lonely job with no one to talk to, no one to confide in. "Wonder if I could call Pam? See how she's doing. Fuck, she's there again."

Reading the Court transcript of the trial gave him the idea that bad boy Johnston did qualify for his attention. The research began with open sources of information. The internet showed 'him' that Johnston was up and running his photo business in the downtown area, about a ten-minute drive from the future control center. Perusing back copies of the newspapers revealed most of the details of the trial and provided the info needed to locate where Johnston lived and worked.

At a store he owned and operated, Johnston had a young female assistant. She worked Tuesday to Saturday. Johnston came and went freely while she was taking care of business. However, the store was open on Mondays as well. Johnston worked alone, tending to the counter and customers. All this information on Johnston was gleaned, categorized and put into a file. Hard copies, easily burned at the end of the operation, were kept in locked drawers. Never know when a curious neighbor may come creeping. The computer was double password protected; info was kept on a USB stick that never left his hands. Better to be safe than sorry. A little more internet digging and 'he' was able to locate Johnston's sexual predator file. Reading the document from cover to cover confirmed that Johnston had to go. The plan, still in its infancy, was taking shape.

He' took a beer from the fridge and sat on the back balcony where no one could see him. Alone with his thought he was weighing what had to be done with the psychological effects this job was going to have on him and his new catalyst. His mind drifted from the intricacies of Johnston's plan to the general situation he could see here on the ground. 'Wonder how Pam is' appeared in his thoughts. 'Dam that woman.'

Johnston's photo and bio data were all available to anyone wishing to look him up. His history was right there for anyone to see. And yet, the thing that was most shocking about this whole situation was that he was the leader of a 'Little men of the Mountains,' a group of young boys that went hiking and did over night camping in the national park built in the mountains around the Town. This sicko had direct and trusted access to the most valuable and vulnerable part of our society, of our own children. His blood pressure rose too high. "Had nobody thought to look this guy up? Wasn't there a law or something that demanded background verification on people who were in direct contact with other people's kids? Where the fuck were the cops in all of this? This is a pedophile's wet dream. God, how dumb can you be?" Frustration was setting in. He downed the rest of the beer, closed the file and went inside.

In a few weeks, he had gathered all the background information on Johnston; his thoughts started focusing on how he was going to get control of this sick man. Monday morning, just after opening, would be the perfect time. Have a delivery company magnetic sign on the door. Pull the van up to the back door. Leave the van there, four-way flashers on and come in the front. Show him the old Swedish camera made by Hasselblad that you bought for twenty bucks at a garage sale. Complain that it's not working properly and can he fix it? This is a classic camera and any camera expert would love to get his hands on one of these. He'll undoubtedly look down and might open up the back to have a look. As his attention is distracted from you, hit him with the taser. The rest is the same. Hog tie, then mouth piece and hood, in the van and off to the control centre. Can't forget to put the "CLOSED" sign on the door and take an extra sixty seconds to clean up the counter and any other mess caused by the abduction. Given all of the surveillance that has been done on Johnston and the fact that he does not seem to have any family or friends in the area, it will probably be a long time before he is reported missing. Probably going to be that young female who opens up the store on Tuesday who can't get a hold of him. He opened his abduction bag and saw the taser sitting there. Make sure that it is fully charged. A memory flashed back of the last time he had used it.

His thoughts inexplicably returned to Pam. "Wow, not again," he said to himself. "Why is this broad still in my head, my thoughts? It's like I'm thinking of her all the time." An old friend returned. The personage who was himself but always talking in the third person about himself took over the conversation. "This is like the tenth time you've thought of her this week. "Why?" His alter-identity asked, and the process continued. "Well, you both went through a major trauma in your lives. She was kidnapped and held for days, not knowing if she would be abused, beaten, raped, then murdered, if she would ever see her kids and husband again?" Your shallow promise to her that she would not be hurt were words and lies to possibly keep her quiet. At least in her mind. Until you did whatever it was that you were going to do. Then, once she was no longer useful, you'd kill her. These thoughts were in her mind all the time. It has to have an effect.

And you experienced the loss of your wife and unborn child, a double kidnapping, then the purposeful taking of a life. You've never done this before. And it wasn't just an ordinary murder; no, you tortured the fucking guy to death. You lived then and still do with the consequences of doing something so terrible that even you can't believe you actually did it. You know that the cops are still looking for you, that the next knock on the door could mean years and years in jail. You're not that old. And you're healthy. It would be a long, long time incarcerated. And now, what are you doing genius? You're looking for your next victim! You, who once was described as a 'marshmallow,' are aspiring to become the next serial killer. The public may thank you for your community service and they are glad these animals have finally received true and appropriate justice, but you still hear Sacks' screams in the night when you're sleeping. You still hear his begging and pleas for mercy. Those cold sweats you wake up from have nothing to do with the temperature. You once asked yourself, "Now, what the fuck do I do?" Well, that new question is, "Now, what the fuck am I going to do?" He reverted back to himself. "I need someone to talk to." The trouble is that you are just as lonely and isolated as your next victim.

It's been a little over six months since he had his encounter with Sacks. He still dreamt of Sacks, still hears the screams of pain, the begging, the promises to reform, whatever. These thoughts and visions don't occupy his day light hours, but in the dark of midnight, when he was fast asleep, they came stampeding into his dreams in abundance. Sleep is a precious luxury that he didn't have. Using over-the-counter sleep aids worked at first, giving him a few nights of peaceful rest, but then the body builds up a tolerance to these drugs and more and more is needed to achieve the same sleeping effect. Then, of course, there are the headaches that come with the abuse of these medications. Eventually, you run out of sedatives to use. Now, these same dreams return as vicious as they were. The thought that this is actually something you did boggles the mind of a normal man. "I wonder what Pam would say if she knew what I was planning?"

"Jesus! She's in my head again. What the fuck? Am I losing it?"

He puts aside the re-occurring thoughts of her. Time to focus. Remember that it is the dumb criminals who get caught. All bases must be covered and then double-checked. 'He' had made some rookie errors with Sacks that nearly compromised himself and his objective. "No more of that rookie shit. Plan your work, then work your plan." Wasn't that one of the things that they drilled into you all the time?

The basic work had been done. With this little bit of information, he now feels that it is time to create a formal plan. The file is building. This is where we're at. As they say in the air force, "Target acquired". Now, he needs a control center. He's been scouting that in the off hours when he wasn't watching or following Johnston or working out in his home made gym. There is a small factory warehouse down by the river. It is kind of out of character when compared to the rest of the buildings in that area. It seems way too small. As well from the looks of the siding and doors, no one has been here in a while. There is grass and weeds all around the entrances. Hell, even the phone number on the sign outside looks like it's been around for fifty years. He has done a double check of the phone number on the internet and the rental company still exists. Time to create my new and hopefully improved control center.

A reasonable cover story is required to rent this disaster. OK. He tells the woman who answers the phone on the first ring that he is looking to store some old furniture he inherited from an old aunt who was a recluse and hoarder. "There are all sorts of cabinets, dressers, sofas and mirrors." He needs a place to store all this stuff.

The answer he receives after his in-depth explanation is just short of "So what!"

"I guess I really didn't need a deep cover story." to himself.

"Do you want to see inside or not?" The sassy girl must be the owner's daughter. "I think I know where the keys are. I can be there in ten minutes."

"Ok," is his nonchalant answer, mocking the secretary to whom he had talked. "See you there." A visit was arranged immediately. A walk around the outside revealed not too many windows, secure siding and a large garage door. Perfect for keeping the van he is going to buy now for the abductions. Inside, he saw that the structure was supported by metal "I" beans. "Lovely," he thought. "You can swing a ton from those things without having to worry about breaking them." The windows had never been washed. It looked like they had been installed dirty. "I don't want anyone peeking in. It's not a show I want the world to see, for now, anyway. Later will be OK. I'll have to remember to paint them." It wasn't a long visit. It was exactly what he needed, and he signed a six-month lease, paid cash and got the keys that very afternoon. She asked no questions. Amazing what cash will do.

'He' still had the plans that he had made for Pam's cell. A little bit of tweaking would be needed. Also, he would have to double the amount of wood, plywood etc., because this control center was going to have not one but two cells. But he didn't see having his guests there for all that long. So maybe he could cut out the kitchen area, really didn't need a comfortable bed. "Ya," he thought, "this place is good, and it isn't going to cost me as much."

Time to start working. "I need a van." 'He' drove over to a shopping center far from his home and parked his car near the grocery store." This center looks a lot like the one I got Pam from. Shit, there she is again. She's a fucking witch, and she's haunting me" said in only a half-serious interior voice." He hails a taxi and gets a ride south, two towns down and finds a used car lot with a nondescript van sitting in the back of the lot. He thinks to himself that, "This place looks shadier than the dark side of the moon. "Just my cup of tea." He pays cash to the driver, gets out of the taxi, and mossies along. He is trying to look nonchalant, like he is window shopping rather than on a serious hunt for a vehicle. He wanders onto the lot.

His first impression of the dealership was one hundred percent on. A sleaze ball of a salesman comes rolling out of the rented trailer, which was serving as an office and approaches him with a rollie-pollie walk, a smile that even his mother would detest and an outstretched hand. The only thing missing was the big fat stogie. "Howdy, buddy," he said. "Arnold Baker's the name. You can call me Arnie; all my friends do."

"Wow, this is sleaze heaven, and he's the gatekeeper," all said to himself. "Hello yourself," he responds, mirroring the sleaze approach. "Bob's the name, and I'm just looking at this van here. Looks like its seen better days. Does it work? With a chuckle and, how much you want for it? Looking for something I can fix up and use. Don't have a lot of money."

The response was classic. "Well, that van belonged to my mother; God rest her soul."

"Oh shit," he says to himself. "This is beyond belief. We're going to the Twilight Zone on this ride." Inside is a laugh so hard it almost sneaks out. He squeezes his checks together. "Really," he says, allowing his new friend Arnie or Mr. Sleaze to continue.

"Yes, sir, she passed away some six months or so ago. I've been keeping that vehicle for someone special, someone like yourself. You look like a fine young man, and I'm sure you'd take care of her just the way my mama would want. Would you care to take it for a drive?"

"Ya, that's a good idea. Ok what's the mileage on it?"

"It's got just over one hundred thousand, but those are all highway miles. That's real easy on all the parts, you know. I guarantee you'll get another hundred out of her."

"This vehicle is guaranteed?" with a slight degree of non-believing in his voice.

"Figure of speech, sir, figure of speech. All my vehicles are inspected by a top-grade mechanic before we put them on the lot, but my personal guarantee is for six months or six thousand miles."

"So, where do you service these cars? There's nothing here?"

"Got a deal with the fellow who owns the garage just up the street. A fine young man he is."

This looks like an outright lie, but he won't be needing the van for more than a couple of weeks so he plays along with Mr. Sleezy. And besides, there is one important aspect he hasn't brought up just yet. The conversation continues until Sleazy has the keys in hand. He gets into the van and sighs a huge breath of relief when the van actually starts on the second try. "See, young feller, just like I told ya. In top shape."

"Yes," he says, "started real good." The little puff of blue oil that comes out of the exhaust confesses that the mileage on this bucket of bolts is higher than the sleaze ball is saying. Not going to be a problem.

"So if I was interested in this, what's the best deal you can give me?"

"Well, son, I can let you drive it off the lot today as soon as we fill out the forms and I do a credit check. Company policy, you know. Can we agree on three thousand dollars?"

The response is, "Oh no, I don't think so, friend. This here baby needs lots of love and care. Gonna cost me some serious dollars to fix it up. How about two thousand? I won't talk about the oil it's burning through the exhaust."

"Don't think I can do a deal like that. It's like giving away my mom for next to nothing. She'd spin in her grave. Maybe I can do twenty-five hundred if you release the warranty. Not even sure about that. But twenty-five hundred and I'd be tempted; what do ya think about that? Can we finalize the deal before lunch?"

"Sounds better, and I think you're ready to come down a wee bit more." He gives Arnie a wink, "But I tell ya that because I'm in a particular spot, I'll give you the two five if we wait a week or so before we register it. You see, I'm from back east, just got in town last week and haven't changed my driver's license and all that bureaucratic stuff. A man of the world, like yourself, understands these things. I wanna leave the dealer plates on it till I get my paper work in order. Already put in for the driver's license, but they tell me it'll take a week to ten business days to process everything. Are you onboard with that idea? Can you help out a fellow world traveler?"

So sleaze ball looks at him and is about to say, "No, sorry, can't do that. Inspectors and all that comes around here regularly. Can't take the chance with my license, you know."

The wheels in Arnie's head are turning so openly that he has to scuffle another chuckle. Arnie wants to get rid of this hunk of junk but is hesitating, leaning towards "No thanks." Time for 'him' to play the last ace.

"Oh ya, one more thing, I'll pay you cash right here, right now, if we can do the deal that way and right away."

"He's holding the money out in front, plain and easy for Arnie to see.

Arnie can't resist the look of twenty-five one hundred dollar bills staring him in the eye. His lips are grinding and salivating. Twenty-five Ben Franklins sure looked good in his hands. The deal goes down instantly. Sleazy has a wall-to-wall smile. All's good.

It didn't take long to get a receipt for the money from Sleazy Arnie. Then he to passes the keys over to him with a wall-to-wall grin on his face. Then 'he' was on his way north to his newly acquired garage. The van spit, sputtered and complained the whole way but eventually made it threw the garage door. A quick look under the hood was quite revealing.

The motor was an older model and still had a carburetor. One look at the air filter showed it had never been replaced; hell, it had never even been cleaned. And if the air filter is this sad, the spark plugs must be just as bad. So, friend Arnie lied about a mechanic checking out the van. What a surprise there.

With basic tools in hand, 'he' changes the filter and plugs. Time to test his mechanic skills. A turn of the key and magic happens. Not only does the van start, the motor is purring like a well fed kitten. It's amazing what a little maintenance mixed with love and care will do.

The final steps in preparing the van are easy. Spray the walls and ceiling with Styrofoam isolation. This will hide any sounds his soon-to-be clients may create as they make their way to his control center. Anchors are put in place to hold the passengers safely. "We're getting readier by the day."

Chapter

XXV

B rian Estor was not your average baby. He was born big and stayed that way all his life, always much bigger than kids his own age. In high school, he was an average classroom student, but on the school's football team as left guard, no one ever got to his quarterback. As big and rough-looking as Brian was, he was really a soft-spoken, polite young man. In any sort of conversation with him, it was immediately evident that he was very well brought up. He was a credit to his parents. Men were sir," and ladies were "Mame" open and held the doors for ladies and older gentlemen. Life was good and clear, with no complications. High school was lots of fun with a little study. But there was football, and that made everything right.

Cassy Trembly was Brian's physical opposite. She was small, petite and beautiful without being pinky-pretty. She was at least a foot shorter than Brian. In mid-semester, she was introduced to Brian's class by the principal as a new transfer. She smiled at the seated students and in scanning the room, locked eyes with Brian. He was big, he was handsome, and he looked intelligent, but mostly, his eyes were on fire and they were focused on her. They were penetrating into her soul. Never before had she experienced such absorption. Silently, she thought, "I can dissolve into this guy." Shivers went down her spine. She looked away not knowing or understanding that she had just met the man made exclusively for her. No one else knew it, but the blush on her face was reserved for him.

Their friendship started immediately. As with any two people who were made for each other, they were together all the time. They walked together, went to school dances together, and, of course, studied together. They were definitely attached at the hip.

The relationship carried over into college. Although they followed different majors, lunch and study times were done together. The college was a good distance from home, so naturally, they shared a small closet-sized basement apartment. It just seemed the natural thing for them to do, to be together.

Brian's chosen career path was construction management. His classes were more along the mathematical line; higher arithmetic, algebra and calculus were the backbone of designing and building unique homes. With a motivated and logical brain, Brian was able to ace these courses. There were minor issues with some of the electives, Landscaping design was tough but not as bad as interior design. "Isn't that women's work?" he would ask and get a punch on the shoulder from Cassy, who was never far away.

As he had done in high school, Brian tore up the field with college football. He had been well-coached in high school. He listened well and followed the coach's instructions to the letter. He made first string in his first year at the college. During the second year, his talent improved to the point that he was nicknamed "The Wall." by the school newspaper. The fact that it was Cassy who baptized him with this moniker was quickly forgotten when you could see "The Wall" in action.

The idea of "the Wall' caught on, and at times, friends would pretend to forget his real name and just call him "The Wall." It became very popular around the campus and later would help him in his business. Cassy had taken a step into marketing but just didn't know it. In the end, Brian graduated with distinction.

Cassy wanted to be a writer. She had always loved creating poems, spent hours reading the great masters and was always amazed at how some people, some talents, could make words sing and rhyme. A favorite was from a little-known Canadian poet named John Magee, who, as an air-force pilot, wrote of his flying alone high in a clear blue sky: "... The high untrespassed sanctity of space Put out my hand and touched the face of God."

"Wow!" The real word artists could make music with ordinary words. She was jealous of this ability and, at a young age, devoted herself to understanding how this magic worked.

But this was a dream world. Not many poets lived well and died rich. Poor Robby Burns used to write his lines in the grim on the windows of a Scottish pub. Not a good future there. Yes, she was a dreamer, but there was a realistic aspect to her as well. To balance her whimsical side and to be more practical, she studied journalism, the making and reporting of an event of minor, medium or major importance. "Any writing is good as long as people are reading it and either being moved or informed."

Sometimes, when Cassy was working on a creative assignment, she would sit in the park with Brian. As she played with words in her mind, he would stare at her endlessly without talking. She accepted this for a little while but eventually gave him the unspoken question mark. He would just laugh and comment that "with math, two plus two is always four, all walls, like our children's teeth, need braces, and an asphalt roof should be put on in hot weather. Rules of the trade by Brian Epson. How many times are you going to twist those words around to make new sounds? They're the same words."

"Men just don't get it."

They graduated together. It was no surprise to anyone when they announced their engagement.

It was a very strange feeling for this young couple. Having graduated, what do we do now? Where do we start? Important decisions had to be made concerning their future. The only sure thing is that whatever we do, we do together.

First discussion and decision. Return to our home town. All our friends are there. There, we have a support system if and when we need one. But mostly because the local newspaper has a need for a young ambitious reporter fresh out of school. This could also be seen as as fresh young reporter who we do not have to pay that much. But the negative possibility was ignored. Cassy had a job. There would be cash coming in. But would it be enough?

Their collective education debt was reasonable but was still a monthly payment after graduation. Brian didn't yet have a job, so it was a one income family for now.

But Brian Epson was a popular young man. Like many people "It's all in who you know that gets you ahead." Well, one of his high school football team mates introduced Brian to his uncle, who just happened to own a construction company. With Brian's popularity, great grades in school and the possibility of getting a fresh young mind onto his team, the uncle hired Brian on the spot. Now, there were two incoming salaries.

After three more of these paychecks, Cassy and Brian moved out of his parent's basement and rented a sad-looking little house. Oh, it was beyond sad. The white picket fence was more yellow than white. The grass hadn't been cut for weeks. The exterior desperately called out for a coat of paint; the windows were blind, and no light could pass through.

Inside was even worse, if that was possible. In the upper corners of the living room, the paint had started to curl. Cob webs abound. First, outside impressions of the filth of the windows were confirmed and even down graded from 'yuk' to 'beyond belief'. The kitchen asbestos tiles were worn through from the finished side to the black backing, the part that sticks to the floor. The bedroom was just as bad, but at this point, it seemed that the whole place needed some care. Brian jokingly asked, "Do we fix it up or burn it down?" But it was their first place, and it was theirs. Cassy started singing, "There's no place like home. Where do we start?"

Years passed quickly for the young couple. They didn't stay long in that first place and often described it as only slightly larger that the apartment they had shared while in college. The land lord was doubly happy to have them as tenants. Happy when they rented the place because they fixed it up at their own expense and happy to nullify their lease when they wanted to leave because it had been so well cleaned and renovated that he could now get considerably more rent from it. Happiness all around.

Cassy and Brian went to Maine for their second anniversary. Collectively, they blame "Larry the Lobster for getting Cassy pregnant. "It's Larry the Lobster's fault," they insisted to all the laughing friends. In reality, both were ecstatic with joy and that little fear that comes from knowing that you are now going to have a little person totally dependant on you for everything, I mean everything. "Am I prepared for this?" It was more of a Brain question. "I didn't study baby upbringing at school, ever. Is there a manual that comes with the kid? Like a nine month book we could call 'Daddies Bringing up Babies for Dummies' or something like that. I mean something to tell me what to expect, what to do."

As a couple, they visited the doctor. He reported that all was going well and normal. He expected that this would be a natural birth but that the baby was going to be big. The pregnancy progressed.

Twenty weeks later, Cassy and Brian found themselves in the birthing room at the hospital. Brian was going to participate in the birth of his son. It wasn't long before that little person started coming into the world. Brian watched in awe as baby Richard was birthing. He could see the head. Then, an alarm sound came from one of the machines. Then, a second one sounded. Brian looked around. There was blood, lots of blood, on the table and floor. The machine attached to the baby was screaming. Emergency code calls went out over the floor's intercom. Extra doctors and nurses started running into the room. They all huddled around Cassy. Brian couldn't see anything. All he could hear was doctors giving orders, watching as nurses grabbed the instruments and turned back to the bed. The matron nurse escorted Brian to the waiting room with not-so-gentle hands.

Two hours later, a doctor came to see Brian. "I'm sorry. It's touch and go for Cassy. She's lost a terrible amount of blood, and her type is rare. We need to find more donors fast. Our blood supply people are canvasing other institutions for extra packets. Baby Richard was in distress with umbilical cord complications. We think that the baby is going to be ok. We got to the problem on time. There won't be any permanent damage. For now, there is just a red mark around his neck, but that will go away, and he'll be fine."

Brian replied, "But you're short of blood?"

"Yes, Cassy is AB Positive. Only around three percent of the population has this blood type. It's rare. But don't worry, we'll find all we need for Cassy."

"One thought entered Brian's mind. Cassy needs blood. In the wee hours of the morning, Brian called every friend and acquaintance he knew, begging for blood. Such was his popularity that on that single day, the hospital established a record for the number of donors in a twenty-four-hour period. For Brian, it seemed like an eternity. But in the end, fast work by a large team of nurses and doctors saved both mother and child. The outcome of this battle was that Cassy could no longer conceive.

Baby Richard was recovering well from his trauma and growing stronger each day. By week two, he was released, and the proud parents took the little guy home to a loving household. All was good.

The intervening years were typical for a young boy growing up in middle America. At around the age of nine, Richard discovered photography. His first photos were good but lacking in imagination. Brian bought him a book made for kids who were interested in the hobby. Richard read the book cover to cover. He started experimenting with close-ups and portraits of friends' cats and dogs. In short, he immersed himself in it.

While trying to get a portrait of some birds down at the pond, Richard dropped his new camera. It hit a rock, and the body developed a small crack. Richard took it to a camera shop to get it fixed. There, he met Johnston.

Johnston started stalking Richard immediately after Richard's visit to his store. He was sure that he had his next victim. It was two weeks later, while Johnston was following Richard that Johnston approached him as if it were a coincidence. Johnston lured Richard into his van and was never seen again by any of his loved ones.

Chapter

XXVI

He was sitting on the back porch, beer in hand, thinking about the next steps he had to take to fulfill this mission. Grabbing Brian is going to be a hell of a lot harder than Pam. This Brian character is big and strong. Not only does he work at a physical job, he exercises regularly. I've seen him running on Saturday mornings when he's not working overtime. There are weights in his garage. I don't really want to admit it to myself, but this guy could probably take me, and that's not good. And Pam quietened down after a while. Will this guy accept restraints? No don't think so. But there's Pam again.

After the mission with Sacks, 'he' cleaned up the sites he had used and prepared to leave town. He sold the van to a young couple who were driving to Alaska and needed a mobile home, a camper, something they could live in. They expected their trip to last six months, depending, of course, on the funds they had and would make as they worked their way north.

Three beers later and feeling lonesome and melancholy he called Pam's bank and asked for her.

He got through immediately.

"Pamela Renny here; how can I help you?"

"Hi Pam, how are you?"

"I'm fine, sir. Can I help you with something?"

"Ya, I just called to apologize."

"For what, sir? Do I know you?" But the seeds of recognition were growing.

"Ya. We spent some time together a while back. I think that you'd remember at least my voice."

"You!! You bastard, why are you calling me? Why don't you leave me alone? You got what you wanted; leave me out of any future plans. You son of a bitch."

"Ya, like I said, I called to apologize about punching you. It was stupid and totally unnecessary of me to be that rough with you."

"A punch? Are you only apologizing for a punch? You tasered me, locked me in a cell, and made me pose in photographs for your sick project. Then you exposed me to your murder room. I still have nightmares about the tooth necklace."

"I'm sorry that I hit you as hard as I did." Getting more excited, "Fuck, you had your hands tied behind your back; you still had the blindfold on your head, for Christ's sake. Why did you run? You scared the shit out of me."

"I scared you, asshole, what about me. I thought you were going to kill me. I had to try and get away."

"Ya, Ok, I understand. But how are you otherwise? Are the cops still watching you, protecting you from me? You know I'm gone, right? I left a few days after I released you. How are the kids doing?"

At this point, Pam calms down and continues the conversation in a very strange way. She remembers all the conversations they had while she was his prisoner. They were quiet talks about everything and he was such a good listener. He rarely interrupted and always had a sympathetic response to worries. His voice was soft and kind of soothing. Not like he was a murderer or anything.

He doesn't understand what's happening, but it almost seems like she wants to carry on in this chit-chat. "Weird, but it is nice to hear her voice again." Silently

"How are Robbie and Carl? Still eating you out of the house and home. And is Bev still playing soccer?" trying to lighten the mood and keep it friendly.

"Robbie's dead, and so is Tom too." She says this with a totally monotonic voice.

Surprise and confusion and stuttering, and in a stumbling voice, he asked, "What happened?

"Accidental shooting, collateral damage is how the newspaper called it. They killed my little boy! They killed him!" There's a pause in the conversation as she recomposes herself. "Carl got an exceptionally good report from his teacher. We were celebrating by going to MacDonald's downtown. I don't know if you've been following the local news, but there are two rival gangs fighting for that particular corner where the MacDonalds is. They sell their drugs from there. The Druids and the '09's, they call themselves. The day that we went there, there was a gun fight between them. Tom got hit in the head by a stray bullet. The doctor said he was dead before he hit the sidewalk."

"Robbie got hit in the chest. They rushed him to the hospital, but he died on the operating table. They killed him. We were just walking along then he's gone. They killed him. The bastards killed him."

There was a long silence as the two absorbed this reality.

After the pause, Pam asks, "Why did you phone me?"

"I don't know. You keep coming up in my thoughts. I'm alone on this mission of mine. I don't have anyone else in my life. Believe it or not, I think of you as a friend."

"Wow, and I thought I was in bad shape. What are you going to do now?"

"I've found another 'Sacks' who deserves the same treatment. I'm arranging that right now, but honestly, I don't really think," and he stutters, "I'm sorry. I can't get my head around this. You talked so much about your kids that I almost feel that I know them."

"I...I'm sorry, shit, wow." Then he falls silent. The line is still open, but there is silence between them.

Finally, he asks, "How are you coping with this? Shit, this is unbelievable."

There's a long pause. "Oh, it gets a lot worse. Tom and I weren't doing so well in those days. I suspected that he may have had a girlfriend. He was very secretive; we didn't talk at all unless it was about the kids. He didn't make love to me for weeks at a time. He spent more time sleeping on the couch than with me. Our fights went from bad to worse, and then nothing. We were like two strangers living together. We agreed on a separation followed by a divorce. But we didn't have the money for the lawyers. He's the only man I've ever been with, so it was a giant adjustment for me. After his death, I found out he had a gambling problem. He owed money to a loan shark, had taken almost all our savings from the retirement account and had pawned some of my jewellery and even his wedding ring. I had no idea that he even gambled until the security department at the bank called me for a special meeting. I was hoping to get a raise. I thought that that was why I was called into the meeting. When they told me of the debt that he had racked up on his credit card, I almost died. Our credit cards are attached, so his debt became my debt. We don't have that kind of money. We live almost from paycheck to paycheck. If one of us should loose their job, we'd be in serious trouble. We might even lose our home. I had no idea that he even went to the casino, never mind loose twelve thousand dollars. We had a terrible fight that night. I told him to leave. He didn't. The argument got worse. At first we were talking, then our voices got louder and louder until we were shouting at each other. The conversation ended there:"

"Then you came along and pushed the problem to the back burner. The Police thought that it was he who had arranged to have me kidnapped so that he could play on the public's sympathy and raise the money that way. A 'GoFundMe' type of thing. I think that some of the detectives still think that he was involved somehow. But that's all moot now."

"And Robbie, my little boy. I can't describe the pain. It seems to be never-ending. I still wait for him to come home from school, wait for him to come to breakfast singing some weird song. I didn't cry for two days. I couldn't accept that he was gone. Now it seems that all I do is cry."

The Bank has a health plan for its employees. I go to see a psychiatrist to help, but I walk into his office, lie down on the couch and cry. I cry for almost the full hour, take a few minutes to try and compose myself, then leave. We didn't talk for the first five or six sessions. He tells me that the pain will eventually go away. I don't believe him. Even at our last meeting, I cried for forty-five minutes. Almost seems like I have an endless supply of tears" She says this with a small chuckle. The air goes quiet again. No one is talking, but the line remains open.

He is totally out of sync. This woman who he has come to, what would I call it, if not love but with whom he can empathize, is loosing it. How much of her pain belongs to him?

"I'm sorry, Pam. I can't continue right now. I don't believe it. Can I call you back later, maybe at home?"

"Ok, after 7 o'clock," and she hangs up.

He sits in his chair, wondering why this tragedy is affecting him so deeply. "Maybe I'm closer to this woman than I thought." He leaves the house and goes for a run. Fresh air and the evening sky may help. He comes home still troubled. Maybe some weight exercises will help.

It's past seven-thirty when he finally calls her at home. She answers in a quiet, beaten voice. The voice of someone who is severely down, maybe even suicidal. "Hello." Nothing else.

"Hi, it's me."

"Ya, I recognize your voice this time. Where are you? Are you near here?"

"No. I'm not very far, but no, I'm not in your town anymore."

"Ah"

The silence on the open line returns.

"I can't believe what you told me this afternoon."

"I can't believe it either."

"Do you have someone to talk to besides the shrink I mean, like a friend or family?"

"No, both Tom and I were only children. We moved here from the East Coast to get work. There was nothing at home, so we started a new life here. Our parents passed away years ago, and with three kids, it's hard to make friends. Life seemed to be work, school, support the kids in soccer or ballet or whatever they were into. By the time we finished with all that, we didn't have the time or the energy to develop friendships with anyone. That was supposed to come later."

"Did the cops find out who did the shooting?"

"There were over eight hundred shots made that day. That's the number of casings they found. One kid, a minor, according to the police, had a small machine gun. I can't remember what it was called, but apparently, it's a very popular gun."

"Maybe an uzie?"

"Could be, I don't remember and don't care. One of these bastards killed my little boy, and no one is going to pay. Listen, can we talk about something else? Anything else?"

"Well, I could tell you about me if you want."

"Ya, Ok, it would be nice to talk about something else; even the things you do would be a relief."

"Well, my life is almost as lonely as yours. I wake up at night in a sweat and don't sleep well, and I guess I just have to accept that these stupidities exist and that the system doesn't really care. The authorities could stop this absurdity if they wanted to but the desire's not there. Eventually, I want to get on with my own life and go back to the way it was. Except my wife and child are gone. How do you restart your life when the reason for living has been snatched away from you?" There's more dead air.

She pauses, then says, "You never talked about that. What happened?" The conversation has taken an even larger shift to the friendly, sympathetic side. It's almost as if these are two old friends catching up after a long period of no communication.

"Same as everywhere else, I guess. Irresponsible people doing irresponsible things driving irresponsibly. He went through a red light, and "T" boned her car. My wife and the baby she was carrying died instantly. We already knew it was a boy and had chosen Nickolas for him. She was thirty-three weeks pregnant when she died.

The drunk driver was later found not guilty of criminal homicide because the police could not prove that he was drunk when the accident occurred. He said that immediately after the accident, he ran into the woods. He said that it was from shock and thought that he was going to be sick, to throw up. He said that while in the woods, he had taken a drink of whisky to calm his nerves. Then he said he came back to the scene to see if he could help. The police gave him the test, and he was way over the legal limit. But they could not prove that he had not taken a drink while in the woods. Reasonable grounds for dismissal. So, the test they gave him wasn't admitted into evidence. I guess 'irresponsible' is the word of the day. Sure fucked up my life."

There is a common thread running between these two people. They have a common history. The connection is becoming more and more apparent as the conversation continues. He lost his wife and unborn child to an injustice. It is very evident that he justifies his kidnapping but is sensitive to her point of view. He apologizes for the rough treatment at the end.

Her world has learned that life is not a bed of roses. She'd been kidnapped and threatened with death. One of her children and husband were shot dead. Finding out your husband may have a girlfriend, was a compulsive gambler and put you into unbelievable debt has battle-hardened her almost to the point of having no emotions, no feelings. There is nothing that shocks her anymore. But the conversations she had with her captor while she was his prisoner were warm memories. She realizes that now. He would sit and listen, sometimes for hours at a time, as she ranted on about any and everything. She figures that by now, there is not a lot about her that he doesn't know. And yet, he was never judgmental and always took her view as accurate and gospel.

And his voice, when he did speak, was soft, almost musical and a pleasure to listen to. As much as it surprises her, she admits that she could easily be friends with this man. There is a small period of dead air before she asks lightheartedly.

"Do you have a name?" A common history can be a binding thing.

"Yes" he responds and then leaves the question hanging for a few seconds like he's going to continue keeping it a secret. Then, in a teasing laughing voice answers, "My name is a small drum roll please, Donald. I was Donnie to my mum, Donald when I was in trouble and Don to my friends. Now I'm just 'He.'"

"Thanks. It's nice to have a name to connect to a voice. So, who was Donald's last name secret before he became he."

"Don was just an ordinary guy. Only child to loving parents who brought him up well, then passed away. No siblings. Only wanted his wife and kid, never made trouble anywhere, quiet person living his life like everyone else until the accident. Always been madly in love with kids. They're so innocent and always truthful. You know, one of my neighbor's four-year-olds once called me 'Old man.' Hell I was only twenty or so at the time when she said this. I had to laugh. It's all in the perspective; where are you looking at it from? But now, look what I've become. A vigilante, by myself, screaming at a crowd of deaf people. Fuck I'm getting depressed just thinking about this."

"And now I'm on another 'mission' I call them. Figure I'm about halfway done. But this one is much more dangerous. There's an element in it that scares me, and I have to find a way around it. How are Carl and Bev taking Robbie's death?"

"They're kids. They know that Robbie's not coming home, but I don't think the reality of it has really sunk in. They don't understand it. Bev asked me the other night if Robbie was mad at them for something, and that's why he won't come home. How do you explain to a child that some bastards took her brother away, that they killed him? Robbie and Bev were really close. Death is hard to explain to a child."

"If you're that worried about this, what did you call it, this mission? Why not just call it off, quit, go home."

"I can't. The guy I'm after is just too bad. He needs to die. It should be all over within a week or so. Then I'll take a break. I can't sleep. I'm tired all the time. I hear screams at night. I'm beginning to believe that I was not cut out for this work. And really, I don't have a home anymore. How are they treating you at the Bank?"

"Good, I can't complain. I was off for six weeks and then had to return. I didn't want to lose my job. The Bank manager is a really nice man. I'll tell you more about him later on. I have to go now. Bev is getting home from Girl Guides. Goodbye."

Reluctantly, he hangs up the phone as well. I need to get back to work, finish this shit up and then maybe live in peace for a while.

Chapter

XXVII

It's time to assess the situation. He has a pen and paper in the van with him. He's watching Brian at a construction site. He's carrying three asphalt shingle packs up a ladder. "Those bloody things weigh sixty pounds each," He says to himself. "Don't they have lifts for that now?" Back to the job at hand.

The garage is ready. Johnston's room is ready. Well, there really isn't too much to it. No need to get too extravagant; he won't be there that long. It is just four walls and a locked door. No need for luxuries.

The outer room is more comfortable. But security measures are in place. Extra strong doors and locks are installed for Brian. It's as comfortable as he can make it, considering the money invested and the amount of time it will be used. But it does have a microwave, a fridge with some basic food stuffs in it. Brian can have a coffee as I tell him what's going on." So it meets both possible requirements. If Brian gets mean and ugly, the security is there. If, on the other hand, he's reasonable, then there are a few comforts. Either way, he expects Brian's visit to be a very short one.

On the Brian front, well, that's still a problem. The more he thinks about it, the more he is convinced that he needs a better way to capture Brian. As he is thinking this, Brian grabs three more bundles and goes up the ladder like he has boxes of tissue paper on his shoulder. He drops them on the roof and three workers come over and move them up to the line. Brian comes down the ladder and looks southward, waving.

He doesn't realize it at first, but his solution drives up in a red minivan. The van parks in the driveway, and Carry gets out carrying two lunch bags. The one for Brian is considerably bigger than the salad-carrying bag she opens. They sit on a stack of lumber, eating while the other workers come down, grab their lunch pails from their cars and wander off to eat and rest.

It's interesting to watch the couple as they eat. They are constantly touching each other, laughing at whatever, and the smiles are ear-to-ear wide. They are looking at each other like the world around them doesn't exist. And then it hits him. Grab Cassy, and Brian will follow. And as an added bonus, Cassy has a handle. She has a ponytail. Eureka. Problem solved.

The plan is now concrete. Grab Johnston, then Cassy, and lure Brian in. Explain what is happening to Brian and Cassy. Then, let them loose on Johnston. Very carefully free the couple and then dispose of the body. Do the after-clean-up and leave town. "Maybe go back and see Pam." without her knowing I'm around. We'll see. Seems simple enough. "I wonder where Murphy's law will come in."

Well I think that Murphy must be out of Town or some other place. After realizing that the best way to control Brian was through Cassy, it became a much simpler task. All I have to do is take Cassy, and Brian will follow like a little puppy dog. Or so my plan goes. At times, I have to remind myself that I am playing a dangerous game. I cannot afford any mistakes. One screw-up, and I'm in jail for a hell of a long time. And for sure, I don't want Brian to get a hold of me. I plan the work, and now I'm going to work on the plan. Think it out carefully. Don't panic and die.

Task number one is to establish a routine for Cassy. Until that's done, anything else would be speculative. So, with this in mind, I arrived at the Elson home slightly after eight fifteen in the morning. I'm thinking that if she has a job, if she is still a reporter then she'll start work around nine o'clock. You can drive from one side of this Town to the other in less than thirty minutes, so she'll probably not leave before eight-thirty. From my perspective, arriving fifteen or twenty minutes ahead of time gives me a chance to find a nice hiding spot and enjoy my coffee.

Surveillance is a tough job. It involves hours of waiting, going close to comatose, and then when your target moves, bang, its a hundred miles an hour in your head. Doing this kind of work is even more difficult when you try to do it alone. Well, today I'm alone. Been that way for quite a while now.

Where the Elsons live poses another problem. Their house is in a development where everyone has their own garage or driveway. There are no cars parked on the street. Therefore, any car parked on the street will immediately stand out. Within ten minutes, some noisy busybody will call the cops. The solution to this is simple. Back off.

Fortunately, this was the way this development was built. There is usually one funnel road where all cars entering or exiting the development must pass. The funnel road will dump out onto a large street but more often a boulevard with traffic lights.

So the one car surveillance team must find a spot where he can see the intersection without standing out and be in such a position that he can fall in behind the target car in a normal traffic flow manner. Screeching tires is not a good idea. There are often clues as to which way the subject is going to turn. If the target car is in the right lane, then he will probably turn right once he has a green light. There is a sign at their corner indicating 'No Right Turn on Red.' If he's in the center or left lane, then expect a straight-through or a left turn. It is doubtful that they will go straight through this intersection as this leads to another housing development. A left turn from this position is ninety percent guaranteed. The light usually stays green long enough to pull this maneuver off, and you can easily get in behind your subject.

With this in mind, I took up a position across the boulevard in a lengthy strip mall. I managed to get a good spot next to the convenience store The traffic was light this time in the morning. I settled into a cozy position and took the lid off my overheated, stale coffee. I didn't have time for one good sip. The red minivan arrived at the intersection. The light was red. I could see Cassy driving. She was first in line, alone in the van and in the left lane. I was expecting a left-hand turn. Wrong!

She came straight through, pulled into the strip mall, and drove behind me as I momentarily panicked, thinking she was coming to see me and maybe say hello. Hell, I didn't know what she was doing. Spinning around to see what she was doing, I spilled the coffee on my lap. Burned my dick. Damn, it was hot. Wasn't there some woman who spilled very hot coffee on herself and then won a massive lawsuit? Hell, I could be very rich and don't even know it. I just can't imagine showing up in Court with photographs of a scalded scrotum and petrified penis begging for compensation. I laughed at myself till I cried. I'm my own biggest fan. But back to work.

She pulled in two cars away from me. She went into the convenience store and came out a minute later with a cup of coffee. She got into her van, continued up towards the other end of the mall, and pulled into a spot. She got out and used a key to enter a yoga shala. Just another word for studio, but I'm feeling smart today, so I thought I'd impress myself. Bingo. Well, that was easy. Only now, it also looks like I peed my pants. I'll have to return home. All in all, a good day's work, and it's not even nine o'clock yet. But the day wasn't over. I had to know more about her movements.

I returned to the strip mall after changing my peed-in pants, found a decent spot to watch her place from and considered my possibilities. It would be easy to pull my van up next to hers and use the same technique I used on Sacks and Pam. The trouble is all the participants of a Yoga class finish at the same time. Are they all going to come out together? I can't do anything if there are ten or fifteen other women around. They'd swarm me like bees. Maybe, being the owner, she'll stay behind to clean up and then close up. Going to have to wait and see.

I stayed around for the next five days. It appeared that Cassy had a very faithful following. The same ladies showed up Monday, Wednesday and Friday at the same time. There was a second group that came on Tuesdays and Thursdays. Cassy was busy all the time but finished early in the afternoon. On Mondays, Wednesdays and Fridays, she finished at three thirty. Tuesdays and Thursdays, she finished at two in the afternoon. Tuesday at two was my target time.

On Monday, I would grab Johnston and bring him to the control center. I would have to give him a little welcoming gift. I still had my Babe Ruth bat. Tuesday afternoon, it would be Cassy's turn. Hopefully, Brian would follow closely afterward. That same evening, I would let Brian and Cassy set upon Johnston. If what I think is going to happen happens, then I'll release Brian first, then Cassy. I'll dispose of the garbage and call it a day. Next day or so I'll reserve for cleaning up my control centre. I don't have any plans after that so maybe I'll wander back and peek in on Pam. Our conversations are the highlight of my weeks. Don't know where this is going to go, but I am mobile and can be in Canada in a couple of hours. I might go there and relax for a while. I do need to decompress a bit. I can see myself free by the middle of next week. Maybe then. For now, no decisions are required, so I'll go with the flow. It's Thursday so I have all weekend to ponder my future fate.

I arrived home at my temporary residence to find a note on my door. The neighbors were having a little social get-together Friday afternoon. We used to call them 5 to 7's. People used to arrive at five but rarely left at seven. It was more likely around nine o'clock when the guests finally left. I was invited. "Sounds good," I said to myself.

I called up Dick's wife, Joan, and accepted the invitation. "Is there anything I can bring?" I asked.

"No, thanks. The ladies have taken care of everything, and we'll have your favorite BarBQ chicken wings. I kind of noticed you paid particular attention to them last time so we picked up a couple of extra packages. I hope you'll enjoy them."

"Oh, I will, and thank you. I'll see you at five on Friday," and hung up. It is amazing how many good, friendly people could exist besides the likes of Sacks and Johnston and the thousands of others like them. Boggles the mind.

It's Thursday. If my memory is right, Bev has girl guides tonight. It would be a good time to call Pam. I need some good conversation. At seven-thirty, I dialed Pam's home number. She answers before the second ring.

"Wow, that was fast," I say.

"I kind of thought you'd be calling tonight. How are you?"

"Well, I'm almost finished here. All the plans are in place, everything is ready, and if all goes as planned, I'll be free from here by next Thursday or Friday,"

"What do you have planned after that?"

"Nothing, really. Like I told you last time, I don't think I'm cut out for this shit. I'm thinking of going somewhere to rest and relax. I need a new life plan."

"By the way, any news from the cops on Tom and Robbie's killer?"

"I called the detective and he told me that they were at the end of their leads and that nothing had changed. They have narrowed down the suspect list, but unless one of the gang rolls over, there is not much they can do. They know that the bullets that killed Tom and Robbie were from a gun used by the 'O9s because there was only one of that type of gun. The 09's had it. They do not have enough evidence to charge anyone. Those bastards are not going to pay. And they are at it again. There was another shooting last week. Luckily, no innocent victims. Only two bastards from one of the gangs were killed. I hope they all die. I hope they all rot in hell." Someone has to stop these guys. They're terrorizing the City, and cops are helpless. There's a slight pause. "But enough about me and my problems. You still having night mares, trouble sleeping?"

"Ya, it's not getting any better. How are you doing?"

"Not well. You remember that I told you that my boss was sympathetic to my problems. That he was going to help me. He called me into his office last Thursday. He closed the door. Usually, that's not a good sign, but this time, it was great. He told me that he knew that my finances were going downhill fast. We, well I only have one income now. It's really unbelievable how much kids cost. He said that he had been reviewing my loan loss ratio and that it was the best in his office. In fact it was the best of any branch in the whole bank. Using this information, he was going to give me a double raise. I was to go from L.O.4 to L.O.2. Sorry, that's bank jargon for 'Loan Officer.' It would mean a very nice raise. I would be able to stay afloat and maybe even put a few dollars aside. I left his office feeling that my cursed year was over. Finally, I could see the light at the end of the tunnel. Then hell broke loose, and now I don't know what to do."

"So what happened?"

"My boss was so good they transferred him to head office, effective immediately. Friday, they called him in the morning, and he left that afternoon. My paperwork was still on his desk. The new manager showed up Monday morning. He's the new definition of 'asshole' An arrogant little prick like him has never existed before. He thinks he's god's gift to women. He wears this three piece suit and has a flower in the lapel. His shoes must cost a month's salary. He doesn't know it, but he looks like a pimp. The shoes are Italian leather and shine like they're glowing. But mostly it's his look, his arrogance. The 'I know all' look and the way that he looks down on everyone, even though he's only about five foot seven. He's the son-in-law of one of the big shareholders of the Bank. His father-in-law is also a good friend of the CEO's. He's a pig."

"A pig?"

"Does the pig have a name?"

"Ya Calls himself William Bishop, now get this 'the third.' Not Bill or Billy, we have to call him Mr. Bishop. There's a rumor that he had to leave his last position because of harassment complaints. Nothing ever went public, but two women left the Bank suddenly and without any comment. Seems, according to the rumor mill, that they were paid off and agreed to keep quiet. And, of course, in most cases like this, there was probably an NDA agreement.

"You called him a pig. Those are pretty strong words coming from you. Did you know one of those women?"

"No, but I have first-hand knowledge that he is a pig.

"A pig, really?"

"Ya, a pig. He called me into his office to discuss the memo that my old boss had written. He starts off the conversation by saying, "This is very interesting. Mr. Ryder wants to give you a substantial raise. Says here that you are one of the finest and most loyal employees he has ever had the honor to work with. That's quite a compliment coming from a man as strict as Ryder is. Tell me, did you provide Mr. Ryder with other services or other favors? Not many people get on his good side as you seem to have done." he said.

"Then stupid me, I didn't really catch on to his subtle hints. Mr Ryder had always been very professional in his dealings with me and with all the employees. He was a good, fair boss. It never dawned on me then and there what he was referring to or alleging. He comes from behind his desk and sits in the chair next to me. Again, I don't understand or realize what he's doing. He skips the chair closer. Now, he's in my comfort zone; he's too close. Then the pig says that it must be lonely for me since my husband died, that living without a man must be hard for a woman such as me. Then, without as much as a wink, he said that if I wanted that raise, I would have to offer him some special service. That's what he said: 'Special services.' And then he reached out and rubbed my breast. I was flabbergasted. I couldn't speak. I just sat there. He continued to touch me until I got up and left the office. I ran crying to the washroom. I couldn't speak, couldn't talk. I just stood there gasping for air. My god, what did I ever do to have these things thrown at me? I'm still flustered, still in shock. I need this job desperately, but how can I do anything? If I complain, I lose my job. I do nothing, and this pig is after me. I'm nauseous. I can't think straight; I'm yelling at my kids for nothing. They think I'm going crazy. Do you know anyone who committed suicide?"

Then he could hear the tears start to flow, the gasping breath and the low tone moan of a desperate soul." He replies to her question.

"No, suicide never happened to anyone close to me, but I have seen some pretty depressed people. I knew a man once who changed so much when he was depressed that even though I knew him in his depressed state, I didn't recognize him. It actually altered his face beyond recognition. Think of your kids. What would they do without you? This will pass. I promise you, this will pass. Suicide is not an option. You're still needed here." He stops talking for a couple of seconds, then asks, "Pam, are we friends?"

The phone line emits only static until seconds turn into minutes. Then, in an undecided, unsure voice, she says, "Yes, I think so. You know more about me than anyone. I really enjoy our talks when we can talk in generalities, about politics even about the weather. Our conversations are so easy. I look forward to your calls; yes, I think we could be friends."

"Even after I kidnapped you, and you know the rest of it?"

"Yes, I understand that, but still, you kept your word. You never hurt me. Not as bad as Tom or this pig, anyway. And these talks do me a lot of good. I think I get better results talking to you than when I talk to the shrink. I look at him, and all I can see is his eyes ringing up the billing hours, listening to this distraught, stupid woman tell him her problems. He seems excited when the hour is up, and he says, 'See you next week. It's like I hear a cash register ring up a sale when he says that. So yes' I think of you as a friend. Yes, for sure."

There is another long pause in the conversation. "You know what I'm doing, Pam, what I've done?"

"Yes, you explained to me many times. I've seen the video. I've been in your murder room and all the shit you had in there. I know you killed Sacks. But honestly, it really seems like a hopeless cause."

"Ya, I know. I'm trying to rid the world of sickies and help save people I don't even know. The effort is killing me. It's very slow, but

I feel myself dying inside. I see what I've done, and there's really no change anywhere. So much for world appreciation. Now, a friend is in trouble. Really, my only friend. Who would I be if I didn't come to help? I'm coming."

"What, no. What can you do? No, no, stop. Oh my god, you're not going to 'Sacks' him, are you? I can't be part of that. Already, I'm in trouble. I wouldn't be able to handle you killing him for me, especially the way you did, Sacks. Please, please don't do anything, please. I'll deal with it, please."

"Can't leave you like this. I'm coming. I see myself as your godfather, your guardian and I will not let this pig give you any more trouble. We'll talk soon." Then he hung up.

"Oh god. What have I done now? I've sent a professional killer after my boss."

"Now, what the fuck do I do?"

Without realizing it, she has just mimicked his words.

Chapter

XXVIII

One thing that is for sure is that plans, once made, can and will be changed. And it seems the more definitive the plan, the higher the likelihood that it will be altered. It's said that all war plans are junk the moment the first shot is fired. Thus, the Johnston file had to wait a full week, maybe more. The plans were rewritten to help Pam first. Saturday morning, he would return to Pam's neighborhood. "It will be good to see her, even if she doesn't know I'm there."

He attended the Friday night cocktail hour with the neighbors. There was a lot of repetition of the last party's complaints and jokes. Dick was as quick as usual and had some interesting information on changes that were being made to the tax code. Seems a couple of other middle-class tax advantages were being shut down. The group could expect a higher tax bill next year. Fewer deductions and fewer places to shelter money for the future. His part of the conversation was to announce that he had a good lead up north and that he would be leaving for a few days to see if this lead played out as he had hoped. They wished him good luck. The party ended after eats and people said their good byes. The wings were delicious. Another weekend had started.

Saturday morning, bright and early, he was on the road. Pam and her problems were now his, and he knew how to deal with them without getting her in trouble. A soft approach was best. "I don't want to get her in trouble. Anything too serious, then the cops would get involved that we don't want. Gotta be soft but firm. "

On Monday morning, he was in place to see the Bank open. There was Pam. Wow, what a beauty. The rest of the staff arrived, but no one who looked like a manager entered. Closer to eleven than nine o'clock, an obvious little prick came strutting down the sidewalk. He had on a white suit and a red rose in the lapel today. It wasn't hard to tell who he was. A little shit of a guy with a face only a mom could love, you know, the type. Even when you don't know the guy, you want to punch him square in the face and knock that smirk clear to tomorrow, even his walk was disgustingly arrogant, nose up and that smirk. The manager had arrived. After less than 10 seconds, he had built up a massive hate for this guy. Mr. Arrogance entered the Bank. So it was him and not just another self-important prick. "See you tonight, buddy. We're going to get very much acquainted."

Pam's Bank closed at five in the afternoon. She came out fifteen minutes later, got into her car, and drove off. Her godfather was further west, just beside the park. Close enough to see but far enough that no one would get suspicious. No one would think that he was casing the bank for a robbery. The park was the direction 'arrogant ass hole' had come from. This was where he was going to meet his Waterloo. As I said earlier, surveillance is a waiting game.

It wasn't long afterward that 'ass hole' came out, locked up and walked towards the park. The nose was held high and looked like a live punching bag. Godfather started walking towards him.

There is one thing about a punch. If it comes from a guy who regularly hits on a bag, arms become strong, and knuckles become callused. His body is used to the shock of a solid hit. If he is in good shape and if the recipient isn't expecting the punch, then there is a good chance that the contents of the stomach will be projected up the esophagus and out the mouth. The receiver will fold in two, roll over and fall to the ground. All wind has been pushed out of his lungs and he'll just lay there gasping for air like a grounded trout. It's really funny to watch, as long as it's not you doing the gasping, doing a fish impersonation.

The arrogant asshole approached Pam's godfather without realizing the trap he was in. As the two men approached each other, AH, because that was what godfather was calling asshole now, looked up into the godfather's eyes and saw something he didn't like. "What was it?" he said to himself. "It's as if he recognizes me."

At two feet to thirty inches and with the left foot forward, godfather advanced the right foot, made a fist and, rotating his hip and shoulders into the punch, let his fist fly out and into AH's stomach.

There was no preparation on the receiving side. Godfather's fist sank deep into AH's stomach till Godfather was sure he could feel the back side of AH's spine. AH folded into the shrubs, arms holding his stomach. Bile and semi-digested lunch matter ejected from AH's mouth as he struggled for air.

"Do you know who I am? William Bishop the Turd? Get it? 'The turd, you little piece of shit. "The turd, come on, that's funny. Why aren't you laughing? At least a little smile," he said as he knelt beside AH. A bit of bile drool slid out of AH's mouth and down onto the rose. "I said do you know who I am? Answer me, ass hole."

There wasn't really an answer but a hint of a nod indicating no from AH?

"I'm Pamela's godfather. You're fucking with my family. You don't fuck with my family." Godfather reaches into AH's breast pocket and takes out his wallet, looks at the driver's license, noting the address "You married?"

A small nod," Yes." So this is what's going to happen. Hey, I'm talking to you." A little slap across the face got AH's attention back. Bile was drooling down AH's face. The rose was destroyed. "You will support Ryder's recommendation; you will not harass my Pamela in any way, as an employee or as a woman. You mess her up, and you'll pay. You don't fuck with my family. Maybe Mrs. Ass hole would like to know what her husband is up to. Maybe her father wants to know what his son-in-law does at work. Are we clear?" Another slap for good measure, and, well, it just felt good. "You don't fuck with my family. "And oh ya. If you're stupid enough not to keep our agreement, well there are other means slightly more pervasive. I think you get the point."

This nod indicated that he understood. There was a little moan that came with the nod. AH seemed to be recovering.

"Good," Godfather says. "We understand each other. No one has to know about our little arrangement. That way, your wife doesn't know, her father doesn't know, and you'll keep your job, and the cops don't know, and everybody's happy. It's a win-win situation, isn't it? Wouldn't you agree?"

There's a nod

"It's a pleasure doing business with you. I'm glad we have this understanding," and he throws the wallet on the ground, leaves the park and heads for the motel.

At precisely seven thirty, he calls Pam. She answers immediately. "Is it you? Is that you, Don?"

"Yes."

"You didn't do anything stupid; you're not getting me in trouble, are you? I really need this job. I'm not going to get arrested tomorrow? Am I? You didn't kidnap him, did you?"

"No, no, and no. You're not in trouble. I just had a friendly talk with him. Seems there was a small misunderstanding. Everything is fine now. You'll see. He's a changed man. Did he do anything nasty today?"

"No, the auditors were with him all day. He did look at me once, and I don't know, but I felt chills go up and down my spine. All manager transfers are followed by an audit to make sure the books are clean. It's a control method."

"Well, the next time he does something inappropriate, tell him your godfather says hello."

"What does that mean?"

"Just tell him your godfather says hello. He'll back off after that. Oh, and ya, hey, you're going to get that raise. Congratulations."

"Oh god. You're gonna get me fired. Are the cops coming to arrest me? Oh god."

"Ok, Pam. Stop. Everything is going to be Ok. I'm not going to leave you like this. Nothing bad is going to happen. Period. You are going to get that raise. Period. He will leave you alone. Period. Believe me, trust me. I'm going to stay here for a few more days, enough time to make sure that asshole keeps our agreement. Ok? We'll talk tomorrow night after you get back from work. I won't leave you alone here. I'm with you. Do you understand?"

Some but not all of the panic is out of her voice when she replies, "What did you do to him? How do you know I'll get the raise? Oh god, am I going to jail?" The panic voice is returning.

"Get some sleep. Do you still have the sleeping aids that the shrink prescribed for you?"

"Yes."

"Take two when you go to bed. It'll help you sleep, and you'll see that tomorrow, he is not going to bother you. I have to go; good night." There is no use continuing the conversation with Pam today. She's too strung out. Tomorrow will be better.

After the call to Pam, he goes to the motel bar and orders a beer, sits alone and contemplates his next moves. Wonder if I'll have to re-visit 'the Turd' or if I can get back to my principle file with the soon-to-die, Mr. Johnston. He's run out of quarters for the jukebox, and the beer is empty. Time to hit the sack. Might have to do a lot of driving tomorrow night, hopefully.

The next morning comes quickly. The beer helped him sleep, and dreaming of him and Pam together made this the best sleep he had had in a while. "Wonder if dreams can come true?" he asks himself.

It's going to be a quiet day. "I need to wait and see the results of the discussion I had with Turd. Won't have any news till tonight. But to be sure that all the players are in the right place, he returns to his watcher spot just after eight-thirty. Pam arrives on time, looking gorgeous. "Is that a new dress?"

William Bishop the Third, also known as 'the turd,' comes walking along, but more on time this morning. White flower today, but he doesn't know which kind. Into the bank, he goes. So everyone is where they should be. Time to take a drive around, maybe do a small workout. I wonder what the old neighborhood looks like today.

With that thought in mind, he drives to the old control center where he held and killed Sack's sickie. "The world is a better place without you, Sacks. I, on the other hand, am not doing so well. I'm still having nightmares because of you." Now he's talking to Sack's spirit: "I won't let you win, pervert." The rest of the day was spent driving around. He skipped the gym. Supper was a hamburger from a fast food joint. Seventy-thirty could not come fast enough, but it did eventually arrive. He pushed the number from his phone's friends and client list. Pam answered immediately.

Her voice was more upbeat when she said, "Hello."

"Well?" he says without specifying what

"Well, what?" is Pam's response.

"Don't screw with me; I've been waiting all day."

"I don't know what conversation you had with him, but he stayed in his office all day. I had to go in and get his signature a couple of times. Each time, he called his secretary in. And this is funny. I reached over to show him where to sign one time; he backed up from his desk as if I was going to hit him. I'm sure I saw fear or dread in his eyes. He looked at me like I was the devil's wife. He's petrified of me. What a great feeling. All in all, it was a good day."

"There are lots more to come, Pam. Honestly, do you think I need to stick around? I've got other shit to do. Oh and by the way, is that dress you had on today new? I don't remember seeing it before. You look good. Any news on your raise?"

"There is no news on my raise, but these things usually take a couple of weeks. No, it's not new. I haven't worn it for a while. Do you like it? How close have you been?"

"Ya, suits you very well, and I've been very close. I especially like your perfume."

"My perfume, you've been that close?"

"No, just kidding, but I do like that dress."

"Well, then I'll wear it when you finally ask me out for supper."

Oh boy. I wasn't expecting that, but the suggestion is more than welcome. "I'll finish what I'm doing and give you a call. Do you have trouble getting a sitter for the kids?"

"No, there's a thirteen-year-old next door who is always looking for money. She's always available." There is a pause in the conversation which seems to have now come to an end. Then Pam says, "I wish you wouldn't go. I feel safer with you around even though I've never seen you."

"I feel that I have to finish this job. One more try to get the world to listen. I'm behind schedule. I'll call you next week, just a check, up. But I don't know if I'll be able to talk. And Pam." There was a short hesitation.

"Yes"

"I'm glad we're friends," and he hangs up.

It occurs to him that he is working his way towards a personal void. Once this job with Johnston is done, he does not have any future plans. But on the other hand a beautiful woman has invited him out. So maybe it was a really good day after all.

Chapter

XXIX

Is there a possibility of a future? Don't know. But it does look promising. And considering that I don't have anything else on the go, this will have to do. Back to the job on hand. Johnston has been free for far too long. Brian and Cassy are ready. The plan is feasible with minimum risk to me. The control centre where all of this justice will take place is ready. I'll grab Johnston just after he opens his store, say 0930hrs. This military talk gives me a feeling of a well-organized operation. I'll get him to the control center and then return for Cassy.

Cassy will finish her class at around 1400hrs. Should be able to grab her at around 1430hrs and bring her to the centre. It'll take maybe thirty to sixty minutes to talk to her and call Brian to get him where I need him to be. I'll have to convince Cassy that there is more than just me in on this. Otherwise, picking up Brian will be a problem. Monday cannot come fast enough.

Monday morning was bright and sunny. Temperature in the mid-sixties with a promise of sunshine all day. I was up bright and early. At 0845hrs, I was set up watching Johnston's store. Lots of good parking spots around here for a stalker. That would be me. At 0905hrs Johnston arrives, parks his van in the usual spot, walks to and opens the door. This is not going to be a usual day for him, but he doesn't know that yet. He'll find out soon enough.

Coffee is finished, so I leave my comfortable parking spot and drive around the back of the store. Four-way flashers are on, and I walk around to the front and enter the store. I have my old black driving gloves on and the old wreck of a camera in my hand. As I enter, I see that he focuses on the camera immediately. He doesn't look at me at all. He's obsessed with these machines. I put the camera on the counter, and as he's looking at it with anticipating eyes, I hit him with the taser. The rest is easy. Hogtie his feet, handcuffs his hands behind his back, place a duct tape over the mouth, then hood over the head. Grab him by the belt and collar and lead him to the back door. Fast look up and down the laneway, nobody in sight, launch him into the van, attach him to the wall, tape his feet, give him a kick for good luck and return to the store.

I grab my camera, lock the front door, put the 'closed' sign up, turn off the lights and look around to see if I missed anything. All looks good. I exit through the back door. I have to be extra careful now. Even if this all went off without a hitch, my adrenaline is still pumping. I'm overstimulated, so I put extra effort into driving and the speed limit and obeying all traffic rules. As I push the button on the automatic garage door opener, I'm thinking to myself, "This was almost too easy."

When the garage door is shut, I pull Johnston out of the van by his hair. He has a big mop there. I cut the tape on his feet and walked him towards his room with him following behind me, all crouched down and stumbling over his own feet. He's trying to talk through the tape and hood, but all I hear is gibberish. Besides, I'm not really interested in what he has to say.

Once in his special room, I grab the chain hanging from the "I" beam and attach the hook to the handcuffs. Then I ratchet it up so he's on his feet, bending over, and his arms are up in the air behind him. An extra push on the ratchet, one click, and he's up on his toes. There is soft groaning coming from under the hood. His present discomfort will soon be replaced by serious pain. Ya, the plan is in motion. It's lunchtime by the time I'm satisfied that Johnston is securely in place.

On Tuesday, after some fast food, I drive over to Cassy's place and check it out. Everything seems to be the same and normal. In the afternoon, people arrive. It's just past 1300 hrs when they start their stretching. I'm watching through binoculars. These women are bending in ways that would kill me if I tried. I'm sure that there would be an ambulance needed to get me out of the Astavakrasana or eight-angle pose position. It's a good job. I have Mr. Google with me. I couldn't ever guess these exercises.

At the end of the session, they all form a circle, then join hands, run to the centre of the circle and shout. The circle breaks up, and they all seem to be laughing. They then head for the changing rooms. Within fifteen minutes, they have all gone and Cassy is alone cleaning up.

There are a lot of parking spaces in the lot. I chose one next to her red van. There is a Korean specialty store beside her Studio. I enter and buy some noodles, and then start looking around. The staff are busy with re-stocking the shelves and don't pay any attention to me. No security cameras anywhere I can see. Great.

Cassy leaves the studio, and I rush out as casually as possible. I'm taking long, fast strides and catching up to her as she approaches her vehicle. I look around quickly. All clear. As she enters the space between the two vehicles, I grab her. My right arm was around her waist while my left covered her mouth. My van door opens as I have her in the air, kicking like crazy but with no effect. I get her hands behind her back and cuff them. A gag over goes over her mouth, hood over the head and then the feet. Duct tape them, and she's caught.

Very casually, I leave the side door of the van and walk around the back. I pick up my purchases that I had dropped. Take a nonchalant look around. No one seems the wiser. I fasten Cassy to the walls of the van. She's very quiet. Then I drive off. This was another easy one. I used the same precautions I had when driving with Johnston and arrived back at the centre without incident. The easy stuff is over. Now, the toughie begins.

I arrive at my Centre and once the garage door is shut, I open the back door and reach in for Cassy. As gently as I can, I pull her towards me and cut the tape holding her feet together. I guide her out of the van and towards the more comfortable room. I can't hear anything from Johnston. Cassy and I arrive at her chair. I turn her around and tell her to sit. She complies. I take the gag off her mouth. Then I pull up a chair behind her and start a conversation.

"Do you know who I am?"

"No."

Do you know where you are?"

"No."

"First, let me tell you that you are not going to be harmed. Do you believe me?"

"You kidnapped me. We don't have a lot of money. We can't pay a ransom. We only have a few dollars in the bank. Why are you doing this to us?" I notice the plural use of 'us.'

"Good questions. I'm not doing this for money, and like I said, you won't be harmed in any way. I guess, to put it plainly, I'm a vigilante. I need you and Brian to help me right a wrong, a place where justice did not do its job. First, we need to get Brian here. Where's your phone?"

"Why do you want Brian? Are you going to hurt him? Are you going to kill us?"

"Where's your phone...please?"

"My left pocket."

Then, I touched her hip when I was trying to get the phone; she recoiled like I had stung her. "Sorry," I said, "I should have told you I was reaching for it. You need to talk to Brian. He has to come here. Call him."

"Why?"

"I will explain everything once he's here. Call him...please."

"Hey, stupid. I can't call him with my hands tied."

"Sorry," and I cut the tape holding her hands. I leave the left hand free and tape her right hand to the chair. It reminds me of the conversations I had with Pam. She calls Brian.

"Hi, sweetie. What's up?"

"I've been kidnapped!"

"What?" There's a pause. "That's not very funny. What's the punch line?"

"No, I'm serious. Some guy grabbed me as I was leaving the studio. He's got a gun and a taser machine. He wants to speak to you." She raises her hand over her head, and I take the phone.

"Brian," I say, "Cassy is here with me. I'm not going to hurt her, and really, I have a big surprise for you and her. I think you're going to like it. But first, you've got to get here."

"Where's here? I'll go now."

"Not so simple. You see, I don't want you to see me. The surprise I have is," he hesitates for a few seconds before saying, "Well, not quite legal."

"What the fuck, what the fuck are you talking about? Not legal. You kidnapped my wife, for Christ's sake. Legal? What does that mean? I get a chance, and I'm going to kill you, you bastard. I'll rip you apart."

I ignore the threats and the cursing and say, "Look, I can't explain it on the phone. At six o'clock I'll send my partner to pick you up just outside Cassy's studio. It's a dark blue van. Get in the back door. Put the hood over your head. There will be tie wraps there. Attach your hands, then sit against the wall. He'll bring you to me. Understand? And do I really have to say it? No cops, please and no monkey business from you. Remember, we have Cassy."

"Yes, I'll be there, no cops."

I cut the line off there, but before I could hear hard breathing. This guy is mad; this guy is dangerously mad. I put that into the 'to be expected' box and carry on with my plan. But I remind myself, "Be careful."

I tell Cassy what Brian has said and that I'll be picking him up at six o'clock. "In the meantime, would you like something to drink or snack? Do you need to use the washroom?"

A curt "No," and the silence begins. This is really weird. It's not at all like when I lifted Pam. Cassy isn't moving in her chair. She's not saying a word. There's no talking, begging, pleading, nothing. She just sits there starring into the hood, into the darkness of the hood.

It's about a fifteen-minute drive to Cassy's studio. I leave at five o'clock or 1700hrs in my military mind. That should give me time to look around and see Brian arrive.

I tell Cassy that I am leaving to pick up Brian and that we'll be back in about an hour. There's a grunt in acknowledgement. Strange, I think.

I arrive at five sixteen precisely and find a decent surveillance spot across the street. I look around and cannot see anyone looking my way, so I jump into the backseat. No shadow or reflections.

Brian arrives minutes after me. He's driving a work pickup truck. He's too early for my taste, but then again, his wife is missing, and he intends to do all he can to find her. He parks in front of the studio and checks out Cassy's van still parked where we left it. I stay where I am and continue looking around. I'm doing some counter-surveillance. I don't want to get caught. I don't see anything that looks suspicious.

At five after six, I drive in front of Cassy's place and stop the van. Brian gets out of his truck and goes to my back door. He opens it and says, "You got Cassy?"

I answer, "Yes, get in and follow the instructions," which he does to the letter. I checked him our as closely as possible and am satisfied. He's well attached, but just in case, my Taser and gun are close by.

We drive to the centre.

It's not an easy thing to do, but I get him into the room beside Cassy. I sit him in a chair beside Cassy. When she hears us enter, she calls his name, and he responds. "Are you Ok?" he asks her.

"Yes. I'm scared but ok. What's going on? I don't understand," she says.

"I don't know either, but here we are."

At this point, I cut in and say, "Tell me about little Richard." There's a gasp as Cassy leans forward in her chair. "Tell me about him," I repeat.

Cassy asks, "Why? Why do you want to know about our dead son?"

I answer, "Because this has to do with him."

"He died a long time ago. We've moved passed his death."

"He didn't die", I say. "He was murdered."

A very quiet "Yes" comes from Cassy's lips.

Brian interrupts, "This is crazy. Our boy is dead, and there's nothing we can do about it. Are you some kind of crazy person digging this story up? None of this makes any sense."

I notice that Brian's breathing is getting heavier. Raging bull heavy. I have to move this along faster so he listens and doesn't go berserk on me. So I addressed Cassy and said directly to her. "Please answer the question; tell me about Richard."

Cassy starts with his birth and the problems she had with the delivery. She builds up her story to the time he was kidnapped. She skips a lot of the small details, but the storyline is as accurate as it should be under her circumstances.

It takes her a few minutes to say all she has to recount. Brian grunts every now and then, confirming her story. At the end of her little speech, I asked them if they knew a guy named Johnston.

Brian answers, now taking control over their part of the conversation. "He killed our little boy. But that was a long time ago. Why do you want to know, and what does this have to do with us today?"

"I'll explain why you are here, but first, some history."

"What the fuck says, Brian."

"Please listen, and you'll understand. My name is not important. It's what I am trying to do that I hope will make a difference in the world. I think that the justice system is failing and failing badly. Too many criminals are getting off with horrendous crimes. They are not being punished at all. Fuck, they let them walk free. Don't you two agree?"

"Yes, but," they say in unison. "There's not a lot we can do."

"What would you do if you could do something? If you could get revenge on someone who's been really bad, someone who hurt you seriously? Someone who stole your most precious possession. Wouldn't you love the chance to even the score? And with no chance of repercussions. Wouldn't you love that? Think about how good that would feel. You got your revenge and settled the score. Wow, what an opportunity."

Brian answers, "This doesn't make any sense. We live a quiet life. No one bothers us. We're not violent people. We don't have any money. Why? This doesn't make any sense."

"It will in a minute. You'll see. Give me a minute or two to arrange things" I leave them there in the chairs and check the monitor in Johnston's room. He's still hanging where I left him. No surprise there. I enter, "Wake up, asshole. Your time is near." I lower the ratchet, and he stands up straight. He's mumbling something, but the tape over his mouth is solid. Can't make out a word. "You'll make a nice target to a professional-level football lineman," I say it to myself and laugh a little. I remove the tape from around the hood. I attach his hands to the same chain, but this time, they are in front of him. I raise the chain so that hands are over his head but his two feet are still on the floor. I take his hood off. I want him to see it coming. I love these moments filled with anticipation of what's about to happen. I leave the room, closing the door. All the players are in place. Time to set the cat unto the mouse.

I return to Brian and Cassy. I can see that Brian is trying to get out of the restraints. He doesn't hear me, so I say, "Save your energy, Brian. The ropes will be off very soon."

One of the problems I encountered when planning this operation was getting Brian and Cassy into the room with Johnston without letting them loose in the outer room. If I had just cut them free, then they'd be after me with a vengeance. And like I said before, this Brian character is big and tough. I don't want to tangle with him. It turned out that the solution was a simple one. I bought chairs with wheels. Second-hand office chairs. "Time for the surprise," I say. "You first, Carry," and I roll her chair into Johnston's room. Her arms are still tied to the armrests, and the hood is still in place. She can't see a thing, but when we arrive, Johnston finally shuts up. He can hear the activity and is looking towards the door. His eyes open wide when he sees Cassy. I don't know if he recognized her or not, but it seems that he did, even through her hood.

"Just a second," I say to Cassy, "I'll go get Brian," and I leave. Brian probably weighs three times as much as Cassy, and when pushing him, I feel the difference. No matter. He ends up beside Cassy. I walk over to Johnston and ask him "Know these people?" He looks around nervously, not really comprehending what's about to happen. I loosen his chain some more. He can move around a little bit. No problem there.

I leave him standing there and go to Cassy. "Listen, Cassy, you hear me?"

There's a small nod. "I'm going to release your arm now. I'll leave the knife on your leg. Take the hood off and free yourself, and then free Brian. Your surprise will be right in front of you. Have fun."

As soon as I close the door and check the monitor, I see Cassy do exactly as I had instructed. She cuts herself loose and then frees Brian. They hug, embrace and check each other out for damages. They find none.

Brain is the first to speak, "What the fuck is going on?"

"I don't know," is Cassy's reply. Still hugging, they realize that they are not alone in the room. "Who are you?" Brian asks, "You look familiar."

Johnston looks at Brian and looks for an exit. There is none. The only door is behind Brian and it's locked.

Brian continues to look at Johnston and finally figures out who he is. It's fun to see the recognition on Brian's face but tons more fun to see Johnston's face when he realizes that Brian has figured out who he is. Fear has a strange face, but to be locked up in a room with the father of a boy you killed and no exit in sight. That is abject horror.

Brian releases Cassy and, in full lineman's speed, shoulders down and screaming like a banshee, levels into Johnston. He's enraged. "I didn't think that the human body could bend that way," I say to myself. "Was that noise bones cracking?" Brian is a dog who has his rag doll. The punches and kicks going into Johnston almost bring up a 'sorry for your situation' thought in my mind. It gets suppressed quickly enough.

Brian has been at Johnston for what seems an eternity when Cassy grabs Brian from behind and literally drags him off of Johnston. "No, you can't kill him. You can't do this. Stop, stop right now." She and her ninety pounds stand between Brian's two hundred and forty pounds and Johnston. She was holding Brian back. It was evident that Brian has the power, but Cassy is the boss.

Brian stops. His fists and knuckles are covered in blood. I don't know if it's Johnston's blood or Brian's. His eyes are wide open and he's more snorting like a wild animal than a human being. He looks at Cassy and says nothing. She stays between him and Johnston and holds him by his shirt, saying, "Stop, we can't do this. This is not right. Stop right now. Calm down." And to my amazement, Brian stops.

Cassy turns to the camera over the door. "We aren't doing this. We won't hurt him anymore. We've stopped." And they stand together, looking at the blinking red light.

Now what the fuck do I do?

Chapter

XXX

I'm in shock. This is one outcome I had not expected. My plan included them. They were supposed to kill Johnston. I was then supposed to let her go, then Brian. Then, I would dispose of the body. Then, I'd clean up and bid farewell to this Town. It wasn't a complicated plan if only everyone had played their part. I'm starting to think my whole idea of righting wrongs has failed. No one cares. I key the mic. "Is that animal still alive?"

Cassy looks at Brian and, without saying a word, tells him to stay where he is. She backs away from Brian to make sure he doesn't move then goes over to where Johnston is hanging. She puts her finger to his neck and says, "Yes, he has a pulse. Seems to be strong." As she says this, there's a grunt that comes from Johnston, and he spins around. As he opens his mouth to take a breath, a couple of teeth fall out, and drool mixed with blood ooze from his mouth. I immediately think of Pam and her pearl necklace. I key the mic again. "You guys want to finish him off. Think about what he did to Richard. He doesn't deserve to live. Kill him."

Cassy is the first to respond. "No, we aren't killers," and her response finishes there.

I really don't know what to do now. The only solution to this is to carry through with the plan, but instead of dropping Johnston off at the town dump, I'll drop him somewhere else. I feel confident enough that he has not seen me and doesn't remember what I look like. Anyway, by the time he talks to the cops, I'll be long gone. How much work will the cops put into this incident? Just another gay bashing. And will Johnston cooperate with them? Doubtful.

On the other hand, when I first took Sacks, I thought the same thing: that the cops wouldn't investigate aggressively. I think I was wrong at that time, could I be making the same mistake? As the kids say these days, "Whatever." Time to clean up here. I key the mic again. "Ok, Cassy, take the handcuffs from the top shelf and tie Brian to the chair. Both hands nice and tight. Then the hood, please. Make sure I can see the hands on the camera over the door. Once that's done, sit in the chair and put your hood on. Remember that I have a gun. I will reverse the procedure for letting you two go." It's visible that Brian doesn't want to be tied down again. Cassy and him have a long, whispered conversation, which I can't hear. They're talking too low. If I do this again, I'll make sure to have better microphones. I key the mike again. "Hey, none of this shit is optional. Brian, get in the fucking chair and do it now" My raised voice and Cassy's pleading get Brian into the chair. Cassy does her part exactly as instructed.

With a gun in hand, I enter the room. The first job is to check Brian's restraints. They seem ok. The next job is to tape Cassy to the chair. Done. "Ok, listen up. I'm taking Brian back to your studio. I'll release him there. Then I'll come back for Cassy. Same thing for her. I'll take care of Johnston. Maybe I'll leave him in the dump even if he's not dead." There's a period of dead air, no movement as I contemplate what has just happened. "Why don't you want to kill this guy? He murdered your son. Don't you want justice? I just don't understand."

Again, Cassy is the first to speak. "We're not killers. We can't do that, especially after all this time. Richard has been gone for over a year now. We're a peace with his passing. He's with God now, somewhere safe. We had to forgive Johnston in order to get our own lives back. We can't, and we don't dwell on what's happened. If you're so intent on righting miscarriages of justice, why don't you just kill him yourself? He really is garbage. Are you some sort of coward who can't do this yourself, so you kidnap others to do your dirty work? Wow, what kind of cowardly sickie are you?" And with that, she was quiet again. I, on the other hand, was perplexed.

Wow, that hit close to home. "Ok. I don't really know what to say. I thought that you would want a chance to take revenge. If that's your decision, I can live with it. Let's get you two outta here."

The plan to release the Elsons went off as it was supposed to. Johnston I left on the sidewalk in what is commonly known as the "Gay Village." Sooner or later, someone will pick him up. Cops will conclude that it was a gay bashing. My last words to Johnston were, "See you around soon for round two, sonny. Especially if I see cops involved." I don't know if that will shut him up, but it didn't cost anything, and maybe it'll work. I'll know soon enough.

It doesn't take me long to undo the control centre. Most of the wood I took to the dump. The other stuff went in the recycling or garbage of the factory across the street. I noticed earlier that they have a private firm do their pickup once a day. This stuff will be gone this time tomorrow. Items that may have had my prints on them went into a forty-five-gallon drum and were burned. It took me until Friday to do the cleanup, and I returned to my 'normal' house late in the afternoon. On the drive home, I was rethinking my mission, my quest to right the world's wrongs, even just a little bit. Things were not turning out the way I had expected. I'd have to rethink my position.

Arriving home, I found a note on my door. The friends were having another get together, and I was invited. I was starting to enjoy these happenings. They brought a sense of normalcy back to my life. I called and accepted the invitation. Once again, I asked if I could bring anything. Not necessarily was the standard answer, and that's what I got. I was beginning to feel like a leach, always taking, never contributing. So I stopped at the florist shop and bought all the ladies a small floral arrangement. Nothing says thank you like flowers. I wasn't too worried that the guys would hate me for this. I knew I'd have to put up with some ribbing, but that's ok with these people. They are teasing each other all the time.

I arrived at precisely five o'clock. Everyone else has already arrived. I guess they were anxious for some decompression after a week at work. The flowers are a big hit. No surprise there.

Burt was the first to comment, saying that I was putting all the guys to shame for not thinking of flowers themselves. I commented that I've had a good week and that I have the time to do these things. I added that if I had brought flowers for the guys, they would not have appreciated it. That got a chuckle. Little compliments go a long way. Told them a little secret. I picked up the weeds after the bridal group had left the church. Got a second chuckle with that.

Then I asked them, "What's the similarity between a pregnant woman and a burnt pizza?" Puzzled looks all around. Not even any attempts at an answer. "A drum roll, please." Burt drums on the table. "Someone forgot to pull out in time." Good laughter. They'd make a fine audience if I had more, but I only have this last little rhyme.

"My grandma makes me chicken;

It chokes me, there's no doubt;

The next time she makes me chicken,

She'll pull the feathers out."

The two jokes together make a good entrance. The conversation grows more normal now, to subjects they discuss every week.

Sports, then the economy, then to more personal matters. Dick, the host and an accountant, announces that there may be some new codes coming from the IRS. He tells the 'boys' that just maybe we'll get some kind of tax break. Clifford, the mechanic, says that they are very busy at the dealership. Apparently, more people are opting to repair their cars rather than buy new ones. A definite sign of tighter times. But it keeps his department going like crazy.

The evening drags on. I'm in a hurry to leave, but I can't be impolite and leave before the normal breakup time. Tomorrow, I hit the road back to Pam. It's about one and a half hour drive. My van is all gassed up and ready to go. The suitcase is full. Suitcase? Well, that's s joke. It's really a backpack with most of my worldly possessions in it. Don't know if I'll be back this way. I'm just coming down psychologically from the whole Johnston affair, and with the poor results I got from that, I'm not sure what to do now. Well, I do have to come back to say goodbye to this group of friends if I leave for parts unknown. That's how I see them now, friends who help me understand what 'normal' is. They make a great moral compass, something I really need these days. I feel a certain sense of nature here. The party comes to an end around nine o'clock. I thank the ladies for the excellent food that they prepared, especially the chicken wings. Joan tells everyone while looking at me that next week, we'll have another guest. Her recently divorced college roommate is coming to stay for the weekend. She has a twinkle in her eye while announcing this. Is Joan acting as a matchmaker? I hope not.

The next morning, Saturday, I skipped breakfast and settled for a coffee. Driving through town is not the time to think deeply. With the traffic, the lights, and the possibility of a kid running out from between two cars, you have to be really on your toes. I finally got through town and hit the interstate. This highway is long and straight. My exit is eighty-seven miles away, according to my GPS. This old buggy doesn't have cruise control so I push with my foot and hold at slightly over the speed limit. People are passing me but that's Ok; I just don't want to be stopped. I still have the sleazy-ball's plates on the van. He must be really pissed by now. No matter, the future is ahead on this straight road. It's an easy drive, and I relax. It makes a great time to think.

My mind was still reeling from Cassy and Brian's reaction to what I had planned. I've had two or maybe three no 'thank you's' so far on two serious crimes I've committed. Doesn't anyone care? The obvious answer is "No'. Should I take these two incidents and generalize them to everybody, or maybe more precisely, nobody gives a shit, nobody cares?

About a third of the trip, I come to some conclusions. First is that even the victims forget and forgive after enough time has passed. Secondly, my efforts to scare away perverts are not working. Really, it's almost laughable for me to think that single-handedly, I could have a global or even a national effect. That really was a pipe dream. And Cassy was right. I am a coward and cannot kill anyone, even these paedophiles. Then I think of how this has all been affecting me. Sleep eludes me. When I can fall asleep, I hear Sacks and the screams. I've taken so many over-the-counter drugs that my head hurts almost all the time. I'll have to dry out from 'Sleepy Eyes Sleeping Aid' and other products like it and resume a healthier diet. I think maybe it is time for me to give up on this idea and return to a normal life. Yes, no more kidnappings. I'll see Pam, have a meal with her, maybe meet the kids. Maybe we'll hit it off and become more. More of what I don't know and can't bear to imagine. If that doesn't work, then head home to the east coast. Ya, that's it. No more vigilante shit for me. Fuck all of you who don't care. I'm quitting. My little chuckle is that at least I don't have to offer a letter of resignation.

I feel this certain sense of relief. I recall my friend, the third person singular and use him to go over my activities with the goal of determining if I should be worried about getting caught. First job, Sacks. Nothing in the news, even the local papers, have long since forgotten about him. Pam, the other person involved here, seems to be on his side. Maybe she doesn't condone what he's doing, but she won't give him away. And there is no reward to the person who turns him in. "Na, he's safe on that one."

The Johnston operation didn't go as he planned. What are the possible consequences? On the positive side, he made sure that no one ever got a good look at him. Johnston himself only had that short distance from the door to the counter, and he was smart enough to flash the camera, thus diverting Johnston's eyes. The general description that Johnston could give fits half the men in America. In the rest of the interaction with Johnston, he was hooded.

The real danger here comes from the Epsons. How much did they see, and what are they going to tell the cops about their experience? They will go to the cops for sure. He doesn't think that Brian will be much of a danger. He was hooded almost all the time. Couldn't have seen anything.

Little Cassy could probably give a better description as far as witnesses go. She will probably say between five foot eleven and six-two, one hundred ninety to two hundred twenty pounds, causation, very strong. Wore denim all the time. Had a gentle voice.

Will the cops in the two towns be able to connect the two crimes? If they do then he has a problem. They might even start up a task force to trace the killer. On the other hand, if he keeps his word and stops this activity, then there can't be any new leads. The task force will quickly disband.

Any new activity and, of course, the task force remains with new funding, and he'll be called a serial killer. So much for public support. The third person singular advises the first person that, in his opinion, the risk of getting caught from actions already committed are minimal. Any new activity in this area, and the assessment is null. The more I think about this, the more I am convinced to stop this stupidity. My decision is final.

I arrive in Pam's town just around noon. I take a sweep by her place before finding my motel. Her car is in the driveway, but I can't see any activity around the house. I check in and then grab lunch. I'm feeling better already. It's like a giant weight has been lifted from my shoulders. No more kidnapping. No more beating these child molesters, though they deserve every strike. No more looking over my shoulder all the time. Hopefully, the nightmares will subside and then go away altogether. The future looks good. I am super satisfied with my decision and I can even feel myself breathing easier. All the anger has left.

I pick up the phone and call Pam's number. A little girl's voice answers. "Hello, this is Beverly."

I say, "Hi, is your mom there, please?

Very gently, she says, "Just a moment, please," and then she screams into the phone, causing a ringing in my ear. "Mom, the phone's for you."

"Hello, who is this, please?"

"Hi Pam, it's me, I'm back. Everything is finished and I said I'd come by once finished. I was hoping to take you up on the supper date you invited me to. Any time this week is fine with me. I'm really looking forward to it. We have a lot to talk about."

"I'm not really sure who asked who out to supper, but I'd love to. This week will be difficult, PTA and course the Bank is giving me, but on my own time. Really, only tonight is free. Is that too fast for you?"

"No, not at all. There's a nice steak house just up the street from the bank. Is that OK with you?"

"Fine, shall we say seven o'clock?"

"Yes," he replies, "I'll make the reservations. Do I pick you up, or would you prefer to meet there?"

"I'll meet you there. Noisy neighbours around here. Nice, friendly and helpful but noisy as hell. But I don't know what you look like. How will I know you?"

"You're going to wear that dress, the old one I saw you in at the bank?"

"Yes, Ok."

"Then I'll be there and meet you at the door." And with that short conversation, he has his first date in a long, long time.

Chapter

XXXI

The flower trick worked well with the ladies back at the house. So, I picked up a small bouquet to lighten the introduction. I arrived at the restaurant at six forty-five. I had requested a quiet corner but I had to be close to the door for when she arrived. The table was too far in the back, so I hung in the bar just beside the entrance. "Why are women always late?" I asked myself. She arrived at seven ten in that old dress of hers in which she looked like a roman goddess, to me anyway. I hadn't been this close to her since we shared the first control room. At that time, she was in serious distress and dishevelled. Now, she had had time to prepare. Make-up was slightly administered. Posture elegant. Hair glowing in the late afternoon light. I walked up to her and froze. "Now, what the fuck do I do.? We had never been formally introduced, and most of the latest communication with her had been on the phone. How do you say hello to your captive? I approached her, and she solved my dilemma. She took my hand and kissed my cheeks, both sides. "Oh well, out of that awkward situation." I lead her to our table.

The waiter was punctual and arrived with a small bottle of champagne. We toasted our first unforced supper together. It wasn't long before the routine we had established earlier in our relationship took over. My participation was short questions, and small comments with the odd agreeable grunt thrown in. I watched in fascination as this beautiful woman told me absolutely everything about herself, her family, small as it was, and her hopes and dreams for the future. Her almost unbroken dialogue went on all through the appetizer, through the main course and stopped abruptly when dessert arrived. "Now it's your turn," she said to me. "Tell me all. Maybe we could start with your name."

"Well," I said, "As I told you on the phone, my name is Don, Donald Minson, born just outside Pittsburgh. Only child, great parents, what else can I say? I'm not really used to talking about myself. I was an only child with a normal or average childhood. My father worked in a mill in Pittsburgh, and my mother was a stay-at-home mother and wife whose main concern was me. At eighteen, I joined the Army. I wanted to be one of those Delta Force guys. Big and strong and tough. I made it almost all the way through training but got a hit to the head during one of our training exercises. I ended up with a slight concussion from it, and it affected my eyes. My vision wasn't as good as it should be. I didn't meet their standards for eyesight. They had to let me go. I went back to school and took up architecture. I apprenticed with a firm that did work all through Pennsylvania. Duller work has never existed. I got tired of just designing things and then having someone else complete my work. So I quit, got my own licenses and permits and 'hung out my own shingle'. They say that in all those old westerns. I started offering a complete service. I would not only design these houses but would build them as well. People I talked to seemed to think that it was a great idea. It did seem to be starting well. In the first week, I got a nice contract."

"I met my wife while we were both studying. She was into computer design. I never really understood what she did, but she was very good at it. She designed and built a program that allowed businesses to keep track of their inventory more effectively. A small outfit can use free software from the net, but businesses with massive inventories need something special. She built it. They leased it. It wasn't long before she was making three times as much as me, and then, finally, someone bought her out. We made a lot of money with that."

"We lived together for over a year, and when she got pregnant, we decided to get married. We were married less than a year when she got killed. I was supposed to pick her up that day, but I wanted to finish the roof I was on so we could have the whole weekend off. She jumped in with a friend, and as they were driving home, the car got hit by a drunk driver. She was thirty-three weeks pregnant, and she and the baby she was carrying died on impact." There's now a silence at the table. "I've been living with this for over a year now, and still, it hurts." The pause in my recital is left to linger. Pam says nothing. "It's been a short time, and it's been a long time since the accident. Sometimes, I think I can hear her in the next room. At other times, I have trouble remembering what she looked like. A doctor told me that that was normal. I think that that was the first step into my becoming a vigilante. The drunk got away with it.

"I stumbled around for quite a while aimlessly after that. I didn't know what I wanted to do. Then I learned about Sacks. All of a sudden, I had this flash in my mind: "Fix it," and that's what I tried to do."

"Oh God, do we have to talk about him?"

"No, not really, but he is the one who triggered me to do what I've been doing. I saw what he did and how he got away with it. You know the rest. I felt I had to do something, anything. I'm not doing it anymore. Screw it. Let the sickies live. Not my problem. You know that other thing I was working on. Well, it didn't go according to plan, either. A total screw-up. I still don't understand people. Even the victims don't want revenge. On the way here, I had a lot of time to think. This whole thing I'm trying to do is hopeless. No one cares, and it's tearing me up. I'm quitting." As I say this, the breath in my lungs leaves, and I just sit there, resigned. A slow recovery of breath, and I ask, "Any news from the cops?"

She looks at me. I can see that her eyes are bloodshot and notice her speech is slightly slurred. Hell, she's getting drunk. The champagne is starting to work. "No, they know it was the '09s' because only the 09s were using that sort of gun. Other than that, the investigation is dead. Those bastards killed my little boy, and no one is going to pay for murdering him. I hate them. I'd like to kill them all." There are tears in her eyes, so I have to lighten the conversation. "Hey heard a good joke the other day. So this couple are lying in bed together when the husband touches his wife's shoulder. He rubs all around the left side, then works his way down her back, gently passed the hips and down the right leg. He continues up the other side of the same leg. His wife is now in tune with his advances and is starting to purr. He passes her other hips, moves up over her body, and abruptly stops. Now she's in the mood and asks, "Hey, that felt good. Why did you stop?"

His response is a curt' Well, I found the TV remote." Her eyes brighten as she releases a smile and a laugh that brings out her natural beauty. I look on in wonder at how gorgeous she is. I can't think of any other words to describe how beautiful she is. I'm in awe. The air around the table has lightened up. That's good.

There's a long pause in our conversation as the waiter removes the dessert plates and brings the coffee. I notice that she's had three glasses of champagne, well, maybe two and a half. Her glass still has some in it. She's looking down at the table, seemingly in contemplation. She is gorgeous.

Slowly, she looks up at me with a sombre look and asks, "Do you ever get lonely? I've been lonely for so long. And you going around doing this all by yourself? Don't you miss a normal life?"

"Yes, I want to go home, but I don't have one. It died with her. What about you? Do you find it hard being alone?"

"Tom and I weren't getting along very well. We lived together, but there was nothing between us. We used to fight a lot. A couple of times, he even hit me, and I told him I was going to call the cops. I never did because I felt I was part of the problem. But the problems never got resolved. And then he got shot. Now I've got the problem. I'm even more alone. It's ok during the day. I've got work, and in the evening there's the kids with homework and activities, but when they go to bed and I'm there all alone, I feel the emptiness in my life. Even if it wasn't a romantic bed, at least there was someone there. Now it's just cold."

"Don," she says in a most serious, soft voice, "we can't go to my place, but will you take me to yours and just hold me, hold me tight, don't speak, just hold me?"

"Yes, let's leave now." The ride to my motel is quiet. We go into my room without speaking. She puts her purse down beside her shawl and comes to me. Her arms open, and she gets absorbed into me. We stand there, not talking, saying nothing. I started to move around a little bit like we were dancing. She's moving with me. She takes me by the hand and gently leads me over to the bed. She sits down, the mattress creaks, and she starts unbuttoning my shirt. I'm no fool. I let her lead, and before long, we are naked in bed, doing the deed a thousand different ways. Eventually exhausted, I fall asleep.

The sun is in my eyes. I'm in that conscious state between sleep and wakefulness. I lie there without moving not wishing to disturb the euphoric feelings that I have. Finally, I roll over and discover she's gone. I never heard a thing. Eventually, I get up, look around at my dismal surroundings and see a note near the sink.

"I had to get home for the kids. Thank you for a superb supper. The dessert was really out of this world. Bev is in Seattle this weekend for a soccer tournament; Carl is going camping with his troupe. Both will be gone for three days. I'll call you when I finish my last morning interview. It should be around eleven o'clock. And we can discuss some different desserts.

"Thanks again, Pam."

"Ok," I said to myself. This is getting better than I imagined. I looked around my rented room. A place for me to sleep, Ok; a place for a night in the dark, Ok, but a place to spend three days with 'Helen of Troy' here, not Ok.

Now, in the time I had spent here working the Sacks operation, then later watching out for Pam, a lot of my time had been just driving around looking at scenery, basically wasting time. After all, even a serial killer needs time off. To the east, in the mountains, I had once stopped at a small camping ground situated on a beautiful lake surrounded by glorious snow-capped mountains. I remember thinking to myself at the time that this has to be one of the most beautiful places in the world. Breathtaking doesn't describe the beauty.

One side of the lake had camping lots complete with platforms for tents as well as BBQ pits. Near the office were kayaks, canoes as well as paddle boats and wind surfing boards. The farther side had small cabins, which the owners rented out on a night or weekly basis. I didn't remember if the camp was still open or even if there were vacancies. I had to find out. It was still early enough in the day that I could make it there, rent a cabin if one was available and get back to town if Pam should want to have lunch with me. The cabin would be a great surprise for her and give us a chance to connect further.

At ten-fifty-five, I returned to my motel room. Mission complete. I had a cabin on the point of the lake, complete with a dock and a small row boat. The motor was not included. I don't care. At eleven ten, my room phone rang. It was Pam.

"Hi."

"Hi yourself", said the angel's voice. "What time did you finally wake up?"

"Sometime around eight-thirty and poof, you were gone."

"Kids can't show a bad example."

"Are we on for Friday?" I asked.

"Yes, Carl leaves at noon and won't be back till Monday evening, time to be determined by the traffic. Bev joins her team after school and they leave directly from there. She took her backpack and all the needed equipment with her to school this morning. She'll be back Monday night. If they win, she'll be going back next weekend for the finals. I promised her I would go if they win."

"Great" was my understated response. "Do you want me to pick you up at work at home? How would you like to do this?"

"My neighbours are noisy. I'll take a taxi to your place. We can work it from there."

"Sounds fine, what time?"

"Five thirty at your place."

"Good, but we're not staying here. I have a surprise for you."

"What is it?"

"It wouldn't be a surprise if I told you now, would it? You'll have to wait." There's a long hesitation, and she asks me semi-seriously, "You're not getting weird on me, are you?"

"No, us mass murders don't reveal our identity till we have our victims in hand," I respond. "But seriously, it's a good surprise." like any psychotic serial killer would say. Then I laugh. That seems to calm her, and she closes the conversation with, "Ok, see you Friday and thank you."

Friday doesn't come fast enough, but it does arrive. She has a small overnight bag and probably the largest purse I've ever seen. It is enormous. I get a smile and a kiss as I reach for the suitcase. I am a gentleman, after all. I don't even let her enter the motel room. I direct her immediately to the van. Off we go. She tells me about how excited Bev was to be going to this tournament. This will be her first time away from home for more than one night. Carl is Carl rarely shows a lot of emotion but the quickness with which he left the house and boarded the bus showed his enthusiasm. Then she chuckled and said. "They couldn't see that I was just as excited as them about the weekend. I could hardly wait. Where are we going?

"Just a little place I found during my travels. I think you'll love it."

We start talking as we always have. She unwinds, telling me absolutely everything while I respond with grunts, one-word responses and leading questions. Like "Then what happened."

"Or tell me more." She goes on to tell me that at the bank, the manager I had straightened out has been fired and then arrested. Apparently, one of the tellers he touched inappropriately and then got more aggressive with was the wife of a cop. When she told her husband what happened, all hell broke loose. It shouldn't have happened like it did, but the husband was part of the arresting team. The story goes that when the cops went into his office, he resisted arrest. Can you imagine that little punk resisting arrest? He came out folded over. I don't really think that's what happened, but I loved the result. The cop was a tall skinny wirey guy, and we know how small and cowardly the asshole was. A little bit of instant justice, I suspect. I also got a letter from head office that I would be getting a raise effective the first of next month. I'm so excited that finally, things are looking up." When she abruptly ends her monologue, she says something to the effect, "ok, I've spilt my guts; now it's your turn."I respond, "Well, my life is not as exciting as yours. I spent most of the week driving around and eating in greasy spoon places. I did start reading a good book if that counts." Then, I was saved. Look, there's our cut-off." We leave the asphalt and turn onto a gravel road. Immediately, there's a sign indicating three miles to the camping ground.

"Are we going camping?"

"Yes," I say, "I've bought a tent. We'll be sleeping on the ground. We'll get used to the bumps and tree roots. The rocks only bother you for a little while. You get used to them. They promised me that there are no big snakes here, just small garter or grass snakes. They don't bite and sometimes can be really friendly."

I'm getting a look of disbelief from her. The silence is thick, and the chill coming from her would freeze an ice cube. "Ok, " I say finally. "It's only partly true. Yes, we are staying in this camping ground, no I did not buy a tent Yes we will have comfortable quarters. No, the snakes are not friendly." As I finish my defense, we turn a corner, and the lake, in all its majesty, shows itself in front of us. She looks on in awe.

"You like it?"

"Wow, so beautiful."

"You see that little cabin way down near that point, the white one with the red trim?"

"Ya."

"That's ours for the weekend."

"Wow, again."

I drive the van down the gravel turned-to-dirt road-style cow path till we arrive at the cabin. She's quiet, but you can see the excitement in her eyes. They're glowing. There's smoke coming out of the chimney. I had paid the caretaker to start a small fire in the fireplace. The light smell of smoke filled the air. Country living at its best. It's not hard to see that she loves this place. We unpack the van and open a bottle of wine. We sit in front of the fire and relax. No talking. Well I relax from the drive while she decompresses from work and kids and the constant demand on her for whatever. Here and now, nobody, nothing, is asking anything of her. Total peace.

The first glass of wine goes down fast. Without saying a word, just a smile and an outstretched hand holding an empty glass tells me she would like another glass, please. See how fast I am. Her wish is granted. As I pass her the refilled glass, I sit down closer and put my arm around her shoulder.

"What took you so long?" she asks. "Normally, I fall asleep after the second glass."

"Thought I'd catch my breath first."

With that said, she curls her shoulders and rolls into my arms. And now it begins.

We fall asleep in each other's arms and pass the night like that. My shoulder gets sore as hell, but I'm not moving. I don't want to wake up from this beautiful dream. We wake up to the sound of loons on the lake echoing their lonesome calls. The mountains are glowing in the sunrise. Heaven looks like this.

Breakfast is bacon and eggs over easy. "Sorry, I didn't bring brown bread; you'll have to eat the poisonous white stuff. But I do have the antidote."

"And I bet it's in a bottle of wine, isn't it?"

"I think you may have a point there. The question is, is it the bottle of red wine or the bottle of white? I think we'll have to try both to find out. Would you like a glass now?"

"Hey, it's still early in the morning. Plenty of time for that. Let's eat and see outside. It's a beautiful day." The eating and cleaning up are quickly finished. She goes into the bedroom and comes out wearing a simple pink summer dress with a straw hat complete with a pink ribbon around the crown. She looks gorgeous. I invite her into the row boat. She accepts and sits at the back. I get to the oars and start rowing along the shoreline. It's pristine. The flora is bright green and moving gently in the breeze. We continue up towards an inlet, where the water enters the lake. As we get closer, we can see a small waterfall. The sun is sparkling in the falling streams, creating a kaleidoscope of colours. We look on in silence at nature's beauty. I look towards her and see that she is enthralled by what she is looking at. Her hair is glowing in the radiant sunlight. The dress has come alive with coloured radiance. I'm looking at her with absolute joy.

I give a gentle pull on the oars, and we glide off to the other side. As the boat turns and she is between me and the waterfall, I think that Monet must have had such a moment that inspired his paintings. I wondered who his lady was and was he enthralled as much with her as I am with this beauty in the boat with me. This place just gets better and better.

It's hard to talk. The beauty of the lake continues to amaze us, and speech is totally unnecessary. We continue our exploring until we arrive back at our wharf. I realize that I'm hungry. "Is it lunchtime?"

I ask, killing the serenity. She responds with a laugh. She laughs so easily. She's got to be made for me. She laughs at my jokes. Now, there are two of us who appreciate my sense of humour.

"Sure, as long as you're doing the cooking. I'm feeling kind of frisky." There's a small pause in her conversation then she says, "Frisky, what am I twelve? I haven't said that since I don't know when. You, sir, are a bad influence on me. What kind of poison are you going to force on me and call it lunch?"

"Can't go wrong with hot dogs."

"You brought me all the way up here on a weekend that was planned last week and you're serving hot dogs?" There's a small pause; then she says, "Great, I love tube steaks."

Lunch is prepared and served. It's eaten on a picnic out by the bar B Q next to the shoreline. We talk about the lake, what we saw how it would be fun to live up here in the wilderness to just try and be one with nature. The sun is high in the sky when we retreat indoors and have our own special dessert.

The dessert was very sweet and satisfying. We decide to go for a short walk to the camping ground office. There are some kids playing in the playground. The girls are screaming on the swings while the boys have created swords out of old sticks and are sword-fighting to save the kingdom. Laughter abounds.

The sight of the kids brings Pam around to talk about her own children. We sit on a bench overlooking the playground. Out of the blue, she says, "Beverly has adjusted well to Robbie's murder. She doesn't talk about him much. I don't think she really understands what death is, what murder is, but in her way, she's adjusting to his absence. " There's a small pause. "Carl, not so much." He puts on a brave face during the day, but at night, I can still hear him crying. When I go into his room, he stops immediately and pretends he's asleep. I just lay down beside him and hold him tight. What else can I do? I still cry myself to sleep many times. Those bastards. Those bastards, those bastards." There's quiet in the air as she empties her soul, shakes her head and apologizes for bringing on a melancholy mood. She smiles, kisses me on the cheek and turns toward the playground.

It was bound to happen. One of the knights protecting the king gets wounded. There is a small gush of blood, causing immediate panic in the motherhood watching their charges. Turns out that a small band-aid and a mother's hug cure-all, and the battle goes on. We wander silently but arm in arm back towards our cabin. There's this swing that rolls back and forth when you push it with your feet. We sit on it and look at the lake, swinging slowly. The afternoon is moving on to twilight, and the lake is becoming still. A few minutes later it's a mirror reflecting the trees on the other side like we were observing a reverse universe.

I leave the swing with a bound and declare in a raised voice, "Amateur BBQ enthusiasts use propane to BBQ with. We want nothing to do with these inept, bungling want-to-be's. We professionals use maple charcoal to give the meat that smoky flavour. Plus there is our secret ingredient passed down from generation to generation and only revealed upon pain of death." I declare.

"You? A professional cook? Hot dogs don't count as a culinary feast, and if the flames get higher on your BBQ, the fire department will be here with their hoses to kill for a second time our poor beef supper."

"Oh, ye of little faith. I've not slain anyone yet. Behold the nimbleness of my swinging spatula."

Pam turns her back on the BBQ and whispers loudly enough for all to hear, "This is a disaster in the making. I wonder if there's delivery up here. We're going to need it. "

"She has no faith," I say to the empty lake. "You wanna bet, sweetheart?"

"Ya, 30-minute back rub, and you're on."

"I accept. Get the body oil out." I say with questioning bravado. "Put forth a good face," I think to myself.

With a spatula in hand and plenty of sauce, I put the "T" bones on the infernal I've created. I let them sizzle until I feel that they are just right. Flip them over, and the grease goes into the flames, and they rise even higher.

"Oh God," she says, "He's going to burn down the whole bloody mountain."

Then I rescue them. "Look at that," I say, looking proud as a peacock, "Done just right. Dark on the outside and darker in the middle." I say this while hiding the actual steaks. "No, really, look, perfectly done to a perfect medium rare." And they were.

Pam looks at me, smiles and says, "A total accident that they came out like that. You have no idea what you're doing."

I grin back at her lack of faith. "I used to be the cook for the church's annual fundraiser supper. We charged a lot but served steaks. I was the cook. I've had lots of practice. Get ready to pay up."

"So you cheated me into this."

"A bet's a bet. Get the oil ready. I feel a tightness in my lower back that needs immediate attention." Then I blow her a kiss.

I was very authentic with the steaks, using maple charcoal, but I put the baked potatoes in the microwave. A certain amount of cheating is allowed, isn't it?" I place the perfectly cooked steak on a plate along with the potato and some butter for the taters and serve it to her. My steak is close behind. Then we enjoy a quiet meal at the picnic table, watching the dragonflies search out mosquito larvae and the setting sun. This place oozes peace.

Supper is finished, and we return to the rolling swing and sit there still in silence. "Beautiful place, isn't it?" I ask.

"Yes, there's a tranquility here that I haven't known for such a long time. I don't remember the last time I felt like this."

Darkness falls, and we flee from the hoard of mosquitoes that are coming out in search of blood. I don't have any I want to offer them. The dessert is a quiet encounter, soft and gentle. She pays her debt, then rolls on her side and falls asleep instantly. I follow close behind. I do seem to be doing a lot of that lately. The nightmares have gone.

I wake up in the morning to the sound of a bloody mosquito buzzing around my ear. He or she works its way to my forehead, lands and dies instantly. I may have just given myself a black eye, but the blood-sucking insect is toast. My movement didn't wake her. I see that Pam and I have been spooning in our sleep. She's gone to the world. I lie there without moving, thinking of where I am and who I am with. I've promised myself that I would no longer be the conscience of the world and take it upon myself to correct all wrongs. I can't do that. No one can. It was just a dream to protect kids. I wonder if Freud would diagnose me as getting revenge for the death of my unborn child. Really a hopeless cause if I'm honest with myself. But laying next to Pam and enjoying all the time we've spent together has brought me back to the real world. It's like my dreams have come true. Can I really be this lucky? Or maybe it is because I've been alone and in self-conflict for such a long time that any kindness my way is seen as love. Can I really be in love with this woman? My immediate answer is yes, yes you are.

With this realization, I look at sleeping beauty. Does she feel the same way? Interesting question. I notice that her breathing has changed. She's waking up. Her eyes open, and she feels behind her to where I am. She gives me a little pat on the thigh. "Good Morning," she says.

"Hi yourself. How'd you sleep?"

She chuckles, "Logs have more life in them than me when I'm asleep." This gained a laugh from me.

"I don't want to get up. Let's stay here, at least for a little while."

"Ok," I respond. "I'm quite comfortable up against you. Let's stay like this forever."

"Nice dream."

There's a long pause, and she asks me, "Don, seriously, do you love me?"

Wow, I say to myself. Has she been reading my thoughts? "Yes" I say, then am quiet. I'm thinking that maybe she wants to introduce me to her kids or family back east. She wants to take this relationship to the next level. Something that shows a certain amount of commitment on my part towards her. I'm willing.

She hesitates and then continues. The conversation is slow. "Would you do something for me that I can't do by myself? I would give you anything you wanted, including being your mistress if you wanted me. I honestly can't think of anything I wouldn't do for you if you helped me. I've even thought of selling my soul to the devil, but I can't find his number." There's a small chuckle for a small joke. Seriousness returns.

"Well, I guess I'd have to know what this favour was before saying yes, but what is it you want to do?" My tone is light, almost playful.

"I want you to help me get revenge for Robbie's death, Robbie's murder. I want to kill a bastard in the '09s. Anyone will do just so long as he dies. If I can, I want to be involved; I want to participate so that fucker knows why he's dying."

"Fuck" I say to myself. "Fuck is right." I didn't see that coming. There's an involuntary jerking from me as I quickly recall the trauma and sleepless nights I suffered after Sack's death. Pam interprets my hesitation as a 'No' without giving me time to absorb and think; she says, "I sorry. I shouldn't have asked you that. I know how difficult it is for you to deal with the aftermath of these things."

"Pam," I say, "I wasn't expecting that. A shock. Let me think about this for a few days."

She breaks our spooning position and rolls over into me. She hugs me gently and puts her head on my bare chest. I can feel her warm tears falling on me.

We'd been talking almost every hour that we were awake and not having dessert, so that there really wasn't much left to say. This elephant in the room cuts conversation to a minimum. After she had asked me to help her with the revenge thing, we agreed that I would give her an answer next Monday. I really did need time to think about this. The drive home was quiet.

We arrived at my motel with plenty of time for her to get home to greet the kids. "I don't know when I'll be able to see you again. The kids will be home next weekend, and there's nothing in the future when they'll be gone." There's a pause, and she says, "You're going to think about it, right?"

"Yes" is my one-word response.

I just go to her and hug. She responds with a bear hug and puts her head into my chest. I don't want to let her go. "This was the best weekend I've had in a long, long time. Thank you," she says. "Will you call me?"

"Of course, at home or the office?"

"The office is better. I work with my door closed, so less chance of anyone overhearing or of being interrupted."

"Ok. We'll talk this week."

In my mind, I'm asking myself, "What the fuck do I do now?"

Chapter

XXXII

I'm a midnight debater. Most people don't know what that is. I discovered this many years ago when in conversation with friends, at work or wherever. Politicians are the opposite. They can answer right away, and for the most part, their answers are accurate. Me? Not so much. I always had to ponder something before I came up with the answer. Someone would say something at supper that I thought was a little off-beat. It would only be later that night, as I lay in bed, that I would come up with the appropriate response. Usually, my belated answer was a good one, but I was always four or five hours late with the response. Realizing this I would rarely give an immediate answer to any important questions. It's just the way I've always been. Normal for me. I needed time to think it through. Now Pam has laid a good one on me. This was going to take more than a little thinking.

It was Monday morning. I had slept at the motel and was up early enough. I thought it was time to return home to my rented house with the all American friends. Along the highway where I had decided that I wasn't going to right the world anymore, I was now thinking my decision over. Would I and even could I repeat the Sacks and Johnston shit over again. Then, a terrible thought came into my mind. It concerned Pam.

I had told her that I loved her. She had never reciprocated; she had never said that to me. Did she have an ulterior motive for the fantastic weekend we had just spent together? Was she just trying to use me to do something that she could not? Was I being set up? I tried to weigh all the factors, and by the time I arrived home, the space between my ears was one massive site of confusion. Not only did I not know what to do, I couldn't even think of a way to solve this dilemma. The only thing I knew for sure was that I loved her. I loved her face. I loved her body. I loved her smell and her touch. I loved the way she spoke with that soft voice. I loved the way she sat, legs tucked under her. Hell, I even loved her dandruff. How ridiculous is that? But did she really love me, or was she just setting me up? She knows my history. She knows that I can do it. But I need a motive. Love would be the motive here. Am I being set up?

To that last question, I had no answer. I posed it to myself several times in different forms. "Given the weekend we just spent together, she should love me, right? Definitely, maybe to that question. And if she was setting me up, this would be the best way to do it. Make me love her then pop the demand. Make an outrageous promise of future benefits, i.e., she's willing to become my mistress. This is not getting any easier, nor am I any closer to a conclusion. I need help here.

Among the friends I have here, Dick and his wife seem to have the strongest relationship. Don't get me wrong, all the gang does seem to be happily married, but Dick and his wife work in the same office. They are together almost 24/7. That has to be hard on any relationship. I regard this as a mature approach to love and life. Maybe a small conversation with Dick will help. I gave him a call, and he agreed to see me that same afternoon. I arrived at his office, and Joan greeted me at the door. "Dick's in the back office near the coffee machine. He's on the phone, but he'll be finished in a minute. Would you like a coffee?"

"Yes, please. This is a nice office. Not too far from home and in a nice neighbourhood. How long have you been here?"

"Well, we bought the building about five years ago and moved in right away. Been here ever since, and we have no intention of moving. I hate packing boxes. It's better since we've been digitized but we do have to keep paper copies for too long. I see Dick is off of the phone. Go on in, and I'll see you later. Oh, by the way. Are you here on Friday? We're having another get-together, and you're invited."

"Not sure about Friday. I'll let you know. Thanks for the coffee."

I went into Dick's office and looked around. It wasn't luxurious but was very cozy and functional. He greeted me with an ear-to-ear smile and offered me a seat. The chairs in here are ultra comfy. I mentioned this to Dick, and his response was funny.

"Oh ya, above all, we must be comfortable," and we enjoyed an ice-breaking chuckle. Dick was the kind of guy who got straight to the point. "You sounded a bit lost when you called. What's up?" "Can I help?"

Wow. I don't know what I was expecting but I don't think that it was starting this fast. A little warm-up would have been nice. But the ball was now in my court, so I had to lay it out as simply and quickly as possible. Of course the real demand from Pam would be hidden. I'd found a different excuse. "First off, thanks for seeing me on such short notice. I know you're busy and don't have a lot of time to spare."

"Well one of the luxuries of being the boss means I can do whatever I want. So taking a break in the afternoon is easy. How can I help?"

"I've met a lady, and I don't know if I'm crazy, but I am madly in love with her. I don't know for sure that she feels the same way. In the back of my mind, I wondered if she had an ulterior motive for being with me. I've known her for a while, but it is only recently that we've become more than friends. We just spent the weekend together at a camping ground. I had a fantastic time. I think she did, too, but when

I said I love you, she didn't respond. That's what got me thinking: what if she doesn't feel the same as me? What if she's just after my money? What if she has something else on her mind? Is she keeping secrets that'll come and bite me later on?"

"What did she do when you told her that when you told her you loved her?"

"Well, we were lying beside one another, and she rolled over and hugged me. Long, long hug, but only that. She didn't say anything, and that's what got me thinking. Am I being duped?"

"You understand that I'm not an expert on this topic. Hell, I have enough trouble interpreting Joan's signals. Especially when we were first together. I fucked up those signals many times. But you do get used to them and they do fade away with time. Maybe fade away isn't accurate. It becomes almost like you can read each other's mind. You seem to communicate telepathically. I don't even pretend to be an expert on women. Hell I don't think that such a person even exists. You've heard the joke about the guy walking along the beach, finding a bottle with a genie in it. Genie says you get one free wish for freeing me. What do you want? I'm in a hurry?"

The guy says I love Hawaii. I want you to build me a bridge to Honolulu so I can drive over any time I want."

Genie says, "Hey, don't be ridiculous. A bridge there would be way too long. It'd take four or five or six hours to drive there. You can fly in ninety minutes. No, that's a stupid wish. Can't be done. What's your second choice for a wish?"

"Ok," the guy says, "I want to understand women."

Genie looks at him and says, "Would you like that bridge to be two or four lanes."

"You see what I mean. Understanding a woman is impossible, especially in a new relationship. What's important is what you think and feel. If you love her as much as you seem to, put it on the line man, go for it. If you come on too fast or whatever, she'll tell you, and you'll know."

"So you're saying go for it."

"Ya, in for a penny, in for a pound."

"Thanks. Sometimes, I think that I've been alone for so long that I'd go with just about anybody just to have somebody. Does that make sense?"

"Oh ya, but your wife has been dead now for well over a year, so it is time for you to move on. You've got to keep her in a special place in your heart, but move on. Find another partner. Find a new love to share your life with. We weren't meant to live alone. Loneliness is not a good thing for anybody. We all need partners. But getting to the point to know if she feels the same way, get her to commit something that is important to her."

"She has two kids."

"Well, there you have it. If she'll introduce you to her children, I think that's showing where you stand with her, very close."

"You're a wise man there, Mr. Dick; you're a wise man."

I left the office feeling great. Finally, I had a plan. It was workable. Best of all it would confirm to me that Pam shared my feelings. I was sure she would agree. I headed home to wait. Waiting is a long process. The clock seems to take one step forward, then two backward. There were some old logs in the backyard that needed splitting. I got my axe out and went to it.

After splitting and piling the wood to dry, I realized I was sweating like crazy. I mean not just a trickle of water down my back but a torrent of sweat. I hadn't sweat this much since boot camp. "I guess I'm working off my anxiety. I need an outlet for my uncertainty, so I'm taking it out on these poor logs. Well if all fails and I crash and burn with my plan, I'll still have plenty of firewood. A great compromise. It took its bloody time, but finally, two o'clock came around.

My plan was simple. I was going to take Dick's advice and ask her to introduce me to her kids. I would suggest that we return to the camping ground for another weekend. It is a perfect place for kids. It would give me a chance to bond with the children and give them time to get to know me. Most importantly, I would listen very carefully to Pam's answer when I called and made the suggestion. If there was hesitation, it would mean a reluctance on her part to involve her kids. I would not take that as a good sign. The longer the hesitation, the weaker my position would be, in her eyes anyway, according to my thinking.

I have to admit that when I picked up the phone to call Pam, my hand was shaking. I realized that I hadn't been this nervous when I snatched Sacks or Cassy. Even getting Brian didn't have me in this kind of sweat. "Dam the torpedoes, full speed ahead." I pushed the appropriate button.

She answered on the first one and a half-rings. "This is Pam, how can I help you?"

"Hi, it's me."

"Hi, I thought you were going to call earlier. I was afraid that you weren't going to call at all. That was a super weekend. I enjoyed every minute of it."

Good sign. "Ya, I was arranging some stuff here. Had to get it out of the way." I lied. I didn't tell her of my apprehensions. Can't give too much away. "I have a suggestion. Let's go back to the camping ground this weekend. You could bring your kids." There my di were cast. Nanoseconds passed. Then milli seconds, no answer. I'm dying here waiting for an answer. "What a great idea," she says. My tears and fears are flushed down the toilet of life. I'm jubilant. I'm ready to dance in the streets. She feels the same way as I do. All that worry, all that time I spent wondering, worrying and tearing myself up for nothing. A simple phone call and I'm back on track. "Am I stupid or what? I knew she loved me all along."

"How do you want to work it? Do I pick you and the kids up, or would you rather meet me there?"

"We'll meet you at the campsite. You'll take care of the reservations and all that stuff. I'll take care of the food. I know you like steak, but what else would you like?"

"I like almost anything and everything, but I'm particularly fond of desserts."

There's a hardy laugh from the other end of the line. Her door must be closed. "Ok, I'll make sure to bring something special." I hear a knock on her office door. She says, "Just a minute, please," I hear her say. "I've got to go."

It's my turn to laugh at her 'something special.' "I'll see you Friday." and the line goes dead. "I'm going to bring some of my own food as well," I say to an empty line.

It's going to be a long couple of three days, so I decided to start looking into the '09' gang. Open media research on the internet tells me a bunch of general info. Apparently, the name of the Club reflects the date that the leader escaped from prison and has been a fugitive ever since. The date was 3 June 2009. So every year on the 3rd of June, there's a massive party. There are more specific stories about how they are fighting with rival gangs for control of the drug trade in most of the western states. The indications are that they are extremely ruthless when it comes to expansion. There are no rules; just win at all costs.

It's not just Pam's town. It's almost a viral epidemic, spreading at unprecedented speeds. They were originally from Columbia, and the gang consisted exclusively of Colombians. Since their rapid expansion, they've grown and other nationalities have joined with their own franchises. Only one franchise per town is allowed according to their constitution. If the town grows big enough and business is flourishing, a second franchise is allowed, but only with the permission of the overall governing body based in Bogota. Bogota establishes the rules of conduct between the neighboring franchisees as well as the boundary lines that each must respect. Failure to adhere to these rules means serious consequences for the offending club. They have an enforcement group somewhere. Nobody seems certain as to where it is, but when called upon, they strike immediately. The common penalty seems to be death.

They moved into Pam's Town about five years ago. Their original incursion was low-keyed. They pretended to work with the local biker gangs, and it was believed by the bikers and the police intelligence units that they had an agreement, a truce where the region had been divided up and that each was satisfied with the arrangement. In reality, the '09s were just building up their numbers and learning the tricks of the local trade. Their plan had always been total control. That was the general idea of who they were.

As I was reading the local paper, I came across an article about the shooting in which Pam's husband, Tom and Robbie, were killed. The headline read "War in the Centre of Town" It was longer than an article, more like an expose. It started with a brief description of each gang. First, the reporter talked about the bikers and their reputation for violence when it came to defending their turf. The bikers had their fingers in drugs, prostitution, loan sharking and extortion, and before the '09s arrived, they were exclusive. The arrival of a competitor was not welcomed by the bikers.

A brief but violent war erupted in which both sides lost many soldiers. The war was halted by mutual consent because the public was demanding decisive action against the violence on the streets. A task force was set up between State and local Police Forces to stop the killings.

It was interesting to note that the mandate of the task force was not to investigate and stop the numerous crimes now being committed by both criminal gangs but to *"Stop the Violence on our Streets."* It didn't take the warring parties very long to figure out that if they stopped shooting each other, the task force would have achieved its objective. Then, the Force would be disbanded. They wouldn't discover and then have to investigate other crimes. Business would go on as usual. The truce was established, but each side knew that this setup was purely temporary. There remained hostile intentions and scores to settle.

On a beautiful Saturday afternoon, one party, the '09s decided that this was the time to settle those differences. The intersection where Pam's family found themselves was in the heart of the contested area. According to witnesses, there were at least sixteen shooters, mostly coming from the '09' side of the boulevard. The conclusion of the Police Chief was that the '09s had ambushed a biker group collecting money from the front-line workers.

Besides the killing of Robbie and Tom, two other people were killed that day. Fifteen others were taken to hospital with various wounds. Two were in critical condition, four were stable, and the rest were treated with minor injuries and then released. Over two thousand empty shells were found by the Police. The reporter goes on to say that it was a small miracle that not more people were killed.

The irony of the whole episode was that not one gang member was even injured. They all got off scot-free. No charges were ever laid. The Task Force continued to investigate, and the State Governor and Mayor promised more intense investigations and a greater police presence. The gangs continued their criminal activity but maintained an uneasy truce without interruption.

The article ended with the usual promises to curb organized crime, and both the Mayor and Governor expressed their condolences to the bereaved families. Attached to the article was a photograph of the '09's clubhouse.

There wasn't any other useful information.

I decided to take a drive by the club house to get a feeling for the general vicinity and to have a look at the building. At this point, I had no idea how I was going to do anything.

I had to make sure that Pam was still on board with this idea. It wasn't a plan yet, just a concept. I didn't know where to start. I didn't know either how she was going to react to something that she put in motion and was responsible for. Killing someone is not easy. I can attest to that with the Sacks story. She knows of the turmoil I am experiencing because of what I did. I will be the actor involved here, but she is the cause. But she wants to participate in some way. She'll have to come to terms with that. Is she ready? That is something we'll discuss this weekend. And then, of course, there is the question of what is she willing to do for me. I should make up a list of questions we'll have to talk about. My thoughts are bouncing all over the place. I have to do some serious organizing of my own mind before meeting her again. And then another factor jumped into my mind for the first time.

That was me and the kids. In my shock and my acceptance to do what Pam had asked, I had missed that important factor. I never even thought of them. How were they going to see me? They warn kids of the 'stranger danger' in school, on TV, on social media and anywhere else kids congregate. I know that being with their mother will take away some of the shyness or hesitation, but I wanted to get close to them as fast as possible. We only have two days together. That's a lot in a short period of time.

I figured I'd help get over that by buying a doll for Bev and a truck for Carl. As extras, I included sand toys for the sandbox for both of them. But the best, I think anyway was fishing rods for all four of us. I thought that maybe we could create a competition of who got the biggest fish, and I had a little prize for the winner and second-place finishers. The fix was in.

The rest of the week flew by. Before I knew it, I was on my way back to the camping ground. The pleasant memories of my last visit here made me want to speed up and get there. I was in a hurry. I had a difficult time not exceeding the speed limit. I don't want to be stopped for any reason. I still had Mr. Sleezy's plates on the van.

I arrived at our cabin just after lunch. We had the same cabin. I wanted to arrive early to make sure that everything was in order. It was. I unloaded the food and extras we would need for two days and started the fireplace even though it was warm enough that we didn't need the heat. A warm fire says welcome and creates a warm, cozy, friendly environment. I thought the environmentalists would forgive me for this one little transgression. I was all set. I had nothing else to do but wait, so I sat on the swing, pushing softly, and looked over the lake. I thought of a beer but I didn't think that that would make the proper impression, even though they were just kids and probably wouldn't notice it. I was more concerned with what Pam would think.

I heard the crunching of the tires on the gravel/dirt road before I realized I had fallen asleep and that they had just arrived. I jumped up like a guilty man, which I was in so many ways and walked towards their van. I opened Pam's door and went for a kiss but was stopped by her hand telling me to cool it. I did. Both the kids stayed in their car seats looking at me and Pam, well mostly me I think.

I said, "Hi Carl, Hi Bev, welcome to my cabin. We're going to have a lot of fun here, and I've got some surprises for you. "Let's get all the stuff together and bring it inside. Ok? Would you like to help?" It turns out that each one of them had their own little backpack suitcases which they had packed themselves with their clothes and personal treasures. Carl had his own terribly worn-out old blanket, while Bev had a rag doll dog that was so old and tattered that it even looked like it was in misery. She called it "Arphie." A human adult would have put it out of its misery a long time ago. But it was Bev's favorite and was a 'no touch' item.

The kids went into the smaller bedroom. Carl chose the top bunk immediately and Bev seemed to be quite content with the lower bed. All was good so far. Pam made it a point to take her suitcase into my or our bedroom so the kids would know we would be sleeping together like adults do. There was no reaction from the kids. I figured it was time for phase one of making friends with these two rug rats. I got the doll and truck out. Of course I had had them wrapped up so as to make a show of it. I was sitting cross-legged in front of Pam, looking like the anxious parent that I wanted to be. They attacked the packages like it was Christmas morning. There would be no reusing that wrapping paper. Both presents were a hit. I had scored one run. More to come.

While all this was going on, Pam sat back in the most comfortable chair with a wall-to-wall grin on her face. "I think they like the presents, don't you?" I said.

"Oh yes, they do. But I'm having more fun watching you with them. I'm wondering which ones are really the kids. Given your performance, you qualify."

"You're making fun of me." small pause. "Are you making fun of me?"

"No, sweetheart. I'm just enjoying the show."

"You're mocking me. I know when I'm being mocked. Ok, kids, let's go outside. There's another surprise for you there." We left with Pam still sitting in the chair. I gave her an infantile distorted face, which involved sticking my tongue out at her and exiting. I offered the sand toys to the kids, and the plastic implements were taken with enthusiasm. Bev ran over to me and without talking or saying a word, he gave me a hug. I melted instantly. Another hit.

On the other side of the cabin from where the swing was, there was an old blow up swimming pool. The plastic no longer held enough air to make the proper side and hold water, but someone had filled it with sand. Both kids made a beeline for the sand, and everything got quiet as they played with their new toys.

I sat down on the edge of the porch, and Pam joined me. "Well, you seem to know how to make friends with children. You swept them away faster than you did their mother."

"Oh, I don't know. I had you with one touch of your touch."

"I don't think using a Taser on my ass counts as good courting etiquette."

"Well it did eventually work now, didn't it?" There was no comeback.

The supper timer arrived, and I started the BBQ. Hamburgers were on the menu for tonight. While I tended to the meat, Pam set the picnic table, got the mustard and relish, the dill pickles and onions etc. She also made sure that the kids had their milk and napkins to keep their faces clean. There was no recognition for her efforts. "The hamburgers are great," said Carl. I get the credit for a delicious supper. The BBQ has magical qualities.

After supper, while Pam and Bev cleaned off the table, I got Carl to come to the fire pit with me. We got an old fashion camp fire going. As the fire was growing, I asked Carl, "What's missing?"

Carl had a blank look on his face. "I don't know."

"Well," I said, "A campfire isn't a campfire unless there are marshmallows. " Right?"

"Ya," he said, catching on real quickly.

"We," I said. "I just happen to have this bag of marshmallows here, and look, I have the sticks to cook them on the fire with."

Carl's eyes lit up. "Wow, that's going to be fun. Ma, look at what Don brought."

Pam and Bev came out of the cabin together. Bev joined in the excitement and ran over to Carl. He had the marshmallow cooking sticks in hand. Pam wasn't quite as excited. She asked with a smirk on her face. "You're going to give the kids marshmallows just before bed. Do you know what kind of a sugar rush this is going to give them?"

"Hey," I responded, "You can't go camping without a small fire and marshmallows. I think that there is a law about that somewhere."

There was no response to my legal argument.

The marshmallow cooking, more accurately described as marshmallow burning, went on for some time. Each child consumed white or colored sugar and a healthy amount of black carbon for their cooking techniques. There was a great surprise when they discovered that if left long enough in the flames of the campfire, the marshmallows would burn. Outside, the marshmallow was carbon or coal black, but the insides were still sugary. Apparently, and according to adolescent tastes, this was delicious.

It wasn't long before darkness fell, and it was time for the kids to go to bed. There were the expected groans and resistance, but her kids listened to her well. They went off to bed laughing and excited about what surprise I had in store for them tomorrow. As much as they protested about going to bed, they fell asleep instantly. I stayed outside, tending the fire. It was our time now.

Pam tiptoed out of the chalet and came straight to me. A kiss that would melt an iceberg was gently placed on my lips. "Thank you for this, thank you for everything. The kids haven't had this much fun in a long, long time." Then she curled into my arms. We stayed like this for a few minutes, watching the fire then she slowly started our lovemaking. She can be quite an aggressive lover when she wants to be, and I was a very willing victim. Until it was my turn, and I flipped over our love-making roles, at which point she became the perfect submissive. We played like this till the fire died down. "Tomorrow's going to be another busy day. We should get some sleep," Pam said. We entered the chalet carrying most of our clothes sometime after midnight, both exhausted and ready for bed. I was very glad that there had been no hungry mosquitoes this evening. We'd be scratching like a flea-infested dog if there had been.

It seems that whenever I sleep beside Pam, my nightmares disappear. I had a great night's sleep and was still in slumberland when I heard the patter of little feet, and Pam slowly rolled off the bed. I was still in that wasteland between sleep and consciousness, trying to figure out what was going on. I'm not used to waking up at the speed of light to respond to hungry mouths.

Bev showed up at the door to our bedroom.

"Hey, Don, are you getting up?"

"Yes, sweetheart. See, that's me getting dressed."

"Don, you're not moving." The honesty of kids.

"Ok," and I rolled out of bed. I looked at my watch. God, it's seven thirty already. I haven't seen seven thirty for weeks. That's what a lazy life will do to you.

I strolled into the kitchen area, and Pam was already dressed, looking drop-dead gorgeous, looking for dishes. "I brought bacon and eggs," I said.

"The kids want cereal. Did you bring any?"

"Ya, bottom shelf beside the dishes." Now, I discovered that I had committed a cardinal sin. I had bought pre-sweetened cereal. I was informed immediately that these were full of sugar and not good for the children's health or their teeth. Now I know. But the cat was out of the bag as it were because the kids had seen the boxes, and now the cereal was out of the box and into their bowls. I got 'the look' from Pam. "Well Ok, this one time." I knew that these boxes would vanish once the kids were out of sight.

Breakfast was over, and we headed outside. The kids returned to the sandbox while Pam cleaned up inside. Once she had finished, she came out and joined me on my perch, watching the kids.

"Let's go down to the big playground. Maybe some other kids there."

"Ok." the simple answer.

We rounded up the kids and strolled down to the campground office where the big playground was. There was a couple of kids the right age for ours, and they made friends quickly. Kids can do that. During the quiet, leisurely walk, my mind was racing. I had a zillion questions for Pam, things we had to discuss and agree on before we went any further. We sat on the same bench we had sat on last week as we admired the bravery of the knights protecting the imagined king.

We sat embraced on the damp wood. The question foremost in my mind jumped out. "Pam, I want you to marry me."

"Yes," she said. There was no hesitation. The answer was immediate.

I continued without hearing. "I don't want a mistress. I want someone to hold, to walk with, to sleep with. Someone who'll share the ups and downs, someone I can build a life with. Someone I can grow old with."

She said "Yes" again on deaf ears.

"It's not enough for me to have a fling once a week or whenever time permits. I'd be sitting around waiting waiting. I don't want to do that. I want someone to hold, someone who'll laugh at my crummy jokes, someone who'll share their problems with me, someone I can share our successes with. A once a week is not enough. I'm not built that way. I want permanence. I want someone who'll always be at my side. And I want to be at the side of my wife, through good and bad. I want a home. I don't want a mistress." By this time, I was speaking so fast that my words were slurred; my brain was making sentences faster than my mouth could say them. Slurs and babbling came out as I pleaded my case to Pam's court. I forgot to breathe. Words stopped when there was no more air in my lungs. Involuntarily, I stopped talking. I pumped up my lungs and was preparing my next salvo when she yelled at me loud enough that the kids stopped playing and looked up at us. "Don," she said, then louder. "Don, I said yes five minutes ago."

"Oh" I said and then was speechless. That was a good thing because she planted a kiss on my shivering lips. I hadn't realized that I had gotten that worked up. I took a deep breath, and as she kissed me, I pulled her to me. Such a sweet embrace. I calmed down.

We sat silently watching the kids until lunchtime. Back to the cabin, we went singing some song the kids had heard in one of their TV shows. I didn't know those words, so I just pretended. They saw through me immediately and then laughed at my performance. I didn't think that it was that bad. Everyone's a critic.

Yesterday was hamburgers, today's hot dogs. They went quickly. Probably more quickly than Pam would have liked, but I told them that there was another surprise after lunch, and this made them devour the dogs at an unhealthy rate. Anyway, no one got sick, so I went to my van and pulled out the fishing rods. "Come on," I said. "There's fish in there waiting to be caught. Carl was all for it. Bev, not so much. "Do I put the worm on?" she asked.

"No, kiddo, I'll do it for you. OK?"

"Ya." One-word answers seem to be in vogue these days. Pam looked at me when I handed her her rod. "Are you serious?"

I gave her the wounded puppy look, and she complied. All parties would play.

The smiles returned all around, and we headed for the wharf. Pam looked at me with a beautiful smile. "Thank you," softly said.

Pam sat in the back with Bev while Carl took up the lookout position on the bow of the boat. I took up the propulsion position on the middle seat with the oars in my hand. We were off into the seas, even if the lake was only a hundred yards across.

"Before we get started," I said, "I have an announcement. Can I have a drum roll, please?" The kids didn't understand what this meant until Pam beat her hands on the seat she was sitting on. Her days as a drummer were limited. I continued, "Whoever catches the biggest fish gets a surprise package. Whoever catches the second biggest fish gets the second prize package. Ok?"

There was agreement all around and the kids adopted serious faces so as to win a prize. "Seriousness brings fish closer," I joked. The kids ignored my joke, but I did get a smile out of Pam, my intended target.

Carl was OK with putting the worms on. Bev held her rod towards me. I took a worm out, and she made a face saying out loud, "Yuk." I worm went on, and she threw the line into the water. Next thing I knew Pam's rod was in my face. "You too?"

"Yes, I'm a girl too, you know."

"Yes," I noticed. I also noticed that my dumb joke condition was contagious. Pam seems to have caught it. The worm went on, and her line went into the water as well. Carl caught the first fish, a ten-inch perch. A couple of minutes later, Bev had a nine-inch bass on her line. The fishing was good. Each of them had caught six fish when it was time to row in and have supper. The official weigh-in was held away from the cabin. Bev had caught to longest fish at twelve and a half inches. Carl was a close second at eleven inches. The prizes were distributed accordingly.

Bev got dresses for her Barbie dolls, while Carl won a box with eighteen action figures. Pam and I didn't catch a thing. You need worms on hooks to catch fish, something we had covertly neglected to do.

The supper went fast. The kids played with their new toys, but you could see that they were tired. We lit a fire and finished off the remaining marshmallows. The marshmallows had lost their appeal to the prizes the kids had won. Both voluntarily went to the bedroom and played with the new toys. Pam and I were free to sit on the swing.

"I think that that was one of the most interesting proposals ever," she said.

"Ya, I was kind of nervous. Did it show?"

Being very polite on such a delicate matter, she diplomatically said, "A little bit."

"We have a lot to talk about. I don't know where to start."

"Let's start with the wedding. When, where and what kind of wedding do you want?" I asked.

"Very simple. We go to the Town hall and get the license, wait the two weeks required by law then go before a Justice of the Peace and get married there. Minimal guests, minimal expense."

That was fine with me. She could have whatever she wanted. All I wanted was her and she had agreed to that. "I'd want to go Monday. We'll go at noon, during your lunch hour?"

"Yes."

We had never discussed where we were going to live once married. We were heading for a scenario where I would be living with her and her kids. It didn't bother me too much about the living ones; it was more about those who had been murdered that bothered me. There were memories of Tom and Robbie everywhere in the house, on the back lawn, everywhere. Even in the objects that didn't have their names on them but, the little things that no one would notice would trigger a memory and cause pain.

"Have you thought of where we are to live once married? I asked.

"No. I just assumed that it would be at my place. You don't have a permanent home, do you?"

"No, but I do have the place I told you about. There are great people living there. They would love you. Your Bank has a branch there. You could easily get a transfer. There are good schools for the kids. We could start our new life together without any painful memories."

"That's a lot to think about. How would this affect the kids? They have their friends there. Their school's there. Uprooting children isn't always a good idea. I don't know. Can we think about it?"

"Sure."

The subject of the wedding had run its course. Some decisions were made. Others were put off to another time. There was still the elephant in the room, and neither of us wanted to bring it up. But our time together was limited, so we had to talk about it. I said, "Last week, you asked me to help you kill an '09'. Do you still feel the same way?"

"I've been thinking about that all week. Yes, I do. Someone has to pay. The cops seem incapable of doing anything. Hell, no one even talks about or even remembers what happened. It was just a month ago. It scares me to be involved in something like this, but if I don't do something, no one will, and these bastards will get away with it."

I didn't have to answer. I had mouthed the exact same words not so long ago when I decided to become a vigilante. "I know exactly how you feel. I said the same things to myself not long ago. And look where it got me. Frustrated, alone, and not having solved a dam thing."

"The difference is that you are doing this for people you don't know. I know the whole story. This was my son they killed."

"Do you think you can handle the trauma that goes with this shit?"

"I'll make myself handle it." And with that, the subject was closed. We or more I had to make a plan.

Sunday with the kids was great. They played in the little sandbox for a while then we went back to the big playground. We went back to the cabin for lunch.

After eating, Carl and Bev wanted to go back into the rowboat, but they wanted to go by themselves. "Oh shit," I thought, "I don't like that idea very much. I was already becoming overprotective. Pam got involved, and after difficult negotiations, it was decided that as long as they had the life vests on and didn't go far from our wharf, it would be ok.

When they pulled away from the wharf, I went and got a lawn chair and sat on the wharf. My staring must have been quite intense as Pam reminded me that nothing bad could happen if I was to look around. She also mentioned that I could blink without too much danger.

She grabbed a chair and sat beside me. "I don't know how to get a '09'. They're always together in gangs or small groups. The smallest group I've seen is four. I'm going to have to watch them longer to find a weak link. He'll show up. I just haven't seen him yet."

"I've waited this long. I never thought that I could do this, get revenge, so I'm not in a hurry. And if you think that it's really too dangerous, maybe we won't do anything. We'll see."

The rest of Sunday rolled on. After supper Pam and the kids headed home in preparation for school and work tomorrow. I sat by the fire and thought about the wedding and what it meant to me, now our future life. Then of course, was the bigger problem: Pam's revenge and how I was going to deal with her request and the promise I had made. The 09's were going to be a problem.

I stayed at the cabin Sunday night and slept on Pam's pillow. Her beautiful scent was still there. It was quiet, and I had time to think things through about where I had been emotionally and where I was going. I noticed that the anger that I had been carrying for such a long time had gone. I was at peace. The future looked brighter. I fell asleep instantly.

The tweeting of the birds woke me up Monday morning. "This is the way to wake up," I thought to myself. I cleaned up the cabin and headed to Town to pick Pam up. I arrived at 11:45 sharp, and she was waiting for me. The license was given out quickly and we had time for a fast lunch. "What are you going to do today?" she asked/

"I have to look at the '09's closer. I think that I'll be spending most of the week on this. Maybe we can steal a lunch together, maybe a supper."

"I'll be home around six o'clock tonight. Come for supper. The kids would love to see you."

"Gee, let me think about it. I'll consult my dance card. Oh, look, I happen to have an opening this evening. I'd love to have supper with you and the kids."

"Give me a break. Even if you didn't come for me and the kids, you'd come for the free home-cooked meal."

"You got me. Six thirty, ok?"

"Yes, that's fine, and leave the crummy jokes behind."

I gave her that wounded animal look, kissed her on the lips, held the kiss a little too long, and she left. "See you tonight." I left with a wall-to-wall smile. Then I went to watch the '09s again. Surveillance is a patience game.

I noticed when I arrived that there was a construction crew working on the front door. They were building an entrance using cinder blocks. It seemed to me that this was overkill, an unnecessary expense on what amounted to a windbreak barrier. They had replaced the front door as well. It appeared to be a solid reinforced metal door with extra struts. I watched without understanding why build what amounted to a fortress entrance.

Then, I went around the block to get a better look at that side of the building. I couldn't see it from my other perch. Immediately, I saw that they had also re-enforced the back door. The workers must have done this while I was away. The back door was held open now by a cinder block. I could see that the door opened out and that it had crash bars on the interior. There was a steel frame embedded into the cement wall. I know construction. That was one solid door. Were they expecting something serious? Maybe a catapult attack.

I returned to watch the workers in front. They were mixing cement for the blocks. The front door was held open the same way. A cinder block standing on the edge kept the front door from automatically closing. The work went on. There didn't seem to be any gang members around. At least if there were I didn't see them.

I stuck around for an hour and a half. There were no motorcycles in the yard. I hadn't seen anybody other than the construction workers, so I decided to call it quits for now and come back tonight after supper. Maybe some kind of life then. Now it's too quiet. We'll see.

I arrived at Pam's at six thirty. Of course, I had some flowers. Flowers are a great way to make an entrance. The kids came to see me like they had known me forever. It gave me a really warm feeling. I watched them play, and then they headed for bed. Again, they went to their rooms without an issue.

Pam and I sat in the living room in each other's arms, but there was no dessert for me tonight. Too much of a danger that one of the kids would come downstairs and catch us. I knew that Pam had to work tomorrow so I invited myself to leave. I had to return to the clubhouse to see what, if anything, was going on. Reluctantly, she agreed, and I left.

I set up again in front of the gang's home base. Tonight, there were a few bikes in the parking lot, but for the most part, the place was quiet. Around 2 a.m. I called it quits and went back to the motel.

Tuesday and Wednesday followed the same pattern. I would arrive just before lunch. I don't get up early. Both days, the workers were at it. The entrance had been finished and they were putting bars on the windows. All this security was puzzling. Did they really think that someone was going to break into their clubhouse knowing how violent these people were? It didn't make sense. Anyone getting caught would probably be killed without any kind of trial. And what was there to steal? Some booze, probably, but the gang isn't dumb enough to keep any drugs here. This is where the cops are going to come when they finally figure it out.

Thursday was the best day. Oh, the surveillance was as routine as ever. Nothing going on. But supper was super. Pam announced that Friday was a ped day at school and that after Girl Guides, Bev was going on a sleepover with her coven, or whatever they call it. Carl was also gone for the evening and wouldn't be home till midnight. And almost best of all, Pam had chicken wings as the evening meal. I was in my glory. She changed into loose-fitting clothing. "To be more comfortable," she said. Fine with me but it does hide all those nice curves. I didn't know it at the time, but she did have an ulterior motive that I would be very happy with. I'd learn that a bit later.

After the kids left for their activities, Pam and I cleaned up and went down to the clubhouse. She wanted to see it and see what was happening. When we arrived, I gave her the grand tour, showing her the work that was now completed in front. We drove around the back so she could see the newly installed doors. I shared with her the fact that I didn't understand why they were doing all these security improvements.

We returned to the front of the place. If there is going to be any action, it's going to happen in front. We parked in my usual spot and settled down for the watch. There were five bikes in front and I figured that meant that there were five gang members inside. Another quiet night.

Pam sat on her side and questioned me on what I thought would be the best way to get revenge for her. I confessed that I didn't know. I can't see any pattern here like I did with Sacks or the Elsons. It grew quiet in the van.

Pam slid over to my side and cuddled. I held her, and she took my hand and placed it under that loose-fitting pullover onto her tummy. "See how loose it is, why you could slide your hands all over the place, up or down and around. If the cops come or if there's a noisy neighbor with a telescope watching us, he won't see a thing." I got the message.

The rest of the evening I felt I was a teenager again, making out with Sally in the back seat of my father's Chevy. It was very enjoyable. Like it was when I had the Chevy, Sally had a curfew from her parents so we had to knock it off, and I had to get her home for eleven thirty. Pam had a curfew from her kids. Particularly Carl. He would be home around midnight so she had to be home thirty minutes before. I really am a teenager again. I drove her home and then returned to watch the clubhouse. Two of the bikes had gone and the other three guys were leaving as I arrived. One of them locked the door, and all left on roaring bikes. I don't know why someone hasn't made a compliant about the roar of these machines. It's super loud. On second thought, the neighbors must know who these people are, and they don't want the come back with a complaint to the cops. That makes more sense. I waited a couple of minutes and made my way back to the motel.

Friday was the same routine. I arrived at the clubhouse late in the afternoon. Stayed a bit, then went to Pam's for supper and to see her and the kids. They were starting to accept me as part of the decor. I liked that idea. After supper, they went off to do homework, so Pam and I sat quietly in the living room. "I'm going to tell them this weekend that you and I are getting married. Do you think that that is Ok?"

"Ya, I think it's time, and I'm anxious to start a normal life again."

"Ok. I just wanted to check with you that it was ok."

"Thanks. You have homework to supervise, and I have a date with some bikers. We'll talk tomorrow?"

"Ok. Love you bye-bye."

I arrived at the clubhouse, and there was a roaring party going on. The music was blaring. There had to be forty bikes. All of them were shiny new machines. Through the windows, I could see people walking around, some dancing. Outside others were sitting around the new doors or on their bikes talking. There must be a great comedian in the group because the guys outside were laughing their heads off.

I took out the photocopy of the newspaper article I had read in the library, the one with the clubhouse photo. I compared that with what I was looking at. The photo showed wooden doors and single pain windows.

Now, I could see steel-reinforced doors and bars on new windows. There was something, a sticker on the windows, that I couldn't make out with my eyes. I took out my binoculars and read one. The windows had a bulletproof coating on them. "They really are fortifying the place," I said to myself. I couldn't see the benefit of staying. I had been there all week and seen the same thing. I figured that Saturday night would be the big party. Everyone would be there. Maybe I could figure out who the leader was, but for now, it was useless to stick around. I was bored and tired, so I went back to the motel. I didn't think that Saturday was going to be as big as it was and I had no idea that I was going to find the Achilles heel to this place and figure out how to get revenge for Pam. But first, I needed to sleep.

I slept on Saturday morning and didn't wake up till just passed eleven. There was a message Pam had sent me at nine inviting me over for lunch. Lunch or breakfast, it's all food. It's just a different perspective, that's all. They could all have lunch while I was having breakfast, but essentially, it was all the same food. We had hot dogs, but she steamed her buns. I was more of a 'toast my buns please' guy but I did enjoy the difference.

After lunch I was sitting on the sofa while Pam was making us a coffee. The kids were in the house doing their thing. I'm not really up to what kids do when they're not sleeping, in school or eating. I don't have any experience here, so I try to wing it and go along with whatever seems to be the right way. Basically, I'm bullshitting my way through, hoping I say yes and no at the right time. So far, I don't seem to have made any mistakes. I'm not sure if it's a good thing or a bad thing that I can lie like that, but for now, I'll accept that it's working and I'm not making a massive faux pas.

Like I said, Pam was in the kitchen preparing a coffee when Bev came into the living room looking at me. She didn't say anything. I smiled, and still, she said nothing. She walked towards me, put her little arms around my neck, and squeezed. She stayed squeezing me with all her force. Now, you can imagine how I melted, but what brought this on? So I asked. I said, "Wow, that was the best hug I've ever gotten. What did I do to deserve such a big big hug from a little little girl?"

"You make mummy smile and laugh all the time, and she doesn't cry at night like she used to when she thinks I am asleep."

Out of the mouths of babes comes the unfiltered truth. "I'm glad that mummy is happy. She makes me happy, too. Do I make you happy?"

"Yes. You're fun and make silly jokes. I'm going to play outside. Denise is waiting for me." And with that, she was gone. I sat there in the depth of happiness. Pam brought the coffee in and saw my face. "What?" was all she said.

"I've just been visited by an angel." A small pause: "You did remember two sugars right?"

"Ya, and a neat way to deflect the conversation."

She was on to me but let it ride.

We talked about all the little things in our life. Well, mostly, it was she who had these little things to discuss. How the kids were doing in school, how the work at the bank was getting to the overload stage. According to her, many of the people she had approved commercial loans for last year wouldn't qualify today. She suspected that the Bank was going to call in some of the loans that she had authorized. Many of those coming up for renewal were going to have trouble making the payments. I don't know if the Bank will even renew some of these loans.

On the good side, her raise had kicked in and she was able to put a little bit away for the future. She saw this as a positive marker. Her life was going to be better.

When she mentioned the tough times coming, I thought of my friends back at the rented house and how they had expressed the same ideas. Times were tough. This thought brought on a new line of thinking. I hadn't seen them now for a couple of weeks, and I was missing the Friday night get-togethers. Especially that apple pie that Caroline Switch makes. I wondered how they were going to take it when I arrived with my new bride and two kids in tow. It was going to be interesting. Then I figured that Dick had probably briefed them on my visit and the advice he had given me. He'd come up with a line like, "Well, you know, I told him to go for it, and I haven't seen him since. I guess whatever he did or said must have worked 'cause he's not back here with us."

I got my mind back to the present. "I think that I'm going to see some wild stuff tonight. The troops are gonna wanna see the improvements at the clubhouse. And Saturday night is party time for the under-thirty crowd."

"Yes. Have you found what I'm looking for yet?"

"No, but I think that tonight is the night. I'm honestly expecting a shit show. I'm sure I'll be up all night." An hour later, I left for my perch in front of the clubhouse. It was just after ten. There had to be at least fifty bikes parked every which way. The music was loud. A kind of rap with a lot of drums keeping the beat going. Not my favourite but I had no choice. The music blared. There was dancing inside and at the entrances. There seemed to be more girls there than guys. Then I figured that the guys were probably talking business while the ladies kept themselves amused and available.

Sometime around eleven thirty, four patrol cars arrived. One of the officers and his cruiser partner went inside while the others stayed outside looking at the bikes. A couple of minutes later, the music died down, thank God, and the cops left. The house became reasonably quiet.

The party went on till passed four. The music was gone, but the crowd inside remained about the same. There were bikes that left, but no sooner had one left than another arrived. This went on all night. One particular guy arrived, and I watched him more closely than the others. That was because he parked his bike right by the door. I realized that there was a spot there for one bike, a reserved parking spot. This must be the boss.

His lady was treated with the utmost respect. When she entered the clubhouse, the others made way for her. She didn't really walk like a normal person. She more strutted into the house. Honestly, it was like the queen of Sheba had arrived.

The guy, I figured, was the boss who was inspecting the new work done on the doors. From my distance, he seemed to be satisfied. He patted one of the guys on the back and gave him a hug. The thumbs-up signal confirmed for me anyway that this was the head honcho. He went inside, and I lost sight of him.

About fifteen minutes later, and light came on the roof. There was a little cabin up there with a door that gave access to the roof. The boss and three others came out and were looking around. The boss was pointing here and there and they were counting off distances by marching. One step equals 30 inches. It's not an accurate way to measure, but when the project is just being conceived, it suits your purpose. I myself had done this many times when giving rough estimates to clients I didn't feel were sincere enough.

And then I saw them. There were two sitting there in plain sight. The answer to Pam's desire to wreak revenge on the '09s. There, on the roof in plain site were two goose neck vents. One would be for the kitchen and the other for the toilet. All we had to do was block the doors and pour gasoline down the vents, followed by a burning flare. It would be ugly inside. All would die. I felt no pity.

I looked at my watch. Way too late to call anybody, even your fiance. When that thought jumped into my mind, I stopped. Yes, she's really going to marry me. I never thought of her as my fiance. That's more kids' stuff.

It was well past two o'clock, and I was tired. I had to stick around. I knew what I had to do, but the '09s had to cooperate. They just didn't know it. Two turned into three and then headed for four. Finally, I saw the second half of what I was looking for. The party participants were finally winding down, sitting around talking. I presume it was business because there were some lively hands flying and gestures indicating excitement. At four fifteen exactly, the whole bunch went inside and closed the door. That would be my striking time when they went inside.

I headed back to the motel. I would tell Pam tomorrow at breakfast for me and lunch for the kids. It wasn't without danger, but the risk was minimal. As well, the authorities, that is mostly the cops, would think that it was the bikers seeking revenge for the ambush. Yes, this was a good plan and would work. The chances of getting caught were also very small. All the right boxes were checked. I went to bed happy in one sense, apprehensive in another and fearful in a third. I still didn't want to spend the rest of my life behind bars, but I was stuck between a rock and a hard place. I also thought that what Pam wanted to do was more dangerous for her than for me. Had she thought of her kids and what would happen to them if she was caught or even worse? Even if I thought that the risk was minimal, Pam could be killed in an unforeseen anything. Maybe an armed gang member who arrives late would see us and alert the gang inside and maybe take a shot at us. Someone inside could want to come out for a cigarette and find us preparing our attack. A police cruiser could drive by and see me on the roof and intervene. The possibilities of something going wrong were almost endless. But each one of these possibilities would be devastating for us, but more so for Pam. After all, she has kids that depend on her.

I wanted to quit this vigilante shit, but at the same time, I wanted to please Pam. Of course, Pam came first, so I would keep my promise to her. '09's would die. And if my plan succeeded, it would be a lot who died. Time for this discussion tomorrow after some shut-eye. Without sleeping aids and without nightmares, I fell asleep quickly, remembering the smell of her hair. I guess that the anger that I had built up was really gone.

I woke up late and then rushed over for some eats. Bacon and eggs with brown bread toast and a touch of peanut butter, followed by a steaming hot coffee. It doesn't get much better than this in the morning, even if it was well passed noon. The kids ate and were gone.

I don't think that they actually chewed anything; just kind of inhaled and swallowed and disappeared.

Pam and I took our coffees and went into the living room. I explained to her my plan, how I was as sure as I could be given the nature of what we were going to do, that we would probably not get caught but that this was drastic, far beyond what I had done with Sacks or what I had tried to do with Johnston. I asked her if she was still adamant that she wanted this revenge. I reminded her of the effect it was going to have on her. I talked about what I had thought of last night. The negative implications if she were caught or even killed in our plan. She was sure she wanted to do this. "I have to do something. This seems the best way." and went on to say that she would help in any way she could. We agreed that I would pick up the necessary items. She had nothing to do but arrange a babysitter for next Saturday and to prepare mentally. As I left her, I said, "Think seriously about what I said if something goes wrong." I left it at that.

The week went by far too fast. I stopped by on Tuesday and Thursday to see the kids and have some dessert with Pam. We were still in the teenage can't keep my hands off of you stage. It was fun. I briefed her on the preparations. Everything was going off as planned. I couldn't see any reason for it to call off.

Chapter

XXXIII

We arrived at the clubhouse around three o'clock in the morning. The scene was pretty much like it was last week. We waited. Sure enough, at ten after four, the people who were outside drifted in small groups inside the clubhouse. The last ones closed the doors behind them. I was wondering if there isn't some kind of secret meeting that goes on at four on Saturday. It didn't matter. This was striking or attack time.

The first thing we did was change drivers. Pam took the wheel and drove over to the back of the building. I took the extension ladder out and laid it on the ground near the building. Next, I took a two-four and wedged it under the back door handle and secured it in place with a twelve-inch spike. No one would be coming out through that door. I contacted Pam on the walkie-talkie. "You good?"

"Ya," she responded.

"Ok," I said. This is the tricky part. Securing the front door. Ready?" I prayed that there would be no latecomers.

"Yes."

With my two-by-four securely in place by the back door, I put the ladder up against the building. Now, I had easy access to the roof. The next part was the trickiest.

I went around to the front door. Everyone was still inside. Thank God no one had come out for a smoke or something. I put the second two-by-four under the door handle. No one came out. I could hardly hear any noise from inside. Seemed to be just one voice. Probably the boss encouraging the troops. I put another spike to hold it in place. The '09s were now effectively trapped inside. They just didn't know it yet. The coup de grace was coming quickly.

I gave Pam the signal. She came out from her parking spot to where I was. I opened the back door and grabbed the green army surplus five-gallon gas tank, two road flares and some leather gloves. The flares went into my back pocket. I put the gloves on, took the gas tank and headed for the ladder. Pam was my lookout. If she saw something wrong, use the walkie-talkie.

I was on the roof removing the first vent with my hands shaking. Pam buzzed me. I looked around with more fear than I've had in a long time. "What the fuck is wrong?" I said to myself. There wasn't any pedestrian or vehicle movement. It was as quiet as could be.

I stopped working the vent and keyed my mic, whispering, "What?"

"I can't do this."

"What?"

"I can't do this, come back."

"Are you serious?" in a loud whisper.'

"Yes, come down. I wanna go home."

"Ok" was my short answer. I was so glad she had changed her mind that I was ready to party with the '09s.

There are some things that a person does automatically. They've repeated the action so often that it is done without thought. I'm one of the guilty ones. Stupid me. Knowing I would be on a ladder tonight, I put on my heavy construction boots. They are great for going up and down ladders. They are heavy. They have steel in the toes and a steel bar in the sole to protect from penetrating nails, but running across a roof with them when you are trying to be quiet is not a good idea. As I reached the ladder, I realized the noise I was making with these heavy things. The people below must hear this sound. I looked down at the boots realizing my mistake at the same time as I was reaching for the ladder. I missed the ladder. Instead of grabbing it, I kind of punched it. It started to slide away from me, and I had to dive and grab it to keep it from falling, leaving me trapped up there. I hit the roof with a loud thud as my two-hundred-pound-plus body slammed into the roof. I've gotta move fast now. I keyed the mic. "Wait, don't move. I have to undo the doors." I came down the ladder like a drunken lumberjack. Well, it was more like I had a controlled fall down the ladder. I put the gas tank down and ran around to the front. Everything seemed to be the same. I lifted the two-by-four that was blocking the door, grabbed the spike, and ran around back. I was huffing and puffing like that wolf in the kids' stories. The back door was released as easily as the front. I ran to and put the wood into the van and secured the ladder to the roof. I just had the gas tank to retrieve. I was halfway there when I heard some voices coming towards me. I jumped into the ditch and didn't move an eyebrow. The gas tank was by the building, and I knew it didn't look like it belonged there. If they spot that, all hell would break loose.

There were three of them, and one had a flashlight. He was shining the light onto the building, looking upwards. He did a scan of the roof edging and then a quick look around. The light flashed over me. I froze. It continued to sweep until the user was satisfied that there was no one there.

One of them said, "I'm sure I heard some noise back here. I thought it might have come from the roof.

"Ah, you're just fucken paranoid." said another. And the two laughed at flashlight man. After a final sweep, the three headed back to the front door and out of sight. I grabbed my gas tank and went to the van. Thank god I had bought a green tank. A red one would have stuck out like a sore thumb. Thank you for your little favors. The doors were locked, and I couldn't see Pam inside. I knocked and whispered her name. She looked out from under a moving blanket and let me in. We drove home without a word.

"I'm sorry," she said and then was quiet. She got out of the van. "Just a minute," I said. "I'm glad you called it off."

"But you went to all that work, and I got too scared. When you went up that ladder, I thought it was too late. I started to shake. It was uncontrollable. I got so scared I think I peed my pants." I had never heard her voice this frightened. So nervous and tight.

"Stop, it's Ok. I'm glad you stopped me. It's over now. No one was hurt. Everyone is Ok. We're home safe and sound. It's over.' I took her in my arms. "Take a deep breath. There, it's over, and you're safe at home. I'm with you. You're Ok." I repeated."

"Don stay with me; stay the night. I don't want to be alone. I don't want to think about what I just almost did. Hold me, hold me tight." With that, she broke into tears and stayed in my arms all night.

I don't know if she slept. I know I didn't. Even now and then, I would think that she was gone, but then there would be a small reflexive jump in her body, and her breathing would change. I would know that she was awake. We didn't speak all night.

We lay there spooning till the next morning. Till the eastern sky started to glow ever so slightly. She rolled over and hugged me. Then she slid up a bit and kissed me. That was very welcome. Then, the kiss got more intense. It went from a peck to a serious lip-on-lip, then an exchange of bodily fluids. Her tongue was slashing inside my mouth. She was squeezing and holding and kissing me so intensely that it was beyond physical, beyond sexual, metaphysical even. It was her soul searching for mine. "I want to be inside you. I want you to absorb me into you. Hold me as tight as you can. Squeeze me hard hard." Then, she and I were quiet.

Chapter

XXXIV

Morning came, and the kids were up bright and early. I left Pam in bed and told the kids that mom wasn't feeling well and that "I, the world's greatest chef, was going to make them the breakfast of the century. And "Are you ready for the world's greatest pancakes made straight here from this box?" They both broke up, laughing at my antics. I had an audience. They would laugh at anything. I was in my glory.

I made a big production of mixing the milk into the whitish powder that came out of the box. Then I made two little round cakes and one crescent-shaped swirl then put more pancake mix over the two small circles and the crescent. I made two and then put them on a plate for the kids. The result was two smiling pancakes all ready to eat. Just add maple syrup.

Pam arrived in the kitchen just as the kids were finishing up. The kids jumped out of their seats and ran to her. She got a big hug. I was very jealous. She looked around in astonishment. I looked to see what she was looking at. It seems that in my culinary preparation of the world's greatest pancakes, I had used almost every pot and pan she owned. "Oh." I said, "I was just about to clean that up."

"It's fine," she said. "It will give us something to do. But first, a coffee."

The kids went out to play, and we sat at the kitchen table.

"I don't know what to say." was her opening line.

"I suggest that we just don't talk about it. We almost did something that we would have both regretted but now it's passed. We didn't do it. Nobody knows about it. Everything is fine now. Is that Ok with you?"

"I guess. It's just that I didn't think that I could come that close to killing that many people. I mean, I don't do these things. It's not me, but I was this close to killing a lot of people. I never knew that that was in me."

"It's in everybody, Pam. Criminals are getting away with everything, and the cops and the authorities seem helpless to stop it. When it hits home it's normal that you want to hit back. It's just the way we're made."

"What would have happened if we got caught or even shot and killed? Who would have taken care of my kids? They would have been all alone. How stupid of me. You warned me about that, and I didn't hear you."

"Hold on now. You didn't do anything wrong. It's not a crime until it's done, and we didn't do it. Leave it behind you. The kids are here. I'm here, and we are all safe. Come here." And I held her in my arms. I could feel her relaxing as the minutes passed. "Maybe you should call in sick tomorrow morning. Then next weekend we could return to the camping ground. Would you like that?"

"Yes," single the word answer.

"What about the kids? Would they like it?"

"Yes, as long as you put the worms on the hooks."

We cleaned up the kitchen. It was true. There seemed to be an endless supply of dirty pots and pans. I accused her of taking in extra washing when I wasn't looking. I got a small chuckle for my efforts.

We finished up the drying and were putting everything away when she asked very seriously, "Will you dry the dishes when we are married, or is this just a fiancé thing."

"Yes," I answered. I love multiple-choice questions. She's not sure what I had said 'yes' to but she let it slide. This got us around to the subject of our wedding. We were now eight days away from being eligible for the nuptials. Pam said, "I think that we should live in sin until we get hooked. Then we'll make it legal. What do you think?"

"Well, I'd save a lot of money on the motel. I'd get three square meals a day and all the desserts I could handle. Can't seem to find a downside to that."

"Don't get so excited. I do have to work the next morning five out of seven days, and then on the weekends, the kids don't sleep in. Desserts will be limited to sneaky times."

"I can be very sneaky when I want to be."

"I think that you could easily be the king of sneaky if you wanted."

He continues the conversation. "There are things we should talk about. Wedding guests? Where are we going to live? I have some friends at my other house. They're super people. I'd like to invite them to the wedding.

"Where are we going to live? " I asked. "There are a lot of memories here. Both good and bad. They may be hard on you. Let's make a brand new start. We could live in my other place for a while. If you don't like it, then we'll move. We'll make friends there and see what happens. The kids can go to school there, and you could transfer. With your reputation, they'd be glad to have you."

Her answer was a simple one. "I think you're right. It's time to put this place and the things that have happened here behind us. We should have a brand new start together." It was agreed by all two of us.

On Monday morning, she went to work. I had some tidying up to do myself. I took a drive over to the Druid's clubhouse. Their place was an old service station. It still had the pumps in front but they looked like they hadn't been used in some time. The old repair bays were still being used. There were motorcycles in all stages of repair. The place was bigger than that of the '09s', but there wasn't the parking lot that the '09s' had. There were two Harley parked on the curb. I sat back and watched. It wasn't long before a big, ugly, bearded biker with full patches on his jacket came out and mounted one of the bikes.

Off he went with me a good distance behind him. It took a while, but he didn't seem to be in a hurry. He finally pulled into a service station and headed for the washroom. This was my chance. He didn't lock the door and was yelling "Occupied" when I crashed in and put my gun to the back of his head. "Don't move" was the standard order. "We have to talk for a minute. Do I have your attention?"

"Ya."

"What's your name?"

"They call me Bear." His response was very calm. Now that I was up closer, I could see why they called him Bear. But the gun in my hand evened us out.

"You going to listen to me for a minute, Bear?"

A small nod of the head told me he was. "I don't seem to have much choice in the matter."

I challenged him on having lost ground to the '09's. "They came and took your territory from you and what did you do? Fuck all. Then they ambush your guys on your territory and get off by saying, 'Oops,' sorry. And what the fuck are you guys doing? Nothing. What a bunch of pussies. You guys looking for revenge?"

Again, a small nod indicating, "Ya, we're working on it."

"Well, I have an idea for you." Then I told him about my plan, the one that Pam stopped me from doing even if those bastards deserved to burn in the clubhouse like they were going to burn in hell. Shit, I was getting myself all worked up again. "Control yourself," I said to myself. "You understand all this shit?" I asked.

A final small nod.

"Nice talking to you. Kindly count to ten so I can get away from you without shooting your leg out from under you." and I left very quickly. I glanced back at the toilet door and it still wasn't open. I guess he counts to ten very slowly. Maybe he can't count that high.

I went back to the motel and collected my things. There wasn't really very much, but it was mine. Then I went to the campground. Again, there wasn't much there but I did want those fishing rods back. Just being at the campground and the memories of dessert with Pam, fishing with the kids, burning marshmallows and listening to the joy and laughter all around me gave me a feeling of having arrived. I was happy content.

Dick and all the gang came up for our wedding. Really, they were about the only guests. The ladies took to Pam like kids to a candy bar. They and a few people from Pam's work helped us celebrate the nuptials. Pam put her place up for sale. She had an instant bite. She was a mortgage specialist so the loan was quickly made to a young family just starting out.

At the end of the school year, we moved back to my place. Pam had already seen it and was polite enough not to say anything negative. "Did you really paint everything white?" It was, at the time, anyway, my place, and it seemed like a good idea. Now, it was ours, and she looked at it with a different light. This was her nest now. She stood in the living room, which is probably the center of the house and turned slowly in circles. I'm sure there was smoke coming out of their ears as she imagined the changes she was going to make. "Hum ya" was all she'd say. "It's gonna take some work, but it is home for now. Let's call it a work in progress. You painted everything white."

I didn't know if it was a question or a statement. I figured silence was the best answer. Turned out I was right.

We were sitting in each other's arms, watching TV, when the news came on. There had been another horrendous gang incident in her old Town. The anchor switched to the local network, and the reporter was on the scene. One glance and we recognized the '09' clubhouse going up in flames. The reporter said the fire had started around four thirty in the morning and had spread very quickly. She said that she had talked to the fire chief and that, apparently, the doors of the house were barricaded from the outside. He went on to say that indications were that the fire had started from the roof. When the occupants tried to flee the flames, they found the doors barricaded from outside. He could not speculate on how many people were inside but the neighbours the reporter had talked to said that they thought that the place was full. There were at least fifty motorcycles outside. The Police were on the scene investigating a suspected arson.

Pam raised her head and looked at me. "You had something to do with this, didn't you?"

Not all questions have to be answered.

Then she looked back at the TV screen. I think I may have heard a slight "thank you."

I have asked myself many times, "What the fuck do I do now?" Well, now I finally had my answer. I settle down with this beautiful woman who loves me as much as I love her. Her kids seem to have already adopted me, so I'll adopt them and make them the family I have always wanted. We'll make a new life for ourselves. "That's what I'll do now. One other thing.

I seem to use the word 'fuck' a lot. Fuck this, fuck that; what the fuck am I going to do now? I use it like it's an acceptable word. It's the first word out of my mouth when I'm surprised. I am smarter than that. Now, with these kids around me all the time, I'm going to have to change that. How about "What the hell am I going to do now?" Not quite. I guess, like me, it's a work in progress.

Ronald Edward Myles

Thank you for reading this novel. I had a lot of fun writing it. I would appreciate your comments and support. I can be reached at:

Vigilante22@Tutamail.com

Vigilante-238